Jack

Imani in N... Goodbye

Best Young Adult Fiction!
~ **Urban Spectrum**, 2004

"This novel doesn't skimp on any of the drama associated with being a teenager in today's hectic society. Hardrick does a marvelous job of recreating a true-to-life world that lures readers into the lives of regular 'can't-wait-till-I'm-grown' teenagers. The suspense that Hardrick captures will always leave you waiting to see what happens next, but the truth is, you'll never guess." ~ **Black Issues Book Review**

"Hardrick's good intentions are obvious; she promotes higher education and clean living. Readers will respond to the dramatic plotlines and Hardrick's flair for dialogue."
~ **Booklist**

"As cautionary fiction, this book is a success. It will attract readers and offer them food-for-thought. Even reluctant readers will appreciate the quick pace of the plot and snappy dialogue." ~ **Voices of Youth Advocates**

"Hardrick spins a drastic tale of life. She draws a picture of what life can be like in any neighborhood—the good and the bad." ~ **Union Leader**

Recommended Reading by the Black Caucus National Council of Teachers of English

House Lofrano

Teenagers Speak...

"From the first page to the last, I was hooked!" ~ K. Stokes

"I promise that this book will not waste your time. This book is for today and a guide to tomorrow." ~ Janice

"It kept me on the edge of my chair." ~ Natasha

"A good book for teens to learn how to survive these days. Do your friends a favor & share it with them." ~ Brendalin

"I visualized what the characters went through and I just had to read it twice!" ~ Khadijah

"Great book for teens, middle school kids and athletes because they can relate to it." ~ Anthony

Adults & Educators Say...

"This is the real deal! A must read for teens and adults."
~ Rebecca Simmons, author of Nobody's Business

"The fast paced action keeps the reader turning pages. A great book for discussions." ~ April Allridge, filmmaker

"The characters and their experiences reflect the readers' experiences and the universal and critical concerns of today's youth. The result is a teacher's dream – students interested and self-motivated to read and discuss a book."
~ Charlene Baskerville, educator

"*My students were eager to read this novel daily! Our discussions were fueled with well thought out opinions."*
~ Ms. Blaise, educator

- Also Available -

Imani in Young Love & Deception

Recommended reading by **EBONY** magazine, this entertaining story covers hot issues that teens face. Sex, teen pregnancy, STD, alcoholism, low self-esteem, dating, and love intertwine in this fascinating contemporary young adult novel.

Meet the teenagers drawn together by love, lies & deception...

Imani (16 years old) – "Mom says college is my way out. I ain't Cinderella and this ain't no fairy tale. I can't depend on some rich boy to rescue me...I've got to rescue me."

Bhriana (17) – "All of the girls know that I can get whatever guy or guys I want. They can't compete with me."

Tyler (16) – "My father's got more than my back, try my whole life. I wish he would cut me some slack."

Fatima (17) – "How did I get Chlamydia? I thought that was a nasty girl's disease. You know the girls who have sex with a lotta guys. That was just my first time."

Steven (18) – "Either I'm drunk, she's drunk, we're both drunk or I'm imagining she wants me. Who cares, just take advantage of it."

"This fast paced page-turner keeps you on edge until the end." — Angela Kinamore, Poetry Editor, ESSENCE

IMANI

IN

NEVER SAY GOODBYE

Jackie Hardrick

EP Enlighten Publications

IMANI IN NEVER SAY GOODBYE

Published by Enlighten Publications

Library of Congress Control Number: 2003108282
ISBN-13: 978-0-9706226-2-4
ISBN-10: 0-9706226-2-7

Enlighten Publications
P.O. Box 525
Vauxhall, New Jersey 07088
books@enlightenpublications.com

For information regarding special discounts for bulk purchases, please contact Enlighten Publications at 866-862-8626 or books@enlightenpublications.com

Cover design by Stephen Swinton

Printed in the U.S.A.

10 9 8 7 6 5 4 3 2

Dedicated to
my mom,

Melba Hardrick

You are the strongest person that I know and the glue that holds our family together. We thank you for your love & support. I thank you for shaping my character while allowing me the freedom in becoming the person that God intended.

Love You Always...

Acknowledgments

I thank God for His continued partnership and guidance in my quest to enlighten and inspire my young adult audience. I thank Him for opening doors and bringing competent people my way to aid in the mission.

Thank you Mom for your endless support and love. You never discouraged me from pursuing any dream or endeavor. And for that, I am forever grateful.

Much love to family & friends: Jeanette, Glenn, Tyler, Tré, Dean, Gwen, Edward, Uncle Gene, Aunt Ruby, Aunt Bert, Cyndi, Angel, Alicia, Cynthia, Ruth, Wendy, Jerry, Michelle, Sharon, Bhriana, Timothy, Brandon, Aisha, Marianela, and St. Louis crew: Pier, Gail, Ralonda and...

Cornelia & Celeste Layton: I love you like family. I thank you for your dedication & support not only professionally but also in all aspects of my life.

Stephen Swinton: You are a Godsend and a creative genius. I pray that Swinton Design Studio's borders are expanded, indeed. As your client base grows, do not forget me (smile).

Hazel Witherspoon, Lisa McFarlin, Impact 21 Toastmaster Club, Pastor Lawrence Powell, First Lady Vanessa Powell, Minister Tanya Johnson, Terri Davis, Allen Brannon, Erica Bell, Rebecca Simmons, Beverly Harris, Useni Perkins, April Allridge, Alexandra Gina, Newark Public Library, Union and Vauxhall Public Libraries, Ocean County Public Libraries, Montclair Public Library, NJ Books (Newark, NJ), Watchung Booksellers (Montclair, NJ), Here's The Story (Union, NJ), Dr. Margaret Timmons...if I overlooked anyone, please forgive me—all of you have been a blessing!

I thank every customer, school, teacher, church, book club, library, organization and youth group that purchased and "talked-up" my first contemporary young adult novel, *Imani in Young Love & Deception.* I wish you much success in your endeavors.

Peace & Blessings...Jackie

Bamboozled

You keep callin' & callin' me claimin' to be
my answer to love, joy, friendship, protection & peace.
Snow, blow, crack, weed, PCP, LSD, Ecstasy–all y'all got me
trippin' and out here wheelin' & dealin', stealin' & killin'
and I'm
        fallin'
                I'm fallin'

Around the clock you be callin' me & I ask "How high?"
"Sky high" you say & even promised I could fly–you lied.
Just one more shot of heroin, another smoke, hit, sniff
& to get it I turn more & more tricks
and I'm
        fallin'
                I'm fallin'

Money's gone, friends gone, family gone, & I'm hurtin'
so where are you now, "friend"? You lied to me–again.
For once come clean and tell me the truth!
How many like me have you bamboozled or duped?
And they're
        fallin'
                like I'm
                        fallin'
                                we're all
                                        fallin'...

—*Jackie Hardrick*

IMANI

"Sit your sorry self down!"

"Who's Coach talkin' to?" Imani mumbled as she gazed down the bench and stopped at Dominique's glassy blue-green eyes. Imani shook her head. "Dang, his own daughter," she mumbled.

Imani's varsity basketball team, Westmoore High "Jaguars," blew a 20-point lead. Their rivals, Claremont High "Cougars," tied the score with ten seconds left in the game. The Jaguars' fans, most dressed in their school colors of sky blue and white, stood silent as if they could not believe what happened. On the opposite side of the gym the Cougars' crew, adults included, stomped on the metal bleachers and rooted their team on.

"Imani!"

"Yeah, Coach!"

"Don't get cute out there. Execute that play just like I told you. Understand?"

"Got it!" Imani yelled back. She walked onto the court and glanced at Dominique who sat at the end of the bench. All of the other players were on their feet. "Stay focused," Imani uttered to herself as she tried to block out Dominique and the rowdy Cougars' supporters. "Don't panic. Just knock down two and go home."

The referee blew his whistle and play began. The Jaguars inbound the ball at mid court. Imani shook off her defender and received the pass from her teammate Terry. She glimpsed up at the clock and saw that nine seconds remained.

"You can't get around me," Imani's defender said.

"Watch me," Imani told her. Imani noticed that the girl did not play her tight. Imani nodded her head. *Yeah, she's scared I'm gonna fly by her.* Imani used all the energy she had left and propelled her 5'8" frame up high. She launched a shot over the girl's outstretched hands. The ball caught all net a second before the buzzer.

The Westmoore fans roared and all of Imani's teammates swamped her. She peeked between the gap of sky blue and white jerseys and looked at the bleachers. Her smile widened when she spotted her boyfriend, Tyler Powers, and her parents. They beamed back at her. She signaled that she would meet them outside.

Imani ran to the steam-filled locker room and then hurried and got dressed. She wanted to spend time with Tyler before her 9 p.m. curfew.

"You keep playin' like that and your scholarship to Howard is in the bag," Terry said.

"Girrrl, I hope to take my game to another level before this season is over. I can't take any chances."

"I know that's right, Girl," Terry said and then exchanged high fives with Imani. Laughter from the other side of the stuffy room caught Imani's attention. She glanced over and saw a foursome huddled together. Imani zeroed in on their conversation.

"Yeah, if Dots wasn't the coach's daughter, she wouldn't be starting. It's her fault we almost lost."

"Yup, and Domino ain't got the skillz to be startin'," Brenda, the only black girl in the group, said.

"She thinks she's so smart. Always sucking up to the teachers and raising her hands. She's the only one who aced that Chemistry exam and just messed up the curve for everybody else," a tall and lanky brunette said.

"Well, her chemistry ain't mixin' with this team," Brenda said. "Plus, Dots thinks she's cute with those blue eyes and good hair."

"What's good hair?" the brunette asked.

"Hair that don't need a perm. See how it lays flat on her head? Her edges are real straight too."

"Like mine?"

"Yeah, but that's an ordinary thing for white people," Brenda said.

Imani knew if she heard their loud conversation, Dominique had too since she was closer to them.

"Excuse y'all," Imani began so loud that she caught everybody's attention. She pointed at the four girls. "But uh, *we* all did our part in almost blowing that game." Imani scanned the faces of all of her teammates. Her eyes ended on Dominique.

Her complexion was so pale that she looked white. The brown freckles stood out against her translucent tone. If you did not know her mother, who looked Caucasian too, you would swear that Dominique was adopted because she looked nothing like her father.

Coach John Wilkens was deep dark chocolate with jet black eyes and tight curly black hair. With that mixture of dark, light, and freckles, they teased Dominique Wilkens with the names Dots and Domino.

"And start callin' Dominique by her real name. Do you know how bad it feels when someone calls you out of your name?" Imani waited a couple of seconds but no one answered. "Well, I do. A crazy girl at this school last year called me Imooni, Ipooni, Irooni, ghetto jock chick, and everything else but Imani. So I know how much it hurts."

"If it bothers her, she should say something. She answers to Domino and Dots," the team's tall center said.

"It's no big deal, Imani. They can call me Dots, Domino, or whatever. It doesn't bother me," Dominique said and then looked down at the cement floor.

"You sure?" Imani asked.

Dominique shook her head but did not make eye contact with Imani. "You can go on. I'll be all right."

Imani did not believe her but decided not to press the issue. She turned and headed for the exit. The cool October breeze greeted her as it brushed against her warm face. Imani took a deep breath of that fresh air and enjoyed the high she always got after she won a game.

"Hey, Queen," a familiar male voice called out from behind her. His voice was as intoxicating as the air she inhaled. Without hesitation, Imani turned around and hugged the guy with that deep voice.

Like Imani, Tyler was a senior at Westmoore. He was 6'4" of fineness with a smooth bronzed complexion and chestnut hued eyes. However, Imani dated the star basketball player for more than his good looks.

"My girl's game was off the hook. Number 12 thought she had you on lockdown but you got her number and called her. But oops, no answer," Tyler said and then hollered. Imani smiled and shook her head.

"See you're too cool to brag, but I'll brag for ya 'cause I read that girl's lips. She was trash-talkin' my Queen big time. But you handled your business."

Imani knew that her milk chocolate face turned a shade or two as she soaked up Tyler's compliments. When she first met him last year, Tyler spoke highly of her skills on the court. He never held back the props and always showed his support.

"You so crazy," she said and then kissed her boyfriend. Imani could have lingered in that moment. However, she feared that her parents would bust them. Imani removed her lips from Tyler's and scanned about the crowd. "Where's my mom and dad?"

"They left. They told me that they had a stop to make and for me to bring you home."

"For real?"

"Yup, but your dad reminded me of your curfew."

"Can you believe that? Here I am a senior and I still hafta be in the house by nine. That's why I can't wait to live on campus."

Imani and Tyler slipped into Tyler's new black sports car that he received for his 17th birthday. The interior smelled of new leather. He turned on the radio, strapped on the seatbelt and shifted into gear. Imani and Tyler waved to their fellow classmates and fans as they crept through the congested parking lot. Then the couple headed out of Hillsdale, an affluent suburb home to both Westmoore and Tyler.

As they drove on, the scenery changed from a serene community with large homes and mansions to abandoned buildings, congested streets and commotion from every direction.

"I'm too hyped to go straight home," Imani said.

"So where you wanna go?"

"Let's stop by my church's recreation center. I want you to meet somebody I've been working with."

* * *

Tyler followed Imani's directions and made a right turn on Spruce Street. He parked in a lot behind the one level white building where a guard was on post. Imani waved at the burly man and he frowned.

"Who's the dude?" he asked Imani as his eyes drifted from Tyler to the car then back to Imani. "What you got yourself mixed up with, Imani? Don't be bringing the wrong element up in here."

"If you stop long enough for me to answer, I'll tell you who he is." Imani pointed to Tyler and said, "Deacon Fields, Tyler, Tyler, Deacon Fields."

"So what you runnin', Boy?"

"Cut it out, Deacon Fields. Tyler's not runnin' any games. He's my boyfriend from the other side of town so stop assuming he's a dealer or a thug."

"If he's your boyfriend, how come I haven't seen him with you in church? Your parents know about him or are y'all creepin'?"

From the frown on Tyler's face, Imani knew that he was annoyed. She rubbed his back. "Deacon Fields has known me all my life, so he's just lookin' out for me."

"Good lookin' out," Tyler told the middle-aged looking man.

"My parents know Tyler. So if this interrogation is over, we're going inside."

Deacon Fields shook Tyler's hand and Imani heard knuckles crack. She smacked Deacon Field's large brown hand and told him, "Okay, he got your message." As Imani turned and walked away she heard, "Your other boyfriend in there is gonna get thrown outta here if he doesn't clean up his act!"

Tyler massaged his hand. "I thought your father had a monster grip, but he's got nothing on that guy and what other boyfriend?"

"At least you know your car is safe." Imani laughed until she noticed from the grimace on Tyler's face that he did not find that humorous. "Give me your hand."

Tyler extended his right hand and Imani guided it to her lips. Tyler drew it back. "Don't be kissin' all over my hand and you got some other guy up in here."

Imani ignored his comment and kissed his hand anyway. Then she massaged it between her hands. A smile replaced the frown on his face. "I'll be right back," Tyler said and walked away.

"Where you going?"

"I want the deacon to shake my other hand."

"You so crazy. Come back here," Imani said and motioned in her direction.

Tyler held open the metal door and Imani strolled through the metal detector and greeted the armed guard who stood behind a desk.

"Yo, Man, you waitin' for an invitation?" the guard asked Tyler who seemed surprised by the security check. "If you decide to walk through, sign in here," the guard told Tyler and pointed to the visitor's log. "And Imani, I don't wanna hafta shoot your boyfriend in there. But if he steps up to me one more time, Imma let a bullet loose in his behind."

"Time out," Tyler began, "who is this boyfriend everybody's talking about?"

"Well that got him through the detector. Now sign in and go through those double doors and check him out for yourself," the guard said.

The hallway led to a huge gym filled with kids of various ages, sizes, shapes, and shades of brown. The decibel level was high as they engaged in half court basketball, volleyball, Ping-Pong, and soccer.

"Yo, Punk! You betta check yo'self. I'm the man up in this piece."

Imani knew that voice. She spotted him and his wild Afro. Clumps of thick brown hair sprouted out in every direction. Imani yelled, "Tariq! Leave Jimmy alone and get over here!"

The 4'11" brown skinned boy's angry expression changed to a toothy smile as he trotted over to Imani. "Yo, Imani, wat up? You know I don't let nobody diss me like that but you 'cause you my woman."

Imani stared at Tariq. His long lashes accentuated his large mahogany eyes. "I'll tell you what's up, Tariq. If you don't check your nasty attitude at the door, they are not gonna let you in here anymore. Why you always startin' something?"

He tilted his head to the side and frowned as gave Tyler a look over. "Who's he?" Tariq asked and then he stepped up to Tyler.

"Not again," Tyler said and then chuckled.

"Yo, Imani, I know this fool ain't laughin' at me. I don't need my brotha to take you out, Punk. I got you."

Imani grabbed a hold of Tariq's pecan colored ear and led him out of the gym. As they approached the front desk, the armed guard patted his gun as he eyed the pint-sized boy. Once outside, Imani released him and he rubbed his ear.

"Imani, I swear if you wasn't my woman I would whoop your–"

"Boy, shut up and get over here." Imani watched as Tariq stomped his foot and then sat next to her on the cement step. "Do not say another word until I finish."

Tariq sucked his teeth and rolled his big eyes.

"The only reason the staff let you come in here is because I keep telling them to give you another chance. But, Tariq, you're out of chances–"

"They be buggin' 'round here. I'm a man, and they gotta respect me!"

"You're 12. You are not a man. You're a 12 year-old boy who needs to listen to a man."

"Don't tell me that's where that punk you brought up in here comes in. I gotta brotha who's more man than that clown could ever be, and I ain't lookin' for no daddy. I ain't even lookin' for my old man."

Imani pulled her shoulder length braids back from her face and thought for a second. *Wow, that's a great idea. I can hook Tyler up with him. Yeah, Tariq could use some male bonding.* "Hummm, let me ask you something? Why do you like me?"

That question made Tariq smile. "Now you talkin' 'bout sumptin, sumptin." He held onto Imani's hands. "Look here, Beautiful," he began in a deeper tone, "I love you, Girrrl. You fine and got skillz. You even be teachin' *me* stuff on the court. Ain't that a blip? A girl, I mean a wo-man, schoolin' me?"

"That's it?" Imani asked.

Tariq's smile disappeared. "No, that ain't all. See you be mad at me and stuff like the knuckleheads 'round here, but we can still rap."

Imani could not believe she caught him in a serious moment. He brought her hand up to his lips and kissed it. "Plus, you an older woman so you understand that I can't be caught up with one female. You let me have other honeys on the side. See what I'm sayin'?"

Imani slipped her hands out of his moist little palms and wiped them off on her sweatpants. She explained to Tariq countless times that she was too old for him. Imani encouraged him to talk to girls his own age. It sounded as if he took her advice.

"It's like this, Tariq. I don't date guys who have other women on the side. It's all about me or I'm out. Now we can be friends and I'll be here for you, but I can't be your woman if you got all those other honeys."

Tariq rubbed his upper lip as if he stroked a moustache. "So hold up. You want me to trade in all my females at school and just be with you?" He shook his head, stood up, and walked around in a circle.

"Yup. So what's it gonna be, Tariq? All of them or just me?" Imani asked and then crossed her fingers.

"See, Boo, it's like this. Me and my brotha Big Mike don't roll like that. He gotta female for every day of the week. Seven different flavors, Boo, you see what I'm sayin'?" He stretched out his arms to the side. "Yo, Imani, you're leavin' a brotha no other choice. I gotta cut you loose. But we friends, and I'll be lookin' out for you." Tariq sat down next to Imani and grabbed both of her hands. "You ain't gonna get all soft and start cryin' are you?"

Imani shook her head "no." If she opened her mouth, she would have laughed.

* * *

It was close to Imani's curfew as Tyler drove her home. She filled Tyler in on her conversation with Tariq and tried to convince Tyler to be Tariq's mentor. Every time she asked, he said, "no." She tried another angle. "If you won't do it for Tariq, do it for me."

"Oh come on, Imani. Why you gotta go there? That demon is not gonna listen to me. Plus, I can't win the state championship if I'm doing time for murder."

"Murder?"

"In the first degree," Tyler added.

They stared at one another but could not keep a straight face. In between laughter, Tyler said, "Okay, I'll try but I can't promise you for how long."

"That's cool," Imani said. She leaned over and kissed his cheek. Her long fingers glided over the wavy texture of his hair. She loved to play with the tiny slick curls that formed on the top of Tyler's head.

"You're teasing me 'cause I gotta keep both hands on the wheel, right?" he asked.

"All I'm doing is stroking your baby fine hair."

"The key word is stroking. You are stroking me and I can't stroke you back."

"Oooh, Tyler Powers. You're so naaasty."

Tyler laughed and then glanced at Imani. "What? Wasn't 'stroking' your word?"

Imani laughed. "Yeah, but it's how you said it."

Tyler parked the car in front of Imani's apartment building. Although it was close to 9 p.m., groups of school-aged looking guys and girls hung out on the steps and around the doorway of the red brick building. The temperature dropped. Yet, they did not seem fazed by the cold air.

"Look how bold they are," Imani began, "they sell drugs out in the open."

"I guess they're not afraid of doing time," Tyler said. He reclined his seat and Imani did the same. Tyler stretched his long arm behind Imani's headrest. Imani tried to relax but there were too many distractions. In addition to the drug deals, cars raced through the narrow street. The couple tolerated those who stopped and checked out Tyler's car. Some pressed their faces against the side windows and peered inside.

Imani turned on her side and got a better view of Tyler. "As hard as I try, I can never get comfortable with you coming to this raggedy side of town. I know you say you don't care where I live, but it still bothers me."

Tyler turned on his side and faced Imani. "I come here because you're here, and what do you have to be ashamed of? Look at you. You're gorgeous, smart, funny, and easy to talk to. Then to top it off, you have the nerve to have mad skillz on the court."

"Oh stop," Imani said as she waved her hand.

Tyler took hold of that hand and gazed into her eyes. "I'm serious, Imani, and with the off the hook season you're havin', you're on your way to Howard on a b-ball scholarship. And my father says that college can take you wherever you wanna go."

Imani stared at Tyler's gorgeous face and wondered how someone so young could be so together. "You sound like an old man."

"I am an old man. Your old man," Tyler said and gave her a smile that could melt ice.

"Yeah, you better remember that too. I see how those girls be sweatin' you since you got this bad ride."

"Do you also see how I be duckin' & weavin'? It's like that old MC Hammer jam, 'Can't Touch This'."

"As long as I don't have to use a hammer and go banging some of them over the head."

"You know you're not the violent type," Tyler said.

"You know I'm just playin'. But seriously, I love you and all, but I'm not fightin' other girls over you.

'Cause if I have to fight for you, that means you didn't love me enough or respect me enough to tell them you got a girl and to back off." Imani looked straight into his brown eyes. "I can trust you, right?"

The warmth of Tyler's lips took the chill off hers. He backed up and said, "I thought you knew you could."

"And will you be honest with me, Tyler, and tell me straight up when you want, if you want, you know, when you want out?" Imani's brain told her heart not to go soft. Yet, her eyes did not get that message in time.

Tyler wiped away the fresh tears from her cheeks and then hugged her. "Why would I want out? Huh?"

Imani tried to shrug her shoulders but he held her tight. "Do you remember all of the crap we went through before we officially hooked up?" Tyler asked.

"Ummm hummm."

"All that drama with crazy behind Bhriana and back stabbin' Steven and uh what's his name?"

"Jazz," Imani said without hesitation.

"Yeah, Jazz," Tyler said and then shifted his head from side to side. "All of those nuts took us through major drama," Tyler added. He released her and stroked Imani's braids away from her tear-stained face.

She turned away from him. *Why are you still crying? Didn't he give you all the right answers? Don't you believe him? Don't you deserve to be happy?* Imani asked herself as she stared out the front windshield. She felt Tyler's warm hand on the side of her face. He guided her back in his direction.

"Queen, our love is for real. This is never goodbye."

FATIMA

Fatima dusted salt off her brown polyester pants. "I can't believe I'm still workin' here," she said aloud. She checked herself out in the bathroom mirror and slicked down the edges of her hairline with water. The strands of hair sprung back up. "I'm sick of sweatin' out my perm." Fatima sighed and threw on a baseball-type cap.

The dark brown cap was a close match to Fatima's rich cocoa complexion. She applied mocha pressed powder on her nose and dulled the shine. Fatima was careful not to get the powder on her gold ball nose ring. Her doe shaped ebony eyes stared at the yellow chicken embroidered on the front of the cap. "This uniform's whack but I'm still cute," she told the chicken. She pulled out a tube of lipstick from her pant pocket and spread the burgundy shade over her full lips.

Someone pushed open the wood door so hard that it slammed into the gray wall. "No wonder we're out of fries. Your shift's not over yet, Fatima, so let's move it."

Her high-strung manager turned away and marched off before Fatima responded. When the door closed all the way, Fatima mimicked her boss in the mirror. "We're out of fries, let's move it, drop them fries, we're out of fries..."

Fatima returned to her station and dropped two metal baskets of fries in a deep container filled with bubbly hot oil. Fatima stared at the cashiers' backs. That was the position she desired because Fatima wanted to handle the money and to talk to the customers. She was particularly interested in the cute guys. She would perspire less too because the cashiers stood closer to the door where a cool breeze flowed as patrons came in and out. Fatima mimicked one of the cashiers. "Welcome to Chicken Shack. May I take your order?"

Fatima rolled her eyes and shook her head. *May I take your order? That's a stupid question. I wish one day a customer said, "no." I would love to hear the cashier's comeback.* Fatima chuckled to herself and continued her private conversation until the buzzer signaled that the fries were ready. One at a time, she grasped the long handle and lifted the basket of golden brown fries out of the container. She shook the basket and drained the excess grease. Fatima dumped the thin fries in a bin and then sprinkled them with salt. She shoved the hot fries into regular and jumbo size cartons. Fatima repeated that routine until her shift ended.

After Fatima clocked out, Rachel, the supervisor who hired Fatima last summer, gave Fatima permission to take home a half dozen crispy wings.

"I don't care if they're cold, Rachel. I have to bus it home since Hanif's not here. He's still in North Carolina."

"Isn't that Hanif standing over there?" Rachel asked and nodded her head to the left.

"Oh snap! I'm outta here," Fatima said. She took off in Hanif's direction. "Why didn't you call me? When did you get back? How's your mom? Dang, I missed you," Fatima rattled off. Before Hanif answered any of his girlfriend's questions, Fatima locked lips with him.

Once inside his midnight blue old model sports car, Fatima dominated the conversation. "My girl Imani is wrapped all tight around Tyler. We don't hang like we used to. As much as I hate the Chicken Shack, at least I had something else to do other than goin' to school and comin' home watchin' TV with Grandma and..."

Fatima continued until she noticed that Hanif had not said a word. Physically, he looked fine. A fresh low haircut showed off his big ears. His baby smooth face was clean-shaven as usual. However, that wide smile and crazy sense of humor was absent.

"What's up, Hanif? Is your mom all right?"

Hanif hunched his shoulders as he shook his head. "I dunno. The doctors were runnin' tests, but we haven't heard anything yet. I didn't wanna leave, but she made me come back to school for midterms tomorrow."

"Your brothers can check on her."

"Plueeeze, I spent more time at the hospital with her than both of them put together. She can't count on 'em being around. They're just downright selfish. I'm the only one she can depend on," Hanif said. He slammed on his brakes and threw his right arm in front of Fatima who was inches from the dashboard. "You all right?"

"Yeah, I'm cool," Fatima said as she reached for her seatbelt and fastened it. "Put yours on too."

When Hanif stopped at the next light, he did just that. Fatima caressed the back of his head. "You know that's messed up, right? They're in their 30's and here you are 19 in college doin' more for her than them."

"I know," Hanif said.

"I hope it ain't nothin' serious."

"Me too. But if it is serious," he began and shook his head, "I'll hafta go back home."

"I hope you mean just while she's in the hospital. You're not gonna stay are you?"

Hanif did not answer or look at Fatima.

"What's the deal, Hanif?"

"I don't wanna talk about it anymore."

"Pull over. Go up to the next block and pull over," Fatima demanded and pointed to the spot where she wanted him to park.

Hanif stopped by a huge empty lot where a major department store once stood. Next to the lot was a row of boarded-up buildings. Fatima watched a couple of young girls as they pushed baby carriages. Then she turned to Hanif and stared at him.

"Why are you looking at me like that? I don't know how long I would hafta be there, Fatima. It's not like I wanna leave here. I'm just settling into college and Lord knows I love me some you but," he paused and shrugged his shoulders, "but that's my mama."

Fatima sucked her teeth. "Dang, I can't catch a break. I finally hook up with a guy I thought I could be tight with, but he's more loyal to his mama than me."

"If you had a mother, you would understand."

"Why you had to go there?" Fatima asked as tears filled her eyes.

Hanif looked out the window then back to Fatima. "I can't believe I said that. I'm sorry, Fatima." He touched

Fatima's hand and she jerked it away. "That was stupid, Baby, I'm sorry."

"Whatever," Fatima said.

"I love you. Don't make me choose between Mama and you. Plus, ain't we puttin' the cart before the horse?"

"What?"

"We don't know what's happening with Mama. Who said that even if I hafta go back that we've gotta break up? If we really love each other, can't we make it work no matter what happens?"

"Forget it, Hanif. I don't wanna talk about it either. Just take me home."

When they reached Fatima's apartment building, Hanif escorted her to the door. Hanif grabbed hold of her hand as Fatima inserted her key into the lock. "I am sorry. Please forgive me. I ain't too proud to beg," he said and got down on his knees.

"You serious, huh?"

"Don't I look serious?" Hanif asked and batted his long eyelashes. He cupped his hands in a praying position. "Please forgive me."

Fatima smiled. "Yeah, I forgive you. Now get up," she said and wrapped her arms around his waist. "You wanna come in?"

Hanif embraced and then kissed her. "Ummm I wish I could," he began, "but I got a lot of crammin' to do. Tell Grandma Rose I'll catch her later."

"She talks about you all the time. I think she missed you more than I did."

"That's because we shoot the breeze and talk about the soap operas. Then she talks about how skinny I look and whips up a meal. Ain't no poor college student gonna turn down free food."

"I would break you off a piece of this chicken," Fatima began and waved the box under his nose, "but I'm giving it to your girlfriend in there," she said and nodded in the direction of the door.

"That's all right. I ain't thinkin' about food. Just you and the books, Boo, that's all I'm thinkin' about."

"I gotta hit the books too 'cause your girlfriend right here ain't doing summer school again. My last year too? I be dang if I'm gonna serve time one day longer than I have to. I'm outta there and the Chicken Shack."

"The Chicken Shack ain't that bad."

"Boy, your nose stopped up or something? Can't you smell the grease?"

Hanif sniffed her neck. "Sho nuff and I could sop you up with a buttermilk biscuit." Hanif kissed her neck.

It tickled and Fatima loved it. She squirmed and giggled. When Hanif stopped, Fatima kissed his soft lips. "I love you."

"Love ya back and you're making it hard for a brotha to leave your Fa-ti-ma-licious self."

Fatima repeated the word, "Fa-ti-ma-licious," and then hollered. She laughed until her sides ached and watched Hanif as he strutted off.

Fatima stepped into the small living room. The light from the television reflected like a projector on the wall behind the couch where Grandma Rose sat. The full-figured woman's head was laid back and her mouth wide open. She had a rough manly snore that no longer fazed her only grandchild.

Fatima turned on the black halogen lamp in the corner and it lit up the entire room. She sat next to Grandma Rose and tapped her arm. "Grandma, go to bed before you break your neck."

"Huh? What? I ain't sleep."

Fatima laughed. "As Hanif would put it, you were callin' in the hogs."

Grandma Rose grunted. She pulled a white lace hankie out of her ample bosom and dabbed at her eyes and the corners of her mouth.

"I brought some crispy wings. You sittin' up here sleepin' with your dentures in so you might as well eat."

Grandma Rose laughed. "You always makin' fun of my false teeth. What you got against 'em?"

"Nothing." Fatima smiled and then covered her mouth as she snickered.

Grandma Rose pinched Fatima's cheek. "Ouch!" Fatima hollered and laughed again.

"All right, lil' miss missy thang. One day you're gonna be walkin' around here wid a pair of 'em. I hope to God that I can live to see it."

"If you lived another hundred years, you'll still see these in my mouth," Fatima said and showed off her white teeth. "Now, do you want this chicken or what?"

Grandma Rose frowned and rubbed her stomach. "I'll pass. I haven't had an appetite these past few days and just tired all the time. Maybe I'll break down and go see old Doc Floyd. I hate paying that old man money when all I probably need is some vitamins."

Fatima removed her leather jacket and tossed it onto the empty love seat. She took the box of chicken and went into the kitchen. "I don't care if I ever eat another piece of this crap as long as I'm black."

She heard Grandma Rose as she broke out in laughter. Fatima opened the refrigerator door and a rotten odor invaded her nostrils. "Daaang, what died in here?" She peeked inside and detected a few more boxes of chicken in there. Fatima inspected them and saw that they were untouched. Fatima searched about the refrigerator and noticed moldy fruit and brown vegetables that used to be green.

"Grandma, what are you eating? This fridge is full of rotten food."

"I told you my appetite's gone. And you're never home long enough to sit down to a full meal, so I don't bother to cook much."

Fatima got busy and tossed out all of the spoiled food. Moments later, she returned to the living room and sat with Grandma Rose. "Hanif's back. He said, 'hey'."

"How's his mama?"

"She's still in the hospital, but they don't know what's wrong yet."

"That's the only boy I seen you wid that I like. He got manners and common sense. It's 'yes m'am, no m'am, please and thank you'. His mama done good."

Fatima reached out and rubbed Grandma Rose's hands. Fatima felt the thick veins that protruded beneath her thin skin. "You done good too, Grandma."

Grandma Rose smiled. "Lord knows since the day your mama and daddy were killed in that car accident, I tried my best to do right by you. That's how I honored my poor daughter's death. Ummm hummm ever since you were a baby, I have cared for you like I was the one who birthed you." Grandma Rose patted Fatima's hand. "My report card ain't complete until you march down that aisle in June. Then I'll say I've done good. If you go to college, then I'll say I did real good. You do all that without getting knocked up–"

"Grandma!"

"Don't Grandma me. Just keep your drawls up until you get married and you ain't got nothing to worry about. You know your aunt and uncle done put out your fast-behind cousin and her baby?"

"What!"

"Ummm hummm, both of 'em in that old women's shelter downtown on Washington Street. Aunt June said Mercedes wanted to run the streets and didn't wanna work, didn't wanna go to school, didn't wanna hold the baby's daddy responsible or nothing. So she put her 17-year-old daughter and one month old grandbaby out."

"Dang, that's messed up."

"It may be but Mercedes needs to get off her lazy behind and take responsibility for the mess she got herself in."

"But c'mon. Throwin' out your own blood? You wouldn't do that to me. Would you?"

"Like I said, keep them drawls up."

Fatima's cell phone rang. She hesitated to answer it because she wanted a definite answer from Grandma Rose. She punched the green button. "You know who you called so speak."

"Why you so rough? When are you gonna learn how to answer the phone?"

"Well, if it ain't my girl, Imani. Ain't got time for a sistah no more now that you all up in Tyler's face."

"Girrrl, you 're just mad 'cause Hanif's out of town. Otherwise, you wouldn't be missin' me."

Fatima looked away from Grandma Rose and whispered, "Look at how many boyfriends I done had since second grade and I always took time out for you." Fatima glanced over at her grandmother. It did not look as if she paid Fatima any attention. Still, Fatima did not want Grandma Rose in that conversation. "'Scuse me, Grandma. I'll be right back."

"Chile, don't even bother. I'm getting up and goin' to bed." She eased up then flopped back down.

"Grandma! You all right?"

"Chile, stop fussin' over me. My foot just slipped is all." She rose again and made it up all the way. Then Grandma Rose shuffled off to her room.

"Grandma fakin' like she cool but something ain't right with her," Fatima told Imani. "She hates goin' to the doctor but I may have to make her go."

"She won't be able to fake a doctor out. So yeah, make her go," Imani said.

"Girrrl, don't even flip the script. I was in the middle of tellin' you off and here's the deal. You gotta learn how to spend time with your man and your sistah-friend. So don't make me come over there and hurt you."

"Dang. Cut your sistah-friend a break. You know Tyler's my first real boyfriend, so this dating stuff is new to me. I didn't get started in the second grade like you."

"You right, you right," Fatima said.

"And that poor Bobby Rogers is probably still roaming around the playground looking for you," Imani said and they both hollered.

Fatima doubled over and slid off the couch. Just the thought of skinny Bobby with the ashy knocked-knee cracked her up. "Wooo, Girl. Let's just leave that boy in the playground. Don't mention his name again. You're killin' me," Fatima said and wiped her eyes. She crawled up onto the couch and sighed.

"But on a serious tip, Girrrl, my cousin Mercedes, well you know we all call her Mercy, got thrown out of her house with the baby!"

"Get out! For real?"

"Yup. Ain't that a blip?"

"Hummm, I don't know why I'm so shocked. My daddy would do the same thing. He wouldn't wait for me to have the baby. He'd be like, 'if your behind was grown enough to lay down and have sex, your grown behind is grown enough to support your grown self and that baby. So pack your stuff and get your grown behind out of my house right now!' How was that, Fatima? Am I right?"

Fatima laughed. She caught her breath and said, "Yup, yup. You right you right. That's straight up Mr. Jackson but Grandma? Daaang, I believe she would do the same thing. She warned me twice tonight to 'keep my drawls up'."

Both girls laughed. Fatima kicked off her tan sneakers and reclined on the sofa. She pulled a red plaid wool blanket over her feet and propped her head on a floral throw pillow. "Anyhow, I'm visitin' Mercy tomorrow to see if she needs anything. You wanna come with me?"

"I would if I could, Girl, but I gotta cram for the SATs. The pressure's on because I gotta hit at least 1175 to be considered for a Howard scholarship."

Fatima slapped her forehead and sat straight up. "Oooh, snap. I forgot about that test."

"Forgot? We're taking it the Saturday after next! On my birthday at that!" Imani exclaimed.

"Eeelll that's messed up. Who wants to take that crap on their birthday?"

"It's not like I have a choice. Well, yeah I do. I could take it in December but that would be a one shot deal and whatever score I get that's what Howard would see. But if I take it now, then I can take it again in December to try and get a higher score."

"Ummmp, I ain't sweatin' no scores. First off, I'm only doin' this to get you and Grandma off my back. I don't plan on goin' to college full-time. Secondly, and I wish y'all were hearin' me, I'm going to beauty school full-time. Thirdly, how high you think I gotta score to get into Bedford Community College?"

"Are you finished or is there a fourthly?"

"You makin' fun of me?" Fatima asked.

Imani chuckled. "I don't think fourthly is a word."

"Well, it is now. Fourthly, I ain't worried because my school don't have all those fancy prep courses like Westmoore. It's still like it was when you were here. You're lucky to get your own books."

"Eeelll don't remind me. I shared books with snot-nosed Barbara and that funky boy. What's his name?"

"It's a lot of 'em. Which one you talkin' 'bout?"

"Oooh, I think it was Teddy. You know that boy who was scared of deodorant?" Imani asked.

Fatima screamed and they both hollered. "I don't remember if his name was Teddy, but I know he had the teddies all up in his head," Fatima said.

"Teddies, ringworm, and you name it. Wooo, Girl, thank God this b-ball scholarship was my ticket out last year. Two years in Bedford High was enough. I wish you could have gotten out and gone to a better school."

Fatima caught her breath before she responded. "It's cool 'cause if I was in an uppity school like Westmoore, they would have thrown me out after the first day. Either that or I would have jetted outta there once I saw all them books and all that homework." Fatima reclined and stretched out.

"Why don't you come by tomorrow and take some of my material. I'm cool with English. It's the math that's kickin' my butt," Imani said.

"All of it's kickin' me. I don't even know now if it will even matter."

"Stop makin' excuses and come and get this stuff or I'm gonna call Grandma Rose and tell her–"

"Dang, Imani. You don't hafta threatin' a sistah."

"Now ain't you glad I called? Like you said, I need to stay in touch more often."

"Yeah, Imani, I'm so glad."

Imani laughed and then asked, "So what's up with Hanif? Have you heard from him?"

"Oh yeah, Girl, he's back but I don't know..."

* * *

The Hope House, a shelter for women, was located in the busy downtown area of Bedford. Years ago, the old tan brick three storied building was filled to capacity with abused wives who decided that enough was enough. They mustered up the courage and freed themselves and their children from bondage. However, the times changed. Unwed teenaged mothers and their children packed the place. The young mothers battled against something: the father or fathers of their children, drugs, alcohol, their pasts, their futures, and themselves.

"Who you here to see?" the guard asked Fatima.

"Mercy, I mean Mercedes Newman."

The armed guard dialed a number and announced that Mercedes Newman had a visitor. He looked up at Fatima and asked, "What's your name?"

"Fatima Russell, I'm her cousin."

The guard repeated what Fatima said and then sat in silence with the black receiver to his ear. Fatima assumed that he was on hold. "We don't have anyone on the restricted list for her. I believe you're Ms. Newman's first visitor. They're probably asking your cousin if she wants to see you."

"Oh," Fatima said and nodded up and down.

"Okay, I'll process her and let her through."

The tall beefy guard pushed the guest log in front of Fatima. "Sign here and then empty your pockets and your purse and put the contents in this basket."

"What? Why I hafta do that?"

"Just to make sure you're not bringing any weapons or anything that can be used as a weapon or any drugs in here."

"Daaang, is this a prison or a shelter?"

"Some of the women in there may view it as a prison. Hey look, it's my job to protect them and you. So don't give me a hard time, please."

Fatima followed his instructions and cringed as he fumbled through her feminine hygiene items. He pointed to the metal detector and she walked through it and shook her head. *What has my aunt and uncle done to my poor cousin?* She gathered her belongings and then proceeded into a hallway.

"Ms. Russell," a stocky woman with salt and pepper colored hair began, "Mercedes is waiting for you in the family room. Follow me."

En route to the family room, Fatima bypassed a playroom filled with kids. They stumbled over bright-colored plastic toys on the dark green carpet as they chased one another. There was one tiny television in the corner and the cartoons were on.

"Something stinks," Fatima said and pinched her nose as they passed by a kitchen. The scent of scorched peas or some other vegetable filled the air.

"Yes, that's our kitchen crew at their finest," the woman said and then chuckled. They walked by a large dining room and then arrived at their destination.

"Hey, Cuz," Mercedes said.

"Enjoy your visit," the woman told both girls before she left. Fatima stared at Mercedes. She did not look like the glam-fabulous sistah she remembered. Even when she was pregnant, Mercedes dressed well and the hair was always together. The long black tee shirt over the black bulky fleece sweat pants did not do the short girl justice.

"Can a cousin get some love?" Mercedes asked and opened her arms.

"Hey, Girl," Fatima said then embraced her. She felt the roundness of Mercedes' mid section. Fatima pulled back and examined her cousin. A red and white bandana covered Mercedes' hair. The flawless brown skin, which ran in the family, looked good. A bit ashy around the chapped lips but her skin still looked good.

"How did you find me?" Mercedes asked and flashed a smile. Fatima knew it was a fake one because Mercedes' dimples were shallow.

"Grandma told me but I wished you had called."

"It all went down so fast that I didn't have time to think. But I'm glad you came 'cause I need your help."

"That's why I'm here. What you need?"

"I gotta get outta here. They got too many rules. It's like being on lockdown at home. I ain't even got my own room. The baby and me share a room with two other girls and their kids. You believe that crap?"

Fatima shook her head "no" as she surveyed the small family room. A potted green plant in the corner, a vending machine, a wooden center table and chairs filled the space. "Where's Alexus?"

"Sleepin' upstairs."

"By herself?" Fatima asked.

Mercedes waved her hand. "She's all right. She can't walk or crawl so where she gonna go?"

"Let's check her out anyway," Fatima suggested.

"Yeah, so you can see for yourself why you gotta get us outta here."

They entered the well-lit room that contained three bunk beds. The mothers slept on top and the babies or kids on the bottom. Bright colored crayon marks decorated the beige walls. Three wooden dressers and one closet completed the room. Fatima saw a tiny light brown head poked out from under a pink cotton blanket. "Oooh, there's Alexus. She still ain't got no hair!"

"Shhh, plueeeze don't wake her up. I don't wanna hear her cryin'. All she does is cry, eat, spit up, take a dump, and sleep. My favorite part is when she sleeps."

"My bad," Fatima said and placed a finger over her lips. She wondered how Mercedes' parents could have tossed out their beautiful granddaughter.

"You see this crap hole we're livin' in? The bathroom is down the hall and everybody on this floor shares it so you know it's nasty. I wouldn't step foot in those showers. If you don't believe me," Mercedes said and pointed to the hallway, "go check it out."

"Naaaw, that's all right. I believe you," Fatima said as she eased down on the bed where the small bundle laid. She watched her tiny back as it rose and fell. "I knew Aunt June was pissed off when she found out you were pregnant, but I thought she got over it."

"She did when she thought I was gonna give the baby up for adoption. Then I backed out at the last second and she's been ridin' me ever since. You know how old people be buggin'."

"So what happened?"

"She and Daddy expect me to take care of Alexus 24-7 like I ain't got nothing else to do. They're right there in the house so why can't they watch her when I wanna go out? Shooot, I'm young. You can't expect me to stay in the house all day. Now I can see if they were not around, but they live in that house too."

"What about school?"

"They want me to go back and I will. I just wanted to give myself some time to adjust to the baby. See what I'm sayin'?"

"I feel ya," Fatima said and then inhaled the sweet smell of baby powder. She yearned to hold Alexus. Instead, Fatima rubbed her small back and felt the warmth from her body as it seeped through the blanket.

"I might transfer to Culver High because I hear they got a daycare center right in the school."

"Yeah, that's what I heard too. You should check that out," Fatima said as her cousin eased down next to the bed and on to the hardwood floor.

"Sooo, what's up with Troy?" Fatima asked as she viewed his picture in a black plastic frame on top of a dresser. "Has he been around?"

"He's comin' today. My man is so sweet, Fatima. Troy hooked me up with a pager and a cell phone."

"So what is he sayin'?"

"He's glad I'm outta that house. Whenever he wanted to hang out, my father was like 'you can hang your behind in here and take care of your daughter.' So he got tired of hearin' that and stopped comin' over to the house. And if I lose him, I'll never forgive my parents, and I won't ever speak to them again."

"Stop buggin', Mercy."

"I'm serious. Troy's young too and we both like to party. My father doesn't get it. See what I'm sayin'?"

"Yeah, ummm hummm, I see." Fatima nodded her head. *I bet he does like to party.* Fatima turned from the picture and looked at her cousin. "Is he slippin' you bills or what?"

"Now you sound like my nosy parents. How can I get money from him if all he has is a little part-time gig after school?"

"So I guess the answer is 'no'. He ain't helpin' you out with Alexus."

"He loves me, Fatima, and that baby and that's more love than I'm getting from so called family. So right now, that's enough for me. And if all you gonna do is dog me, then this visit's over."

Fatima felt low. *Dang, you were supposed to help her not piss her off. How would you feel if you were in her sneaks? No, you ain't feelin' Troy. But he's her man not yours so squash the attitude and do the right thing.*

"Mercedes Newman," someone yelled. "Do you wanna see a guy named Troy Jones?"

Mercedes' face lit up and her deep dimples returned. She skipped out of the room and leaned over the banister. "Send him up," she hollered and ran back into the bedroom. "How do I look?" Mercedes asked and then ran to a mirror and checked herself out. "You got any make-up on you?"

As Fatima passed a tube of lipstick and eye shadow to her, Troy entered the room. His hands were behind his back. He smiled at Mercedes and brought his right hand around in front of him. "For you," he said.

Fatima sucked her teeth at the sight of the limp bunch of flowers and then she bit her tongue. *He got those from the supermarket. All dried up and dead lookin'.* She stood and watched Mercedes and Troy as they displayed their affection for one another. When she got tired of that scene, Fatima spoke up, "'Scuse y'all but if y'all wanna be alone, I'm headin' out."

"Don't go!" Mercedes said so loud that Fatima jumped. She glanced down at Alexus. The noise had not disturbed the baby.

"We can't have a man in our room one-on-one."

Fatima and Troy gawked at one another but neither spoke. He turned his attention back to Mercedes. "So how's my woman? You lookin' all right."

Pssst. Standing up there lyin', Fatima thought.

"You know if I could get you outta here I would. But, Baby, ain't no way my peeps gonna let you move in."

Fatima nodded up and down. *Ummm hummm now he's shootin' straight.*

"I know," Mercedes said and kissed him.

"Not bad," Troy said as he surveyed the room.

Fatima rolled her eyes at him while Troy's eyes stayed fixed on Mercedes. *Boy? What room you in? Them cornrows must be so tight that they're makin' your vision blurry. Daaang, I can't stand a lyin' somebody.*

"At least I know where my woman is and I don't have to get past your momz and pops to get to you."

Fatima nodded again. *Yeah, now that's the real deal. He just wants free access to her behind.* Fatima leaned forward so her head would not hit the bottom of the top bunk bed and stood straight up.

"How's that new pager and cell phone workin'?" Troy asked Mercedes.

"Fine."

"I was just wondering 'cause it took you too long to return that last page. Why was that?"

"I was probably waitin' to use the bathroom or changin' the baby's diaper."

Fatima crossed her arms in front of her and moved her head back and forth from Mercedes to Troy as if she watched a tennis match.

"Ummmp, well you're gonna have to work on that. When I page you it's because I want to talk to you ASAP, understand? So either you keep that cell phone on or get quicker with returnin' pages. Understand?"

Mercedes glanced down at the flowers.

"Let me see your phone."

Mercedes lifted up her tee shirt and unclipped the cell phone from the waistband of her sweatpants.

"When you gonna lose that gut? Huh?"

No his roly-poly behind didn't go there. Don't look like he's missin' no meals and he surely ain't delivered no baby. I done heard enough. I'm outta here, Fatima told herself and zipped up her jacket.

Troy snatched the phone out of Mercedes' hand. "Let's see who you been callin'."

"What!" Fatima yelled and then slapped her hand over her mouth. The baby whimpered.

"Shhh, I told you don't wake her. And, Troy, who do you think I've been callin'?"

"I dunno. You free from daddy but not me. I don't want you to think that you have the right to go buck wild. You're my baby's mama and you're mine. Understand?"

Fatima felt her pent up aggression as it crept up her throat. She closed her mouth but her brain could not keep it shut. "I'm gonna try and talk my Grandma into getting your," she flexed two fingers on both hands that symbolized quotation marks, "'baby's mama' outta here and to stay with us. Do you have a problem with that?"

"As long as y'all mind your business and not get in our way, then I don't have a problem with that."

Fatima stepped up to Troy and stared up at him until her eyes stung. She cocked her head to the side. "Don't diss me or my grandma and I won't hurt you. Now do *you* understand?"

DOMINIQUE

Dominique's stomach growled. She glanced at Imani who sat next to her on the cold hardwood floor. It did not appear that Imani heard that noise. Dominique's father rushed in and blew the silver whistle that hung from a light blue cord around his neck. The girls in his gym class jumped at attention. The gym was silent.

"Good morning, ladies."

"Good morning, Mr. Wilkens," the class said. All eyes were on the 6'8" former pro player whose career prematurely ended after a severe back injury. He was bitter when he left the game that he loved. For years, he could not bear to watch a basketball game. At a young age, Dominique showed an interest in the sport and that renewed his passion for the game. He switched careers from accounting to coaching and instructed at middle schools and lesser-known high schools.

Westmoore was his first coaching position for a prestigious private high school. The girls' team was talented enough to take City and possibly the State Championship. If they went all the way, that assured Coach Wilkens' advancement into the college ranks. Another major benefit as staff at Westmoore was that his daughter received a quality education, free.

"The rope climbing test is today," Mr. Wilkens said. He waited until the sighs subsided before he continued. "So the quicker we get through this, then the sooner you can play volleyball."

The group trudged over to the rope. Dominique shuffled along and the soles of her size 10 sneakers squeaked against the pinewood floor. She stared at the rope. "I hate this," she mumbled.

"I want the ladies on my basketball team to go first. Then go down to the other end of the court and practice your free-throws."

"Oooh, maaan, why can't we play volleyball?" Dominique whined. She realized how loud that question was as her father marched up to her. He took a hold of her arm and pulled her off to the side.

"Don't ever question what I tell you to do. I am the teacher and you are the student. You do as I say and I don't ever want to remind you not to disrespect me in front of my class. Are you hearing me?"

Dominique placed her hands on her hips and looked down at her baby blue and white sneakers. *Don't disrespect him? Well, what about me?. Now those girls have something else to throw in my face. I know they're watching and laughing. I know they are.*

"Dominique, answer me," her father demanded.

"Yes, Sir. I hear you."

"Good. Now join the others."

Dominique returned to the group but looked at no one, except Imani, straight in the face. Mr. Wilkens glanced down at his clipboard and called out, "Imani, you're up."

The girls clapped and cheered her on. Imani stepped up to the rope and placed one fist over the other.

"Ready, set, go!" Mr. Wilkens shouted. Imani's long body scooted up the rope and then back down.

"Smokin'," her teammate Terry yelled out.

"Good job, Imani, now get started on those free throws. Dominique, you're up."

A couple of girls snickered. Imani was the only one who encouraged Dominique. "Go, Girl. You can do it," Imani told her as she clapped her hands.

*I hate this rope. I hate this school. I hate those stupid girls. I hate...*Dominique chanted to herself as she approached the tan braided thick rope. The knot in her stomach felt as big as the one tied at the end of the rope. She wiped her sweaty palms on her white sweatpants before she grabbed on to the rope. "Go!" her father hollered. She inched her 5'10" frame about half way up. Her arms ached and threatened to give out on her.

"Keep moving!" Mr. Wilkens yelled.

"You can do it!" Imani's voice traveled from the other end of the gym.

Dominique felt flushed. She knew that her pale face was blood red. Sweat dripped down her temples and armpits. She gripped so tight and tugged so hard on the thick coil that her hands and fingers burned. "Forget this," she mumbled and slid back down the rope. When her feet touched the floor, she shuffled to the other end of the court. Dominique never looked back as her father said, "That's only gonna get you a 'C.' I hope you put forth a better effort in the game tonight."

After class, Dominique ate lunch with Imani in the school cafeteria. Her ordeal in gym did not kill her appetite. Dominique devoured her double pizza burger, large fries, and slice of carrot cake.

"You gotta give yourself credit for tryin'. It's not easy climbing that monster," Imani said.

Dominique did not answer. She picked up her jumbo-sized soda and shook it.

"You made a lot of free-throws so that's good."

"Not as many as you," Dominique said and then sipped the last of her grape soda through the red straw.

"Hey, Imani," Christina said. She stood at the end of the table between Dominique and Imani. Christina was one of the few black girls at Westmoore.

"What's up, Girl?" Imani asked and then pointed to Dominique. "Have you met Dominique?"

Dominique glanced at her and mumbled, "Hi."

Christina nodded. "Yeah, I've met Dots."

"You wanna hang with us?" Imani asked as she tapped on the light blue chair next to her.

Christina looked at Dominique again and then scanned about the cafeteria. "I would, Imani, but uh, I promised ummm Joanne and 'em that I was doing lunch with them today. I'll catch you later."

Dominique watched as Christina sat down with Joanne and crew. They peeked at Dominique and giggled. Dominique pushed her brown tray aside and leaned forward. "Let me ask you something, Imani. Why do you hang out with me?"

"What?"

"If you haven't noticed, nobody here likes me. I'm too white for the black girls and too black for the white girls. So I just don't fit in anywhere. I hate this school and these think-they're-all-that-people. Joanne and her clique roll their eyes at me every time I give the right answer in class. Then her two-faced self wants me to sneak answers to her when we take a test. At least I had a couple of for real friends at Parker High."

"I don't think your complexion or your long hair has anything to do with it. It's tough coming here as a Junior and the new girl on campus. I know because last year I was the new girl. And, Girrrl, I went through some drama," Imani said and then laughed.

"I can't believe you're laughing about it."

"Hey, Imani. You ready to kick some Cleveland butt tonight?"

"Yeah. I'm ready, Mark," Imani hollered back as he sat two tables across from them. Imani turned her attention back to Dominique. "It wasn't funny then but I can laugh about it now because it's over. Christina and Mark ain't say boo to me last year. But they get used to you being around, and then they start speaking to you. I guess that's one of the reasons why I talk to you because I know what you're going through."

Dominique felt the water as it accumulated in her aqua eyes. *Don't blink and they won't fall*. She was humiliated enough for one day. Dominique did not want the word, "crybaby," added to her peers' list of insults.

"My mother told me that I am who I am. You can't change your eye color or skin tone. That's how God made you. So, if some people don't like it, forget them. Somebody out there will like Dominique for Dominique and that's who you hang with."

Dominique blinked and was relieved that no tears fell. She figured that it was safe so Dominique spoke. "Okaaay, I hear what you're sayin' but it's hard. You're so popular now and I wish I could be the same way."

"It's gonna take time, Dominique."

"Well, at least I have you. Thanks for making me feel better, Imani."

That good feeling carried over from lunch and through the second quarter of the late afternoon game. It was in the third quarter that Dominique's mood changed. Westmoore led by 14 points until Cleveland High stormed back and cut the lead to two. Dominique knew her five turnovers contributed to the dilemma. She clapped her hands. *Come on, Girl. Get it together. Dad is gonna yank you outta here. Stay focused, come on, you can do this.*

Dominique positioned herself under the basket and hoped for an easy deuce. Imani made a look-away pass to her and Dominique threw up a hook shot. She missed the shot, but the referee called a foul on her opponent and sent Dominique to the free throw line. Imani walked over to her.

"All right, Girl, take your time," Imani began, "make 'em like you did in practice."

The home team fans booed and shouted, "choke." Dominique tried to block them out and pretended that she was in practice. The first free throw shot hit the front of the rim. Cleveland High fans cheered. Again, Imani approached her.

"Put a little more arch on it. You can do it."

Dominique mumbled those words to herself as she prepared for the second attempt. She arched it and that time the ball hit the back of the red rim and popped into the air. Imani grabbed the rebound and laid the ball in for two. Coach Wilkens called a time-out. As Dominique walked by him he whispered, "I guess you didn't take free throw practice seriously either." Then her father yelled, "Dominique, you're out. Terry, you're in."

Dominique sat out the remainder of the game and watched as Imani led their team to victory.

* * *

It was Friday night and Dominique did not look forward to another boring weekend. She wanted to hang out with Imani. However, Imani told Dominique that she had to study for the SATs.

"Dominique, dinner's ready," her mother said.

"I might as well eat. I ain't got nothing else to do," Dominique mumbled and made her way downstairs to the dining room. Her father sat in his reserved seat at the head of the rectangular glass top table. Dominique sat at the opposite end.

"You have a problem sitting next to me?" Mr. Wilkens asked her.

"No."

Mrs. Wilkens sat next to her husband. "John, leave her alone. It sounds as if she had a rough week. Let the child enjoy her food," Mrs. Wilkens said and then smiled at her daughter.

"It's been a horrible, disgusting, humiliating, aggravating, I-hate-that-school kind of week. I want to go back to Parker."

"You see, Denise," Mr. Wilkens began and then pointed his fork at Dominique, "that's the nasty little attitude I've had to put up with all week. And frankly, I am sick of it. She better shape up."

Dominique turned to her mother and hoped she would defend her again. It was as if Dominique looked in a mirror and saw her own reflection minus the freckles. Mrs. Denise Wilkens was a young looking 46-year-old. Her coconut cream complexion and blue-green eyes matched her daughters. She wore her sable colored hair straight and it landed past her shoulders. She looked like the sweetest person in the world when she flashed that toothpaste commercial-type bright white smile. However, Dominique witnessed her high-powered lawyer mom in a courtroom. That gentlewoman turned into a barracuda.

"Westmoore is a fine school, Baby, and that is where you are going to excel and graduate. We are all adjusting to our new environment. So, give it a little time. Everything will work out."

Dominique pushed her plate of lasagna and broccoli away. "Y'all don't understand."

"Y'all?"

Dominique huffed and rolled her eyes. "Sorry, Mom. I meant to say that you all do not understand."

"I thought you could speak better English than that," Mrs. Wilkens said.

"I don't know about English but she better eat that food and build up some strength. Denise, you should see how girls shorter than her push Dominique all over the court," he said and turned from his wife and looked at his daughter. "I told your mother how you only made it half way up that rope. Down right embarrassed me."

"It is not about you, John. All that we can ask of Dominique is that she does her best. Not everybody can climb that rope up to the top. I know I could never do it."

The sound of the doorbell was music to Dominique's ears. She bolted from the dinner table and answered the door. To her surprise, it was Kelli Nichols. "Hey! What are you doing here?"

"I got your e-mail and you sounded so bummed out that I had to see you, Doms. Now smooches..."

The two girls kissed each other's cheeks and hugged. Dominique yelled, "Mom, Dad, Kelli's here." Her parents came into the living room and greeted Dominique's former classmate and neighbor. They exchanged pleasantries and then Dominique led Kelli to her spacious bedroom.

"You look like, like so different. What did you do to yourself?" Dominique asked.

Kelli unzipped her turquoise and white ski jacket, and it slipped onto the tan plush carpet. She held her arms out and wiggled her narrow hips.

"Ohmagod! You've lost so much weight! And what you got stuffed in your bra?"

"Don't I look totally fab-u-lous? The big boobs are birthday presents. Don't they look natural?"

"Ohmagod!" Dominique exclaimed and then she whispered. "I can't believe you got breast implants."

"No more stuffing my bra with socks. Don't I look fab-u-lous?" Kelli asked as she jumped up and down. Her new boobs bounced about too. "Like wait until I lose another 20 pounds. I'm still too fat."

Dominique squinted as she checked out Kelli's new figure. There was no fat. "What size are those jeans?"

"Ohmagosh, would you believe a size six? Ugggh, that's why I gotta lose 20 more pounds," Kelli said and then dabbed at her nose with a pink tissue.

Dominique examined Kelli's face and it was narrower. Her cheekbones protruded beneath her translucent complexion. Blue eye shadow covered her eyelids up to her arched eyebrows. She always laid the black eye liner on too thick.

"Wait until I get a nose job to straighten out this snout and lose that weight. I'm gonna be like totally perfect. Don't you think?" Kelli asked as she checked herself out in the full-length mirror that hung on the back of the bedroom door.

Dominique shook her head and wondered what was wrong with the nose and figure she had.

"Then I'm gonna sign up with a modeling agency first before I start acting and everybody is going to be like totally jealous of me and ask, 'How does she do it? How does she look fab-u-lous all the time? Don't you hate her? How does she get all of the totally fab-u-lous guys?'"

Dominique scratched her head. *Okay, like, this conversation is totally getting on my nerves. Let's change the subject.* "Sooo what's going on at Parker? Have you made any friends since I left?"

Kelli wiped her nose again before she answered. "Oh, Doms, my social life is fab-u-lous! Ever since I lost weight and found a new clique to party with, I have been sooo happy!" Kelli said and jumped up and down and clapped her hands.

Dominique eased down on her bed. *This girl is making me dizzy. She hasn't stopped moving since she got here. What's up with all that energy?*

"Dominique!"

"Yes, Mom."

"Your father and I are going to the movies. Would you girls care to join us?"

Kelli shook her head "no."

"No thanks, Mom. Kelli and I are gonna stay here and catch up on all the news."

"Okay. And if you ladies get hungry, there is plenty of food down here so help yourselves."

"Thanks, Mom. Have a great time."

The front door closed and Dominique exhaled. She was glad that she had the house to herself. "I would offer you lasagna but I wouldn't want to ruin your diet."

"I eat whatever I want. I just don't keep it in," Kelli said and stuck a finger in her mouth and gagged.

"Eeelll, that's nasty," Dominique began, "you're gonna fool around and become anorexic or is it bulimic? Whatever, you know what I'm talking about."

"Ohmygosh, no way. That won't happen to me. I know what I'm doing. You're such a worry wart." Kelli giggled and then waved her hand at Dominique.

"Just be careful, Kelli. Do your parents know?"

"Get real. They don't have a clue. They're a couple of old fuddy-duddy workaholics with issues of their own." Kelli rolled her blue eyes. "Let's get back to my fab-u-lous life with my awesome new friends. I'm having a blast! They love me, Doms, and I love them. I feel like I finally belong, you know?"

"No, I don't know. I'm dying at Westmoore. I need your secret on how to get fabulously popular. A friend of mine at school name Imani said it takes time. Well, I want to be popular now."

Kelli flopped down next to Dominique on the queen-sized bed. "Oh poor, Doms. I felt your pain and stress right through the computer. When I read your message, I was like, ohmygosh, I've gotta help her!"

Dominique's tears flowed down her cheeks. "How is it that you can see it and feel it just by reading a letter and my parents can't?" Dominique rested her head on Kelli's bony shoulder.

"I dunno. They're old like my folks so go figure. But you've got me, and I'll introduce you to my friends."

"For real?"

"Of course, Doms, but you've got to relax. They don't want uptight people around them."

Dominique lifted her head and Kelli handed her a tissue. She examined the tissue and made sure it was a clean one and not the one Kelli used. "Do you like have a cold or something?" Dominique asked.

"I guess it's allergies or something. This runny nose is kinda gross, huh?"

"It's not like you can help it."

"No, but I can help you," Kelli said and then pulled out a small plastic zip top bag. She retrieved what at first looked like a cigarette. However, it was too short and skinny to be that. "Weed is my secret to relaxing," she said and ran the joint under her nose and inhaled.

"Ohmagod! I can't believe you're doing drugs, Kelli." Dominique stood and frowned as her eyes shifted from Kelli and the joint.

"Relax, Doms, it's not like a big deal. It's just marijuana. Weed is not going to hurt you, and you're not going to get addicted to it. If this was heroin or crack, then that's a different story."

Dominique shook her head. "I don't know, Kelli. What's that stuff gonna do to me?"

"It's gonna chill you out, Girrrl," Kelli said.

That didn't sound right coming out of her mouth, Dominique thought. "You're even tryin' to talk cool."

"I am cool. And if you wanna be cool and hang with me and my friends, you've gotta party like we do. So let me take the mystery out of this," Kelli said and pulled an emerald green lighter out of her back pocket.

Dominique flapped her arms. "Wooo, hey, stop, don't light up in here! I know that stuff stinks, and my parents are gonna smell it when they get back."

"Like, do I look stupid? I got that covered," Kelli said and retrieved incense from the pocket of her ski jacket. "Would it be strange for you to burn incense?"

Dominique nodded "no" and watched as Kelli lit the mini stick. Spiced Apple aroma filled the room.

"Let me walk you through this," Kelli said and handed the incense to Dominique. Kelli lit the joint and placed it between her thin lips. The sides of her face caved in and her cheekbones protruded even more as she took a long drag. Kelli held the smoke in a long time before she opened her mouth. The pungent smell of marijuana fused with the Spiced Apple. "I'm already feeling like mellow and good. Like real good...come on, Doms, try it."

Dominique shook her head "no."

Kelli took another drag off her joint, threw her head back, and howled.

"What's so funny?" Dominique asked.

"You. You're so funny. I can't believe you're afraid of a little weed. I'm having a great time and you're so uptight. Don't I look like I'm having fun?" Kelli asked and laughed again.

Dominique grinned because Kelli's laugh was contagious and because she was nervous. She stared at the girl who used to be a loner like her. Now, Kelli appeared happy. Dominique scratched her head. *Well if a little weed can make such a big difference for Kelli, maybe it can help me too. She wouldn't offer it to me if it could hurt me. Oh maaan, what should I do? Ummm, what should I do? Maybe, okay, okay...maybe I'll take one itty-bitty puff. Just one little puff just like I had one little sip of wine. That didn't kill me. Okay, I'm gonna do this for her since she came all the way over here to see me. I don't wanna hurt her feelings. Okay, I'll try it but I'm not putting my mouth on that used one. I don't want her cold or allergies or whatever's making her nose run.*

"Okaaay, I'll try just a tiny bit of another one. But if I don't like it–"

"We'll try something else." Kelli giggled.

"What!"

"Geeez, relax. I'm just kidding," Kelli began, "all I have is pot." She gave the unused joint to Dominique. She held it between her fingers and borrowed Kelli's lighter. She flicked the lighter and tried to make contact between the flame and the tip of the joint.

"I can't do it. My hands keep shaking."

Kelli must have thought that was hilarious. She laughed until she buckled over and rolled onto the floor.

"Stop laughing at me! Oh forget this. I ain't doing it," Dominique said and then closed the lighter.

Tears streamed from Kelli's crystal blue eyes. "Okay, okay, don't spaz out. I'll help you. Just put the joint between your lips and I'll light it for you."

Dominique's lips quivered so that the joint moved about. Kelli's attempt to light it failed. "Hold it still with your fingers," Kelli suggested.

The joint lit up. Yet, Dominique did not inhale. The red tip hypnotized her. She stared at the black rings that formed as the paper burned away.

"Don't stand there and waste a good joint. Hurry up and take a drag. The munchies are setting in and I'm ready for some lasagna."

Dominique closed her eyes and inhaled just a bit.

"Don't blow it out just yet. Hold the smoke in your chest as long as you can."

Dominique tried that and she gagged and coughed. Again, Kelli was on the floor. Dominique took a deep breath and rolled her eyes at Kelli. *I'm gonna show her that I can be cool. I am going to do this,* Dominique said to herself and then took a long drag. She was determined and held the smoke just as long as Kelli did.

"That's how you do it!"

Dominique released some smoke and then took another long drag off the joint.

Kelli cheered her on. "Keep going, Doms. It's halfway finished...don't stop now...smoke it all..."

Dominique was light-headed and her legs felt like elastic bands. She eased down onto the carpet. "I feel sooo good...sooo relaxed...sooo happy," she said and laughed until her stomach ached.

"Like, now do you trust me?" Kelli asked.

Dominique giggled and said, "Yeah."

"Good. Let's get some food. I'm starving."

Kelli opened the bedroom door and Dominique caught a hold of her arm and spun her around. When Kelli faced her, Dominique said, "Let's trade. I'll give you all the lasagna you can eat for another joint."

Kelli did not hesitate. She pulled out two joints and placed them in the palm of Dominique's hand. "I can get as much weed as you need. Just call me."

TYLER

It was a beautiful fall day laced with a crisp breeze. Inside the packed Westmoore gym, it was hot. Saturday afternoon games drew hundreds of spectators with one local newspaper reporter and a photographer in attendance. Tyler put on a good show for the media because he knew that college scouts sought fresh talent for their schools. Good press would get his name out there. Other than the publicity, the game bored him. It was a blowout with the Jaguars ahead by 18-points midway the fourth quarter.

"Tyler, you've got two more minutes and then I'm pulling you out. Then, Paul, you're in," the coach said.

That was cool with Tyler. He had racked up 25 points, 10 rebounds, and 10 assists. He showed the new guy, Paul Logan, who the man was at Westmoore too.

Play resumed and Tyler brought the ball down court and dished it off to his man on the right. His defender probably assumed that the Jaguar star was tired because Tyler stooped over and rested his hands on his knees. Tyler peeked under the outstretched arms of number 18. No one was under the basket. He blew past his defender, soared into the air and yelled for the ball. Tyler caught the ball with one hand. *Slam!* The Westmoore fans roared. The opposing team called time out. Tyler smiled all the way to the bench.

"All right, Show Time, good game," his coach said and patted him on the head. Tyler sat on the bench the remainder of the game and played it cool as the photographer snapped what seemed like a hundred pictures of him. Tyler could not keep a straight face. He beamed all the way to the locker room.

"Great game, Man. I hope you saved some for Cliffside," one of his teammates said.

"I got a little something left for them," Tyler said as he turned on the shower. The warm water pulsated out of the showerhead and massaged his sore muscles.

Paul stopped in front of Tyler's stall. "I heard before I came here that you hog the ball. I see it's true."

Tyler wiped the suds from his eyes. *I'm butt naked and this guy is coming up to me like he wants to start something.* Tyler turned the shower off, grabbed a white towel and slung it around his waist. "What's your point?"

"My point is that I didn't transfer here to ride the bench and to watch you show off."

"Imma ask you again. What's your point?"

"I just told you."

"No, you didn't," Tyler said and walked away.

Paul grabbed a hold of Tyler's arm. Tyler glanced down at Paul's hand and then back up to Paul's face.

"I wasn't finished," Paul said.

Tyler jerked his arm away. He tightened the towel around his washboard abs. Tyler was within inches of Paul's face. "This is the point. I know your rep too. You were the man at Jefferson but this is Westmoore. You're not good enough to start here. I'm doing my job out there and you can call that 'showing off' or whatever–"

"Yeah, it is showing off, showboating–"

"Whatever, Paul, but look here. I'm the captain and if you don't like the way this ship is sailing, then jump off. But don't you *ever* touch me again."

"That's right," their center said. Tyler and Paul glared at him until he strolled away.

"I didn't mean to grab you, Man. But you were gonna walk off like I wasn't even talking to you."

"That's because you weren't say anything, Man. Just blowing off steam and I don't have time for the drama. My girl is waiting for me," Tyler said.

"Maybe Coach will have time because it's not fair that 80% of the plays are designed for you."

"Eighty percent? Wow, so what does that tell you?" Tyler asked but did not wait for an answer. He moved on.

That conversation with Paul did not kill Tyler's high. He floated out of the locker room and into the arms of Imani. "You brought your 'A' game today," she said.

"I was on and it felt so good. Sorta like this," Tyler said and locked lips with Imani.

"Ummm hummm I know that feeling," Imani said and they both laughed.

Tyler hugged Imani and looked over her shoulder. "I thought I saw Fatima and Hanif."

"They're here somewhere."

A group of Westmoore cheerleaders bounced over to Tyler. Some hugged him or kissed Tyler on his cheek right in front of Imani. "Great game, Tyler," the tallest of the crew said. Maybe I'll see you at Paul's party tonight."

"Nope. Can't make it. Got other plans," Tyler said and then kissed Imani on the lips.

"Oooh, I see. Well, catch you later," she said and they all took off behind her.

"You just did that to get rid of them didn't you?" Imani asked.

"You know I don't need an excuse to kiss you. But it worked!" Imani punched his arm and they cracked up.

"Then Girlfriend got the nerve to call me violent," Fatima said as she and Hanif walked up to the couple.

"Sweet game, Man," Hanif said.

"I know you heard me scream after you slammed. But your woman was sittin' there actin' all cool like that wasn't no big thang. Like her man does that all the time," Fatima said. Everyone laughed except Hanif.

"I wanna celebrate. Y'all hungry?" Tyler asked.

Everybody said, "yeah," except Hanif.

"Yo, Man, you all right?" Tyler asked.

All eyes zoomed in on Hanif. "If y'all wanna eat, I'll hang too," he said.

"Anywhere but the Chicken Shack," Fatima said.

The foursome settled for the West Side Diner located in Imani and Fatima's neighborhood. They sat at a booth in the back and ordered their food. The sodas came first so the group sipped on them while they waited for appetizers. Tyler shook his head.

"What's the matter?" Imani asked.

"I'm in the shower and Paul steps up to me."

"Hold up. I'm tryin' to get a visual of that. Was Paul naked too?" Fatima asked and then grinned.

"I can't believe I'm sitting right here and you tryin' to picture Tyler and Paul naked," Hanif said.

"Oh you so sensitive. I'm just tryin' to liven things up. Y'all look so serious," Fatima said.

Imani sucked her teeth and rolled her eyes at Fatima. "Go ahead, Tyler."

Tyler told the story and then added, "I feel the weight of the whole team on me. That wouldn't be so bad if this wasn't senior year. Maaan final exams, SATs, college applications, deadlines here and there and–"

"It makes you wanna holler," Imani said.

"Sounds like a song, 'makes you wanna holler'," Fatima sang. Everyone stared at her. "Oh, forget y'all."

"Man, I remember senior year. It was a trip, but somehow you get through it," Hanif said.

"This is so depressin'," Fatima began, "can we talk about something other than school?"

"I'm with you, Fatima," Imani said and then looked at Tyler. "How's your future step mom?" Imani asked and then giggled.

"Not funny. I hope they don't take it there. But if they do, Candice better not expect me to call her mom 'cause that ain't happening."

"Is she tryin' to move in and take control?"

"Nooo, Fatima, my father don't play that. She doesn't even spend the night there. Now if they're getting their freak on when I'm not home, then that's another story," Tyler said and then chuckled. "If I wasn't sittin' here, I would swear that my father's a virgin."

Everyone either choked or shot soda out of their mouths across the table. "Ya'll tryin' to kill me?" Fatima asked. "I'm here chokin' and y'all laughin'."

"Oh, Girl, you all right," Imani said.

"That's probably what I get 'cause I was just about to talk about somebody."

"Who?" everybody asked and leaned in closer.

"That dang cousin of mine. Only been with us a few weeks and I'm ready to put Mercy's behind out. Check it. I don't like doin' work around the house either. But dang, I do it."

"It's not an option in my house," Imani said.

"Yeah, some of us ain't got a maid comin' in like somebody else at this table and I ain't droppin' no names," Fatima said and all eyes landed on Tyler.

Tyler shrugged his shoulders. What could he say? He knew that he was lucky when it came to his limited household chores. He kept his room clean and took out the garbage. That was it. The maid, cook, and gardener took care of the rest.

Fatima continued and said, "I may be fussin' while I'm washin' them dishes or scrubbin' those floors but I do it. That girl won't do nothing!"

"Don't she have a baby?" Tyler asked.

"You wouldn't think so by the way she acts. The baby be cryin' with a funky-shoulda-been-changed-two-hours-ago-diaper on and she's on the cell phone with that good for nothing Troy."

"What Grandma Rose got to say?" Imani asked.

"I don't think she has the energy to fuss no more. Most of the time she just stays in her room. We moved the TV in there and Mercy complained about that so bad that Troy bought her one. I talked Grandma into makin' a doctor's appointment 'cause I know she ain't feelin' well."

"Speaking of sick, you know Dominique?"

Everyone except Hanif nodded in the affirmative. "She's been acting strange lately. One minute she's laughing like crazy when nothing's even funny. Then she's depressed or yelling at her father. He sends her to the locker room to chill out then she's back on the court giggling and actin' stupid."

Tyler nodded his head. "Coach Wilkens ain't no joke. I'm glad he coaches the girls and not us."

"You got that right. And Dominique's days on the team are numbered if she keeps that crap up. Daughter or not, he'll yank her right off and I'm off to the ladies room so excuse me," Imani said and then slid across the black leather seat and out of the booth.

Tyler waited until she turned the corner. "Finally," Tyler began and leaned forward. "Check this out. I wanna throw Imani a surprise birthday party at my house. Too bad it's the same day as the SATs but there's nothing I can do about it."

"That's whacked. But hey, just another reason to get our party on," Fatima said and snapped her fingers.

"Can y'all help me out with calling her friends and getting some food and stuff together?"

"Daaang skippy! You know I'll hook my girl up," Fatima began, "but wait, is this gonna be a laid back corny so called party or a wild off the hook type thang?"

"W-e-l-l-l, since I'm on my father's turf–"

"And he's crashing it." Fatima said.

"Yeee yup."

"Eeelll, I knew it," Fatima said and then shook her head. "Well, since it's an old folks party, I might as well invite Imani's peeps."

Hanif remained silent as Tyler and Fatima went on with the details.

"So can you do that, Hanif?" Tyler asked.

"Maaan, I wish I could but I won't be here."

"Where you gonna be?" Fatima asked.

"We'll talk about it later."

"Nooo, we'll talk about it now."

Tyler saw Imani out of the corner of his eye. "Shhh," he said and everyone was silent. Imani stood at the head of the table and stared at them. "What's wrong?" she asked and slid back into the booth.

"If you have something to tell me, Hanif, you can say it in front of them."

Hanif tapped the end of his silver fork on the table. He fixed his eyes on it and said, "Well, Mama called and she's gotta have surgery. They don't know how long her recovery is gonna be, so I don't know how long I'll hafta be in North Carolina."

"Dang it! I knew it!" Fatima screamed.

The people behind her said, "shhh."

"Oh shhh, yourself. I ain't talkin' to you."

"Come on, Fatima, let's get outta here so we can talk in private," Hanif said.

"I got the bill, Man," Tyler began, "y'all go 'head."

Tyler and Imani left the Diner soon after their distraught friends. "If I had to go away, would you react the same way as Fatima?" Tyler asked.

"Yup."

"Even if you knew I was coming back?"

"Yup."

"Would you wait or start seeing other guys?"

"Would you start dating other girls?"

"I asked you first," Tyler said.

"My answer is no. What's yours?"

"Why would you ask me a question like that?"

"What? You brought this whole thing up not me."

"Let's change the subject," Tyler said.

"Yeah, let's."

Tyler and Imani remained quiet for a while. Tyler turned on the radio and Imani reached over and turned it off. "Have you spent any time with Tariq?"

"Not yet," Tyler said.

"Why not?"

"No time."

Imani huffed and then asked, "Can we stop by the Center? He's probably over there now."

"Oh, you're mad at me and now you wanna see your other man," Tyler said.

"Okaaay, now you're being ridiculous and I don't wanna talk to you," Imani said and turned the radio back on. Neither spoke for the duration of the ride.

Once inside the gym, Tyler spotted Tariq. Imani approached him first. "Tariq. Does your mother know you're here?" Imani asked.

"Does his mother know he's here?" Tariq asked and pointed at Tyler.

"Ha, ha...very funny," Tyler said.

"And just because I cut Imani loose don't mean I won't cut you if you hurt her. See what I'm sayin'?"

"Tariq. Don't make me pull you outta here again. Check the attitude and answer me. Does Ms. Greene know where you are?"

"Yeah, she knows. I got the twins with me too," he said and pointed in their direction.

"Are you keeping an eye on them?"

"You talkin' to a man with a lot of experience. I know what I'm doin'."

"Yeah, well, I'm gonna make sure they're all right while you and Tyler do whatever guys do," Imani said. She rolled her eyes at Tyler and marched off.

"Oooh snap, she gave you that look she gives me when I piss her off," Tariq said. He balled up his fist and stepped up to Tyler. "So, Sucka, what you got?"

Tyler smiled and walked away. He went over to a bin and took out a basketball. He bounced it a few times between his legs and then dribbled towards the basket.

Tyler took off into the air and slammed the ball with one hand. He passed the ball to Tariq. "What you got?"

Tariq smiled at Tyler like he just discovered that Tyler had an edge to him. Tariq dribbled the ball between his short legs, bounced the ball behind his back from his right hand to his left and dribbled some more. He stopped and hit a jump shot.

"Not bad," Tyler said and retrieved the ball and dribbled out beyond the arc. He fired a 3-pointer that caught all net.

"Daaag, this brotha tryin' to sweat me," Tariq said. He launched a jump shot from the free-throw line. The ball hit the backboard and then went into the hoop.

"Your delivery's pretty smooth," Tyler said. "Let me show you some more moves that you can work on."

Tyler lost track of time as he worked out with Tariq. An hour passed since the last time he checked his watch. "I gotta get out of here. But it's been real, Man." Tyler exchanged high fives with Tariq.

"Hey, Man, I'm throwin' a birthday party for Imani next Saturday at my place."

"You askin' me over to your crib?"

"Yeah."

"Why?"

"I know you care about Imani and she likes you. Sooo, are you there or what?"

"Can I bring somebody?"

"Yeah, who?" Tyler asked.

"Maaan, I got so many honeys it's gonna be hard pickin' just one."

"So you got it like that, huh?"

"You know it. But I ain't got no ride."

"I got you. When I pick up Imani, I'll swing by and get you and your girl if that's all right with your mother."

Tariq frowned. "You jokin', right?"

"Nope, and I need your number so I can call her."

Tariq grinned. "You playin', right?"

"Nope. No number no party."

A little boy and girl ran ahead of Imani in Tariq's direction. They grabbed on to Tariq until he picked them up. The twins looked nothing like their older brother. Ryan and Robyn had sandy brown hair, hazel eyes, walnut complexion and chubby cheeks.

"How old are you guys?" Tyler asked.

"Five," they said together.

"I think it's time for you to take the twins home," Imani said. "Tyler, can we drop them off?"

"What kinda ride you got?" Tariq asked as he lowered the twins onto the court.

"Come on and you'll see," Imani said and they all left the gym and headed for the parking lot.

"Oh Lord, three of 'em," the security guard said as Tariq and the twins walked by.

"Forget you, Man," Tariq said.

"Forget you, Man," the twins said in unison.

When they reached the sports car, Tariq's big eyes widened. "This ain't even your ride, Tyler."

The twins repeated what their brother said and Tyler laughed.

"What you sellin', Man? You gotta be runnin' some kinda game to be profilin' in this."

"No games, Man. My father sprung for it."

Tariq ran his hand over the smooth and shiny black surface. "Whatever game he's runnin', I want in."

* * *

When Tyler arrived home, Miss Candice Rollins and his father sat on a sofa in the entertainment room. Miss Rollins was 32 years old but looked 25. To Tyler, she was an overdressed and prissy cutesy doll. He never saw her dressed down in jeans or sweats.

"You can come in, Son."

Mr. Andrew Powers was a handsome older version of Tyler. However, his good looks and buffed body were not the keys to his success. Mr. Powers studied hard in school and was the first in his family who attended college. He worked his way out of poverty and became the owner of several Power Walk men's shoes and accessories stores. Mr. Powers promised his wife before she died five years ago that he would take care of Tyler and provide for him the best life possible.

"Great game, Son. I left after you put on your warm-ups. I knew the coach would sit you out the rest of the game."

"Your father told me about that...what did you call it, Andrew?"

"Monster slam."

"Yes, that monster slam. However, I am more impressed with the fact that you write poetry."

"You told her about that, Dad?"

"What's wrong with me bragging about my son? It's all good."

"The movie is almost over but you may join us," Miss Rollins said.

Tyler dropped his duffel bag and scratched his head as he stared at her. *Check her out. 'You may join us' like she lives here and I'm the guest. She's getting too comfortable around here.*

"Come on, Son," his father said.

Tyler waved him off. "I already know what's gonna happen. I'm going upstairs."

"Wait a minute. Who did you hang out with after the game?" his father asked.

"Imani, Fatima, Hanif, and this new kid Tariq."

Miss Rollins laughed. "My goodness. The name parents give their children today. Whatever happened to simple names like Mary, Jane, John, and Michael?"

"I know what you mean, Sweetie."

Eeelll, Dad, you're callin' her "sweetie"? Man, she's got you hooked. Barbie's gotta go, Tyler thought as he stared at the 5'7" slender woman. She wore a pale pink cardigan with pearl buttons and light gray cuffed pants.

"I truly look forward to meeting this Imani and her parents," Miss Rollins said.

"Whatever," Tyler mumbled.

"Your father told me that you are planning a birthday party for her."

"That too? C'mon, Dad, keep me out of your conversations with her." Tyler picked up his bag.

"What's the big deal, Tyler?" Mr. Powers asked.

"I can help decorate. I was thinking pastels and white or maybe some floral patterns."

"Imani's not into pastels or that flowery stuff."

"Okaaay, I guess she is not the feminine type. Well, how about your school colors?"

"That's cool."

"What about the cake? Surely she would not mind flowers on top of that?"

"I got the cake covered," Tyler said.

"Sooo," she began and motioned her hands as if she tried to pull information out of Tyler. "What kind?"

"A round portrait cake with a picture of her jersey with her name and number on it."

"Surely you jest," Miss Rollins began, "that's not appropriate for a young lady."

"It's appropriate for my lady."

"Watch your tone, Tyler," his father said.

"She should mind her business."

"Wow. That was rude," Miss Rollins said.

Mr. Powers stood and stared at his son. "Now, you're talking to me and this is my business. So just how much time are you putting into this party? The SATs are coming up. Are you ready? I'm a little concerned here," his father said.

Tyler felt as if he was on trial. The interrogation irritated him. The high from the game faded. "I got that covered too."

"Andrew, I was going to offer to bring food to the party. However, I don't know if I should even mention it now," Miss Rollins said.

Tyler huffed. "Daaa, you just did," he mumbled.

"Candice is a great cook. She's teaching me a thing or two in the kitchen. I may even let our cook go."

"Oooh, Andrew," Miss Rollins said. She stood next to Mr. Powers and they exchanged kisses.

Tyler turned his head. "I can't stand this," he mumbled. Tyler peeked with one eye and saw that they separated. "Bring what you want but I'm ordering food."

"How much are you spending on this party, Son?"

"It's coming out of my allowance," Tyler said and then turned and headed for the staircase.

"All right, big spender. Just remember that you have a car now and it doesn't run off water. So when that needle hits 'E', don't come to me for an advance."

IMANI

All three shook their heads as they walked away from the SAT testing center. Imani inhaled the crisp cold air and exhaled through her mouth. She wanted the pressure that sat above her eyebrows to go away. Tears slid from the inner corner of her eyes and down the sides of her nose. "Just shoot me now," Imani said and Tyler and Fatima laughed. "I swear to God that if I have to take that test again, I..."

Tyler and Fatima must have realized that Imani was serious. The tears were real. They embraced their friend and gave her a pep talk. "Stop buggin', Girl. You know you did all right."

"Come on, Queen, you studied like crazy. I know you scored high. Don't sweat it."

"And thanks for hookin' this sistah up. If you hadn't given me those study guides, the only little circles

I would have filled in on those answer sheets were the ones that spelled out my name. I would have said the heck with the rest of 'em."

Imani laughed at that comment until she felt snot at the tip of her nose. She backed away from her friends and took care of that. It never failed. Fatima had a way of cheering up Imani since they met in second grade. "No more worrying. It's over. And if I have to take it again in December, then that's when I'll deal with it," Imani said.

"Ya dang skippy," Fatima began, "now it's party time! Happy birthday, Girl!"

Imani smiled. "So what we gonna do?"

"Tyler is gonna take us to your place so we can get beautiful and don't sweat the rest."

"That's right," Tyler said and then kissed her.

"Oooh, I miss my maaan," Fatima said. "His mother better hurry up and get well so he can come on back here to me."

"When was the last time you heard from Hanif?" Tyler asked.

"A couple of days ago. The operation went well so now she's in recovery. She don't want me comin' down there 'cause I would sho nuf speed things up."

"Girl, you know you're rough," Imani said.

"I ain't rough. I'm just keepin' it real. She got my man on lockdown and I don't like it."

"Wouldn't you do the same for Grandma Rose?" Tyler asked.

"What?"

"If that was Grandma Rose, wouldn't you do the same thing that Hanif did? Wouldn't you help her?"

"Daaang, why you gotta get all deep?" Fatima asked and then remained silent.

When they reached Imani's apartment building, Fatima retrieved a large box and a garment bag out of the trunk of Tyler's car.

"Let me help you," Tyler said.

"I got it." Fatima walked off towards the building.

Tyler turned to Imani. "Is she pissed off at me?"

"I think she's worried about Grandma Rose. She hasn't been feeling well lately."

"Oh man, I forgot. Then I had to open my big mouth and ask her that question," Tyler said.

"Don't sweat it. I know her. She'll bounce back."

Imani entered her apartment and before she closed the door, her mother asked, "How was the test?"

"Fine, Ma."

"Just fine?"

"Yeah."

Her 6'8" tall father walked into the living room. "So how was the test, Baby Girl?"

"Fine, Dad."

"Just fine?"

"Yeah."

Imani smelled her father's cologne and she noticed that her parents were dressed up for a Saturday. Instead of slippers, they both donned shoes. "Where y'all going?"

"What?" her parents said in unison.

"Why y'all dressed up?"

Her parents, Cora and Robert Jackson, looked at each other. Both were in their mid forties but Mr. Jackson looked older than his wife. Imani attributed that to his full beard and moustache that covered much of his dark brown face.

"Well, Baby Girl, today is a special day. Can't we look a little decent on our daughter's 17th birthday?" Mr. Jackson asked in his baritone voice.

Imani's brows raised. *Oh no, I hope they don't think I changed my mind and gonna stay home with them all night. The last 10 years of shrimp dinner, homemade chocolate cake and vanilla ice cream was more than enough. Not this year, plueeeze.*

"Let's give her our gift now," Mrs. Jackson said.

Mrs. Cora Jackson's toasted almond oblong face beamed with joy. The plus size woman stood four inches shorter than Imani. She was a full-time mom ever since Imani and her older sister Roberta were born. For extra income, she made choir robes, costumes, and other outfits for the members of her church.

"I could use a gift right about now," Imani said.

Her mother left the room and returned with a red wrapped package with a white bow on top. "Happy birthday, Sweetie," Mrs. Jackson said and then reached up and hugged her daughter.

Imani blew on her cold hands and wiggled her fingers. She smiled while she peeled away the red paper and then opened the white box. She pulled out a porcelain black angel. The angel wore a gold cross and held a Holy Bible. The curly hair figurine stood on a square base that read, "DREAM BIG & BELIEVE!"

"We wanted to give you something that you could take to college," her mother said.

"How you like it, Baby Girl?"

"It's beautiful, Dad. I'll keep it forever. Thanks."

Mr. Jackson handed Imani a large red envelope. "Here's a birthday card from your sister."

Imani smiled as she opened the envelope. She pulled out the card and found a $50 bill inside. "Wow, I can use this. I gotta call Roberta. Well, thanks family." Imani exchanged hugs and kisses with her parents. Afterwards she asked, "Did Fatima come up here?"

"She went straight to your room. She acts like she lives here," Mr. Jackson said.

Imani opened her bedroom door and there stood Fatima in black leather pants and a cobalt blue turtleneck sweater. The heels on her black boots were three inches. Yet, she was much shorter than Imani.

"What you got?" Fatima asked and pointed to Imani's hand.

Imani showed her the angel and made room for it on her dresser. "Ain't that cute," Fatima began, "they're getting a little better at gift giving."

Imani rubbed her finger over the angel's smooth surface and smiled. "They do all right with what little money they got to work with." Imani spun around. "And speaking of money, this is courtesy of Roberta," Imani said as she flashed the $50 bill.

"Now you're talkin'."

"That outfit you got on is sayin' something too. You look good, Girl."

"Don't I?"

"I told Tyler you would be all right. He feels bad about what he said."

"No big deal," Fatima said and waved her hand. "I forgot all about that. So I really look good?"

"Girl, you know you're always fly and you're rockin' those boots."

"The Chicken Shack is good for something. It's a nice piece of change so I don't have to beg Grandma for money every time I want a little sumptin sumptin."

Imani nodded her head in agreement but knew that her parents would not allow her to work during the school year. As she surveyed the clothes that hung on a nail on the back of her door, she frowned. "Nothing here I wanna wear." She went to her tiny closet filled with fleece and nylon sweat suits.

"Don't even try it. I ain't even gonna let you out of this room with sweats and sneakers."

Fatima flipped through Imani's wardrobe. "I knew this was gonna happen so check that out."

Imani's eyes followed where Fatima pointed. She gasped at the sight of the huge box. "Ohmygod!"

"I didn't have a chance to wrap it. Sorry."

Imani waved her hand. "That's all right." She removed the top and then peeled back the white tissue paper. Imani's mouth flew wide open. She picked up a bright red chenille sweater and held it out in front of her.

"The sleeves looked long enough," Fatima said.

"It should fit." Imani held the plush turtleneck sweater up against herself. "It's beautiful."

"That ain't all, Girl. Keep going."

Imani removed another sheet of tissue paper. She was so surprised at what she saw that she gasped again.

"Did you think that I was gonna leave it up to you to hook up that sweater?"

"Ohmygod, Fatima, did you really buy these? I mean I know that you didn't steal them or anything like that, but can you really afford them?"

"Your behind won't be settin' off no alarms when you wear 'em. I dropped the bills and got the receipt too. I told you the Chicken Shack is good for something."

Imani laughed. "I was just messin' with you," she said and then lifted up a pair of black suede pants. Imani held them against her waist and the cuff touched the top of her sneakers. "I can't believe they're long enough. They're perfect!" Imani's eyes filled with tears.

"Girrrl, if you make my mascara run, it's on," Fatima said. "Plus, there's one more surprise in there."

"You didn't have to do this. But, I'm glad you did." Both girls giggled as Imani reached back in the box and pulled out a plaid cosmetic pouch. Imani opened it and found lipstick, mascara, eye shadow, and blush. "You're gonna have to show me what to do with this stuff."

"After you put your outfit on, we'll get started on your face 'cause I gotta cover them zits."

"I can't stand them," Imani said as she stared in the mirror. There were a couple on her forehead and one stood at attention on the tip of her nose. Imani went in for the squeeze.

"Don't pop it," Fatima said and slapped Imani's hands away. "Let me try and cover it up."

Imani ran out of the room and changed clothes in the bathroom. When she returned, both girls giggled and jumped about. "Girl, you look goood! If I didn't know how good I looked, I'd be scared of you," Fatima said and hugged her friend.

"Hurry up and do up my face before Tyler gets here. I wanna look good from the floor up!"

Fatima worked her skills all over Imani's face and then added curls to her braids. "I should have bought you some clip on earrings. When are you gonna get these ears pierced? And I don't even wanna look at them raggedy nails. I know they tore up."

The doorbell rang and Imani knew it was Tyler. She did not have time to paint her short nails. Her nails looked clean and that was good enough for Imani.

"Imani," her father called out in his deep voice, "Tyler's here. Don't keep the boy waiting."

"She'll be out in a minute!" Fatima yelled.

Imani checked out her make-up in the mirror while Fatima finished her hair. "You sure this lipstick isn't too red? Is the blush too much? I don't know about the eye shadow. Is it too light?"

Fatima huffed. "You're just not used to lookin' so fly. Deal with it 'cause you look...well um...I was gonna say hot but I don't think your daddy would appreciate that word. So let's just say you look ummm Fatima-ish. Now strut on out there and watch Tyler melt." Fatima shooed Imani away.

Imani stepped outside her door and realized that she did not have on shoes. "I wish that I had some black suede boots."

"Some wishes come true," Fatima mumbled.

"What?"

Fatima bit her bottom lip and then she said, "Worry about the shoes later. Go and greet your fine boyfriend and I'll look for some shoes."

Imani tiptoed into the living room. Tyler sat on the sofa and her father sat across from him. Tyler's eyes grew and his lips formed the word, "wow." Imani imagined that all of her teeth showed because she smiled so wide.

"Nice outfit. Is that what Fatima had in that big box?" her mother asked.

"Yes. Do you really like it?"

"It's beautiful and the pants are long enough too. Very nice," she answered.

"That red is a little bright but it's a nice sweater," Mr. Jackson began, "you can pat off some of that make-up. Otherwise, what can I say? You got your good looks from your mama and me," he said and then laughed.

Tyler joined in and laughed and then Mr. Jackson stopped. Tyler stopped too.

"So what you got there?" Mr. Jackson asked.

Tyler stood and handed Imani a package. He cleared his throat and said, "I hope you like it."

"Thanks. I'll open it in the car," she whispered.

"You gotta open it now."

"What she gotta do?" her father asked.

"Nothing. What I meant was that you would be glad that you opened it now versus later once you see what's inside. That's all that I meant," Tyler said then looked at Mr. Jackson and added, "Sir."

"Okaaay, I'll open it now." Imani removed the red bow and gold paper. She opened the box and yelled, "Fatima! You knew didn't you!" Fatima did not answer but Imani heard the clicks of her high heels. Seconds later, Fatima stood by Imani as she displayed a pair of black suede boots.

"Yeah, I knew, but he picked them out and paid for 'em. And oooh, they nice. The brotha got style and the right size. Size 10. Girrrl, you know you got big feet."

"They look real expensive to me. I hope you're not expecting Imani to repay you in any way if you know what I mean and–"

"Robert! Leave him alone!" Mrs. Jackson yelled.

"Dad! I can't believe you went there."

"Dang, Mr. Jackson, that was bold," Fatima said.

Mr. Jackson rose. The former high school football star towered over everyone.

"W-e-l-l-l, it was," Fatima said in a high-pitched voice as she glanced up at his jet black eyes.

Mr. Jackson bent over and hugged Imani. His beard scratched her face. She hoped it had not scraped off her make-up on that side. He told her to, "Put your new boots on and go and celebrate your birthday." He extended his hand and Tyler shook it. "Drive like you got sense," Mr. Jackson told him and then left the room.

* * *

Imani turned around and looked at the odd combination of people in the backseat of Tyler's car. Tariq sat in the middle with Fatima and a girl named Vicki on both sides of him. Imani did not ask any questions. Yet, she was curious about how the evening would play out. Imani knew from the change of scenery that they were in Tyler's territory.

"Boooy, maybe the first time was a mistake. But if you rub up on my thigh one more time, I'm gonna slap you back to your mama," Fatima told Tariq.

"Why play a brotha out in front of his woman?"

"I ain't your woman, yet," Vicki said.

"Why you wearin' them gloves I got you then?"

Imani turned around again and caught sight of the neon yellow knit gloves.

"Don't get all jealous, Imani. I got you a pair for your birthday." Tariq reached in his jacket pocket and pulled out another pair. "Here you go," he said.

Vicki sucked her teeth. "I can't believe you got her the same ones."

"Thanks, Tariq," Imani said. She stretched them as far as she could over her long fingers and hands. "They're cute." She stared at Fatima and gave her a "don't you dare laugh" look. "So ummm, Fatima, you should have invited Mercedes to hang out with us."

"I left her behind with Grandma Rose and that cryin' baby. Mercy acts more like a baby than her baby."

"Awww, I bet the baby's cute. What's the baby's name?" Vicki asked.

"Cute my behind. Ain't nothing cute about Alexus at two and three in the morning cryin' like she demon possessed. Her sorry behind mother just gonna lay there and wait and see if me or Grandma gonna get up and feed

Alexus or change her funky diaper. Well, me and Grandma stopped that crap."

"So all y'all just let the baby cry?" Vicki asked.

"One of us will get up all right. Get up and shake the heck out of Mercy until her lazy behind picks up that baby. Then we go right back on to sleep."

"I bet she's still cute," Vicki said.

"Is that right? I tell you what. Give me your phone number and when that cute baby starts cryin' in the morning, Imma call you and you can talk her cute self right on back to sleep. Bump that, just come over every morning at about two or three and feed and clean her and spend another hour rockin' her back to sleep. Deal?"

Vicki did not answer.

"Ummm hummm, that's what I thought."

"Don't call me. The twins are a pain in my a–"

"Tariq!" Imani shouted.

"W-e-l-l-l, they are."

Tyler drove up the long driveway to his palatial home. He parked behind one of his father's luxury cars. "Yo, Man, this ain't even your crib," Tariq said.

"This is where I crash."

"You livin' large, Maaan," Tariq said.

Imani watched as Tyler whispered in Fatima's ear. Then he took off into the house.

"What's up, Fatima?"

"I dunno whatcha talkin' about."

"He's coming back out, right? Then we're gonna go somewhere else, right? 'Cause I know we're not staying here especially if his father's home, right?"

Fatima did not respond.

"Tariq?"

Tariq raised his hands. "Hey, a man don't kiss and tell. Right, Vicki?"

Vicki bumped his shoulder. "Boooy, you just did."

Imani turned from Tariq and stared at Fatima until she heard Tyler's voice. "Come on in," he said and motioned to them. Imani glared at Fatima who hunched her shoulders. Imani rolled her eyes at her and then led everyone to the doorway. Tyler kissed her on the cheek as she brushed past him and then she heard, "Surprise!"

Imani's hands shot up and covered her open mouth as she gasped for air. Then for a split second, she froze. "We got you real good. Didn't we?" Fatima asked from behind her. Tariq and Tyler laughed.

"Happy birthday, Imani," Mr. Powers said and Miss Rollins greeted her too.

Imani stood in the same spot and scanned the faces. Dominique, Terry, and most of her teammates stared back at her. Some of the guys on Tyler's team stood out as they were taller than most of the people in the room except for Mr. Jackson.

"Dad! Mom! I can't believe you're here. Wow, I can't believe this and y'all didn't even tell me."

"Well dang, that would have blown the surprise," Fatima said.

Mrs. Jackson walked up to her daughter and embraced her and then everyone, except Tyler, converged on her. When they cleared away, Imani saw Tyler. He looked good dressed in a black turtleneck and black pants. He smiled at her and showed his white teeth. "I can't believe you did all of this for me," she told him.

"I can't take all of the credit. Fatima helped out."

"Yeah, but I have a feeling this was your idea."

"Yeah, maaaybe."

"Maybe nothing. Come here," Imani said as she opened her arms wide. The heat from his body warmed hers. She laid her cheek against the side of Tyler's smooth face. "I love you," she whispered in his ear.

"I love ya back."

She nuzzled her face against his warm neck and inhaled his cologne. The sweet yet masculine scent went straight to her head. For that brief moment, it was as if they were the only two people in the house.

"I thought the party was over there," someone said. Imani and Tyler separated and looked in the direction that the voice came from.

"Hey, Girl," she said and hugged Dominique. Imani detected a strange odor and backed away. She noticed that Dominique's eyes were red and that she wrung her hands. "You all right?"

"Yeah, my hands are cold that's all," Dominique said and then giggled.

"What's so funny?"

"I don't know," Dominique said and laughed again. "I guess I'm just happy to be away from my father for a little while," she said and then broke out in a two-step. However, her pace was too fast for the slow tune that played. She grabbed hold of Tyler's hands. "Imani, do you mind if Tyler dances with me?"

"I was just about to get Imani a drink."

"I'll go with you. I'm sooo thirsty," Dominique said and snapped her fingers. Still, she was off beat.

"Why don't y'all go on. I'll catch you later." Imani winked at Tyler. She strolled behind them and stopped in the living room while they continued to walk towards the dining room. Imani joined Fatima and Terry. "What's up with Dominique?"

"Who you askin'? She's been acting strange since I got here," Terry said.

"Y'all talkin' about that girl with the fake ponytail pushin' up on Tyler?" Fatima asked.

"That's her hair and she's not pushin' up on him," Imani said.

"My bad on the hair. Is she half white?"

"She's as black as you, Fatima. Please don't start no mess tonight. I've got my hands full with Tariq."

Fatima laughed. "Who knew? I was just askin'. But when you come down from cloud nine, you'll see that she is pushin' up on your man and the girl's straight up high. And I ain't sayin' that 'cause she's black."

"High off what? 'Cause, Girrrl, if Mr. Powers is serving liquor, my father's gonna go off."

"Ain't no liquor up in here. I already checked."

"Then what is she high on, Fatima?" Terry asked.

Imani waved her hand. "Don't listen to Fatima. I just think that Dominique's hyper and stressed out."

Terry nodded in agreement.

"Y'all keep thinkin' that. I'm gonna get my eat on," Fatima said as her eyes followed a tall guy who strolled by her. "Hanif must have taken my heart with him to North Carolina 'cause I ain't feelin' none of these fine brothas up in here."

"Hey gorgeous," a guy who wore a Westmoore football jersey said as he glanced down at Fatima. "My name's Erik. What's your name?"

"Fatima," she said as she smiled back at him and then winked at Imani. "It's still there," Fatima said as she tapped on her chest.

Imani pulled Fatima aside and whispered, "What about Hanif?"

"What about him? He oughtta be here with me instead of with his mama."

"Fa-ti-ma."

"E-mon-nee," Fatima began, "all I'm gonna do is rap with this buff brotha. I ain't tryin' to play Hanif."

"All right, Fatima, you better keep your word." Imani watched as her best friend escorted Erik to the buffet table. Just beyond them, Imani saw Miss Rollins, Mr. Powers, and her parents huddled together. Tariq headed towards them. "Terry, I'll be back."

Imani pulled Tyler away from Dominique and brought him to where their parents and Tariq stood. "Hello, birthday girl," Miss Rollins began, "your parents invited us to your church."

Imani shot a look at her mother. Mrs. Jackson smiled. "For Friends and Family Day," she said.

"Okaaay," Imani said.

"You might as well come over for dinner–"

"What! Where!" Imani shouted before her father completed his sentence. All eyes were on her.

"Our home," Mr. Jackson said and gave Imani a look that told her to drop it.

"Sounds good to me," Mr. Powers said.

Imani stared at Miss Rollins. She crossed her fingers behind her back. *Plueeeze say no...*

"Imani doesn't seem too happy about the invitation. Maybe we shouldn't go, Andrew."

"Nonsense, you are more than welcome in our home," Mrs. Jackson said. "Isn't that right, Imani?"

"Yeah, Imani, ain't that right?" Tariq asked and then he chuckled.

"Who's the little guy?" Mr. Powers asked.

Imani slapped her hand over Tariq's open mouth. "He's not little. Tariq's 12 and he's a good friend of Tyler's and mine. Right, Tariq?" Imani asked. She uncovered his mouth but pinched his ear.

"Right. A real good friend," he said in a dry tone.

"Well, Tariq, nice meeting you," Miss Rollins said and pointed to Tariq's hair. "It's so funny. My aunt has pictures of herself when she wore a big Afro way back when. Hers was nice and neat though."

"I like mine like this," Tariq said and patted his mound of wiry hair.

"Dad, Tariq wants to know what kind of game you're runnin'."

"What?" Miss Rollins asked.

Tyler laughed.

"Actually, I think that's a good question, Tariq," Imani's father said and patted the boy's back.

"If I tell you, do you want in?" Mr. Powers asked Tariq and then looked at Mr. Jackson.

"Look how you livin'. Yeah, break me off a piece."

"All right, Tariq. This is how you play the game. First, you gotta graduate from college preferably with a degree in business."

"Yeah, yeah, I'm feelin' that so I can scam people out of their money," Tariq said.

"Nooo, it's so you can learn how to run your own business. And while you're in college, make sure you get a summer job or internship in whatever type of business you want."

"Okay, okay and that way I can get paid and take their money too."

"Nooo, that way you can put that book knowledge to use, make some contacts, and learn first hand how to run that business."

"When you gonna get to the good part about how you got all this," Tariq said as he spread out his arms.

"I don't understand, young man. What are you waiting for him to say?" Miss Rollins asked.

"Oooh, now I get it," Tariq said as he nodded his head up and down. "You frontin' 'cause your woman's here. You want her to think you got all this on the up and up. That's cool. I ain't gonna play a brotha out in front of his woman. We'll rap some other time." Tariq winked at Mr. Powers and then sauntered away.

"What just happened here?" Mr. Powers asked no one in particular but everyone answered, "I don't know."

A chorus of *Happy Birthday* rang out behind them. Fatima rolled out a gold cart with the birthday cake on it. Seventeen light blue and white candles outlined the jersey. "Make a wish," Fatima told Imani.

"Wow, this cake is too cool to cut."

"You make a wish and I'll cut it," Fatima said.

Imani gazed about the luxurious living room with its cathedral ceiling, brick fireplace, artwork and artifacts, rich leather furniture, and plush carpet. Her brown eyes roamed into the dining room and landed on a crystal chandelier that sparkled. She closed her eyes. *I wish my parents and I could live like this.*

* * *

It was the Monday after her birthday and Imani could not concentrate in class. She replayed the party repeatedly in her mind. When the final bell sounded, she was elated. Imani anticipated a great basketball practice because she had tons of renewed energy to burn. She ran straight to the gym and changed clothes in record time.

Out on the court, Terry ran up to her. "Hey, Imani, great party."

"The best," Imani said as she beamed with joy. "I feel like I won the lottery or something because I can't stop smiling. My lips are sore from grinning so much."

"Nothing wrong with being happy," Terry said.

"I am sooo tired," Dominique said.

"You just oughta be. You danced all night at my party," Imani said.

"She didn't look so tired last period. The girl talked and giggled so much that Ms. Walsh told her to shut up or to get out," Terry said to Imani. "And this crazy fool left." Terry turned to Dominique. "Where did you go?"

"The girls' bathroom."

Imani sat on the floor next to Dominique. She whispered, "What's up with you? You doin' drugs?"

Terry joined them and sat on the other side of Dominique. "What's the deal?" Terry asked. "'Cause you were waaay too hyper at the party."

"Dancing even when the music wasn't playing," Imani added.

Dominique appeared to have tuned them out or fell asleep with her eyes open. Her light eyes remained fixed in the direction of the locker room.

"Give me 10 laps, ladies" the coach hollered.

His command snapped Dominique out of her trance. "Y'all cover for me while I go to the bathroom."

"Dominique, lead them out. Let's go!" he ordered.

"So much for the bathroom. Get in front of the line," Imani told her.

"I can't catch a break," Dominique said as she trudged towards the front.

"Today, Dominique!" her father yelled.

Imani lined up behind her and waited for the coach to blow his whistle. When it sounded, Dominique took off at a medium pace and kept that same speed for the first three laps. Then she lost momentum.

"You're killin' me. Pick it up," Imani said.

"I can't. I told you I'm tired."

"Suck it up, Girl. Don't piss him off."

"You take the lead then," Dominique said.

Imani moved ahead of Dominique and stretched out her long legs. She jetted past the coach. When the whistle sounded, Imani knew that he busted them.

"What's going on? Dominique, get back in front."

Imani heard Dominique as she panted. Imani shortened her stride so that Dominique could regain the lead. She waited but Dominique never ran by her. The whistle sounded again. "Dominique Wilkens, get over here. Imani, lead them out."

Imani picked up the pace. As she rounded the far corner, she saw the intense conversation between father and daughter. Imani felt bad for Dominique but there was nothing she could do to help her at that moment.

Dominique rejoined them at the end of the line. A few minutes later, the whistle sounded. "Final lap," the coach said.

Imani felt just as strong on that final lap around the gym as the first one. She raced to the end and the coach blew his whistle once more. "Lay ups let's go," he began, "Dominique, give me more five laps."

"Oh, c'mon. I'm wiped out," she said.

"Dominique!" her father yelled.

"Can't I at least go to the bathroom first?"

"Five laps and then the bathroom," he said and walked towards his daughter.

Dominique took off before he reached her. Everyone watched as Dominique trotted around the gym. A few of her teammates giggled. Coach Wilkens blew his whistle. "Hey! This is not a side show." He passed the ball to Imani. "Since you're the obvious leader of this team, start us off."

Imani dribbled from behind the three-point line at full speed towards the basket. She soared into the air with her right arm fully extended and eyes focused on the rim. Imani heard the coach and her teammates as they screamed, "Dominique!"

The impact knocked the wind out of Imani. She lowered her left hand. As Imani landed on it, something cracked. "Oh God!" she screeched.

"Get out the way!" Coach Wilkens yelled at the players who huddled over Imani. Although the tears blurred her vision, she saw Mr. Wilken's large hand.

"Nooo, don't touch me!" she cried out.

"I know it hurts, I know. Okay, I won't touch you," he said and hollered at someone to dial 9-1-1. "I'm not gonna touch you, but I want you to try to flex your fingers. Can you do that for me?"

Imani squirmed about the cold hard floor. She did not know where the pain came from. Her entire left arm and hand felt as if they were on fire. *You crazy? I can't. I can't. Oh God the pain. I can't move it. Leave me alone. I wanna go to sleep. I wanna go to sleep...just let me go...sleep...*Imani chanted and then laid still. The faces that peered down at her disappeared as her eyelids closed. Their voices seemed miles away.

"Wake up sleepy head," her mother said. Imani smiled and thought to herself, *thank God. That was just a crazy dream. Let me get out of this bed.*

"Oh no, Baby, don't try to get up," her mother said as she eased Imani back down.

Imani opened her eyes and wondered where she was. Her mother was there but so were Tyler and her father. Their somber faces scared her. She took a deep breath and that indescribable hospital odor made her nauseous. "Oh no," she said and glanced about. Her teary eyes landed on her left arm. Imani could not see her brown skin. A white cast covered her arm down to her knuckles and between her thumb.

"Oh God! This is for real!" she cried out. Mrs. Jackson leaned over her daughter. Imani buried her face in her bosom.

"Baby, this wasn't your fault," Mr. Jackson said.

"It was a freak accident," Tyler began, "Coach said that Dominique wasn't watching where she was running, and ummm, well ummm, you know the rest."

Imani stared into her mother's red eyes. "Mom, what did the doctor say? I can play again this year, right?" Imani used her right hand and wiped some tears away. She wanted to know. But then again, she did not want to know. Yet, she had to know. "Mom? Can I play?"

Her mother's lips quivered, yet no words came forth. Imani turned to her father. "Daddy, plueeeze tell me I can play...Tyler...Mom...somebody...talk to me."

Nobody answered her. Yet, their glazed over eyes said it all.

FATIMA

"Ya'll killin' me," Fatima said. She massaged her forehead where the pressure lodged above her brows. "You were in the hospital now Grandma's sick and don't get me started on Mercy."

"What's wrong with Grandma Rose?"

"Her blood pressure is sky high. She didn't even know it. Doc Floyd gave her medicine and sent her home."

"At least she's not laying up in that stinkin' hospital. I'm so glad to be outta there," Imani said.

"And I'm just itchin' to kick somebody's behind so c'mon and let me at her."

"If Dominique doesn't stop calling me, I just might cut you loose. I'm sick of her trying to apologize. There's nothing she can say to make me feel better. She snatched that Howard scholarship right away from me."

Fatima listened to her best friend as she sobbed. For the past couple of weeks, their conversation about what happened led Imani to tears.

"Girrrl, I know you still mad. Gimme her address and I'll go over there right now."

"What good will that do, Fatima? You beat her up and my arm is still broken. I'm out for the season and out of chances to get into college."

Fatima stretched out on the couch and covered her eyes with her forearm. The warm cell phone felt good against her ear. "Your grades should count for something, and I know you tore up the SATs."

"Pssst. I got my scores today and I only got 1000."

Fatima uncovered her eyes. "A thousand! Dang! I knew you were smart. But, dang! You don't even wanna know what I scored. What Tyler get?"

"1375 or something like that."

Fatima shot up to an upright position. "Daaang!" she exclaimed in disbelief. Alexus whimpered so Fatima lowered her voice. "He cheated. I know he cheated. Ain't no way nobody can score like that. I knew Tyler was a brainiac but c'mon, Girl, you know he cheated..."

"'Scuse me, Fatima. But uh, can we get back to me? I only scored a thousand. I needed over 1170. So I can kiss their academic scholarship goodbye too."

"So take it again. You said that's what you were gonna do."

"That's when it mattered. Nothing matters now. I was so stupid to think I could get a college scholarship anyway. I don't care anymore..."

Fatima rolled her eyes even though she knew that Imani could not see her. "Why you cryin' in my ears if you don't care? You know dang well you do so suck it up and take it again," Fatima said and then listened as Imani sniffled and Alexus hollered from the bedroom.

"Get me a job at the Chicken Shack."

"What! You can't be for real." Fatima pressed the cell closer to her ear.

"I'm serious, Fatima. No scholarship means I'm gonna have to work my way into college. Even if I have to stay here and go to community college with you."

"You still takin' those pain killers? 'Cause I swear you soundin' whacked. And, Mercy, pick up that baby!"

"You tryin' to bust my eardrum?" Imani asked.

Fatima exhaled and shifted the phone to her other ear. "I swear y'all killin' me." She took a deep breath and whispered, "Now listen–"

"No, you listen. Daddy can't afford the tuition, so I've gotta do this. How else is it gonna happen?"

"Financial aid. You poor enough to get that."

"I can't count on that covering everything. We're talking about thousands of dollars, Fatima."

"I hear ya but check this. You got one good arm. Ain't nothing you can do at the Chicken Shack with that bum arm in a cast. Why don't you wait–"

"I can't wait. I need time to save money."

"Okaaay, then check this. Your daddy ain't gonna let you work."

"Who said Daddy gotta know?"

"Well, he ain't about to hurt me and when you get busted, don't bring my name in it."

"He's not gonna find out. I'll just tell him that I'm at basketball practice or at the games just in case by some slim chance I can play again before the season's over and I'll know what's going on."

"I don't know about you anymore. You startin' to sound too much like me," Fatima said.

"My Pastor said that God helps those who help themselves. So no matter what, I'm going to college by any means necessary."

"Well all right, Malcolm X. But the Chicken Shack is still out. But ummm, hold up. Let me think a sec'." Fatima closed her eyes and her cousin Shonda came to mind. "There is something that I could probably do but...naw, I don't know about that."

"What?"

"W-e-l-l-l, I was thinkin' about callin' Shonda over at the doctor's office."

"Oh yeah, the office you broke into–"

"Weee broke into last year..."

"I know, I know. Just messin' with you."

"Just say 'no' to those pain killers."

"When these few are gone, that's it."

"Yup, I knew you were high. Anyway, they need a receptionist to work part-time. And since me and Shonda are tight, maaaybe, I could hook you up with them. But ummm, I dunno."

"Don't know what? It sounds good. Call her."

"Nope. Not unless you do something."

"I know you're not bribing me. C'mon, Fatima."

"Nope. I'm not gonna do it unless you take that test again. So you take the SAT over and I'll try and get you that job. Deal?"

"Daaang, Fatima, why you gotta start acting all grown up all of a sudden?"

"Stop stallin'. Deal or what?" Fatima asked as she rose from the couch.

"All right. I'll do it."

"Cool. I'll get back to ya. But right now, I gotta see why Alexus is screamin' like somebody's killin' her."

Fatima smelled the soiled diaper as she entered what used to be her bedroom. She peeked over the side of the crib and saw Alexus' small mouth opened as wide as it could be and tears streamed from the corners of both eyes. Her arms and legs stretched out so that she looked stiff. Yet, her tiny body trembled as she hollered.

"I'll call you back," Mercedes said.

Fatima spun around and saw Mercedes squatted in a corner with a cell phone in her hand and a big bag of potato chips on the floor next to her.

"You got some doggone nerve. Your baby is lying in dodo and hungry and you over there piggin' out and yappin' it up. Grandma's tryin' to rest and you–"

"I was just about to get her when you walked in."

"Yeah, right."

Fatima watched as Mercedes peeled the white tape of the diaper back and pulled down the front of it. "Fuuunky!" Mercedes screamed.

"Fatima, can you clean that crap off her?"

"No! You do it."

Mercedes took a handful of wet wipes in one hand and lifted up Alexus' legs with the other. She scraped the greenish brown mush off Alexus' light brown buttocks with the wipes then got a handful more and cleaned off what remained.

"Can you roll up the diaper and get it out of here?"

"Nope. Act like I ain't even here," Fatima said.

"What's up with you? I expect that stank attitude from Aunt Rose but not you. And shut up, Alexus! I've cleaned your stinkin' behind. Now shut up!"

"Don't yell at her! Yell at that sorry boyfriend of yours. Tell him to get over here and help you."

"Why? You standin' right here."

"It's *his* baby. Not mine."

"I am so sick of hearin' you and Aunt Rose complainin' all the time. Y'all worse than my parents."

"You're free to leave anytime," Grandma Rose said in a husky tone. Mercedes and Fatima's mouths dropped.

Grandma Rose said what Fatima felt. She wanted Mercedes to pack her stuff and go back to her parents. "Move," Fatima said and nudged Mercedes to the side. She lifted the crying baby out of the crib.

"Sorry if Alexus woke you, Aunt Rose."

"It ain't that baby's fault. It's her mama who's about to pump up my pressure," Grandma Rose said and pointed at Mercedes. "Go warm up her bottle. And while you're cleaning the dishes, I'll feed Alexus."

"Dishes? I don't wanna mess up my nails. Troy's coming over. So if you do the dishes, I'll gladly put a bottle in her big mouth."

"Wrong answer," Fatima said as she shook her head. A deep crease formed above Grandma Rose's brow and she planted her hands on her ample hips. "Uh, Mercy, she may not knock you out if you're holdin' the baby." Fatima held the baby up to Mercedes' face. "I suggest you take Alexus and head for the kitchen."

"I was just playin'. I'm gonna do it," Mercedes began, "you've changed, Fatima, and I don't like the new you. I can't even joke with you anymore."

"'Cause ain't nothing funny. Ain't nothing funny about listening to this baby cry all the time. And it sure ain't funny with me goin' to school and workin' at that dang chicken joint then comin' home havin' to work some more when you've been here all day."

"Oh, like raisin' Alexus ain't work? That's what I do all day."

"Stop lyin' and warm up that baby's bottle. There's gonna be some changes around here. You're gonna learn how to care for that poor baby and do some chores around this house. Come January, you're goin' back to school too," Grandma Rose said.

"I guess I have no say over my life, huh? I swear nobody loves me but Troy."

"Oh, Aunt Rose loves you. If I didn't, you would still be in that shelter. I love you so much that Imma give you some choices. You can choose to go with my flow or you can float on outta here," Grandma Rose said and then strolled towards the kitchen. Mercedes handed the now quiet Alexus back to Fatima and marched close behind Grandma Rose. Fatima followed.

"That's it, Aunt Rose?"

"Nooo, you have other options. You can float back to the shelter or go back to your mama's house."

Fatima could not take it anymore. She laughed. It wasn't what Grandma Rose said that was funny but rather how she said it in a calm and cool demeanor. Fatima stopped when Mercedes scowled at her.

"Oh, you're havin' big fun, huh? Did you have fun at Imani's party too? You didn't even invite me. That was messed up, Cuz."

"Were you gonna take Alexus?"

"No. I was gonna ask you to baby sit, Aunt Rose."

"'No', would have been my answer."

"Why? It's not like you had anywhere to go."

"That's not the point, Mercy. You've gotta take responsibility for Alexus. She is your number one priority not going to some party. Now answer this. Do you want to keep Alexus or give her up?"

Fatima kept one eye on Mercedes and brought Alexus closer to her chest as the baby squirmed about in her arms. Fatima kissed the top of her head and inhaled the sweet aroma of baby oil.

Mercedes never answered. Instead, she took the bottle of beige colored formula from Grandma Rose and gave it to her cousin. Fatima tested the formula on her wrist and then placed the nipple against Alexus' tiny lips. The baby turned her head away. Fatima leaned her head to the side and made eye contact with Alexus.

"Come on now. I know you're pissed off that you had to wait so long and I don't blame you. But don't front, I know you're hungry. You gotta eat and grow some hair up here. It's too cold to be bald-headed." Fatima kissed the baby on her cheek. Alexus smiled and Fatima laughed. "Come on and let's do this again." That time, the baby tugged on the nipple.

She drank about half of the formula and Fatima noticed that she did not suck as hard. Her little eyelids eased down over her jet black eyes. "Oh no, Sistah, you gotta burp before you go to sleep on me," Fatima said and hoisted the small bundle upon her shoulder and rubbed and patted her back.

At what point Fatima fell asleep on the couch, she did not know. Alexus was asleep right next to her. "I don't remember putting her down," she said. Fatima walked into the kitchen and the sink was empty. The clean dishes were in the ivory dish rack. "Go 'head Mercy." Fatima returned to the living room and lifted Alexus off the sofa. She tiptoed to Alexus' crib and eased her down onto the mattress. Fatima checked Mercedes' favorite spot, in the corner, but she was not there.

Fatima heard Grandma Rose's snore before she opened her bedroom door. She peeked in and sure thing, Grandma Rose was asleep with her mouth open. Mercedes was not there, either. "Dang it. I bet she out creepin' with Troy."

The telephone rang and Fatima sprinted into the kitchen and snatched up the receiver. "Who is it?"

"May I speak to Fatima?"

"Hey, Hanif, it's me."

"I miss you something awful. How ya doing?"

"When you comin' back?" Fatima asked.

There was silence before Hanif said, "I dunno."

"Then what do you care how I'm doing? It ain't like you can help me from there now can you?"

"Why every time I call we gotta argue? Why you hafta make this harder than what it already is? You know I love you, Fatima."

"But you love your mama more."

"What do you want me to say to that?"

"You don't have to say anything. I know the deal. All I'm gonna say is there's some messed up stuff goin' on here and I need you with me right now."

"What's going on?"

"Ain't it enough to know I need you without you knowin' the details? So are you comin' back or what?"

"Don't do this, Fatima. C'mon and tell me what's happening. I really wanna know."

Fatima huffed.

"How's Imani? Is she all right? Is Grandma Rose feeling better?"

Fatima remained silent. She yanked on the tangled white cord until it reached the couch.

"Fatima, c'mon now. Talk to me."

"I'll talk to you whenever you get here."

"Wow. So whatcha sayin'? You don't want me to call you anymore? Is that whatcha sayin'?"

"What I'm sayin' is that you can't help me from where you are right now. And if you cared about me, you would come back ASAP. That's what I'm sayin'."

"And if you cared about me, Fatima, you would understand why I can't leave here just yet. Mama needs my help and I'm sorry you can't accept that..."

Fatima listened as Hanif explained his mother's condition and the progress she made in rehab. "You know my brothers are useless. They claim they're sooo busy and yeah they got jobs. But shooot, Mama worked two sometimes three jobs and raised us. If it wasn't for the sacrifices she made back then, I wouldn't be in college today..." As Hanif continued and pleaded his case, Mercedes and Troy entered the apartment.

"I gotta go. I'll see ya when I see ya."

"C'mon, Fatima, don't end the conversation like this. Can I at least hear that you still love me?"

"I love you just like I've loved other people and that didn't stop them from leavin' me. So big deal."

"I'm not leaving you, Boo. I'll be back."

"Whatever, Hanif."

"So can I call you again or what?"

"Do what you wanna do just like you're doin' right now. And right now, I'm hangin' up," Fatima said and did just that. She slammed the receiver back on the hook then turned and faced Mercedes and Troy. Mercedes had tears in her eyes.

"Where you been?"

"Hello to you too, Fatima," Troy said.

"Where you been, Mercy?" Fatima asked again.

Mercedes rolled her eyes from Fatima to Troy. "Why don't you trust me?" Mercedes asked him.

"Hummmp. After what you pulled on me tonight, I don't trust your behind either. And you still didn't answer my question."

"Mind your business," Troy told Fatima.

"You're in my apartment so it is my business."

Troy brushed past Mercedes and stepped up to Fatima. She looked up at him and leaned her head to the side. "Whatcha wanna do? Huh?" Fatima asked.

"I wanna talk to my woman without you buttin' in. Can I do that?"

Fatima stepped back. "Go right ahead," she said and sauntered into the kitchen and over to the dish rack. Yet, she listened to their every word.

"That guy wasn't hitting on me. All he asked was did I have the time and I told him. That's it."

"So why were you smilin' all up in his face? I told you about smilin' at other guys. Who you belong to?"

"You."

"That's right. So don't diss me like that again."

"I didn't do it on purpose, Troy."

"Did you wear those tight jeans and that little sweater on purpose? Why you wanna show that gut? Huh? Are you doin' sit ups like I told you or just sittin' around eatin' chips and junk?"

"I don't eat chips anymore," Mercedes said.

Fatima dropped a plastic plate onto the floor. She knew that would get Mercedes' attention. Sure enough, Mercedes turned and stared at her cousin. Fatima mouthed the word, "liar."

Mercedes waved her hand at Fatima and rolled her eyes again.

"What's taking you so long to lose that weight? You used to look good. But you're slippin', Baby. Get it together or else–"

"Or else what? I had your baby, moved out of my parents' house, and now you gonna threaten me talkin' 'bout if I don't lose weight you're gonna walk? I love you, Troy, and I thought you loved me."

"I love you, Baby, but you gotta start actin' right."

"I've been actin' right. I return your pages right away. I call you at three, four, eight, and eleven o'clock everyday. I even slipped outta here tonight because you said you needed me so bad."

A glass plate slipped through Fatima's fingers. It hit the linoleum floor and crumbled into pieces.

"What's wrong with you?" Mercedes asked.

Fatima stepped over the shiny pieces and into the living room. "Hold up. Let me get something straight. You left your baby hangin' to go and have sex with him."

"A man needs attention too," Troy said.

"Boy, plueeeze. I don't see no man up in here."

"Fatima, don't start," Mercedes said.

Fatima scanned her up and down. "I don't see no woman up in here, either. Standin' up here lettin' Troy beat you down with that big mouth of his."

Troy snatched off his black leather gloves and pointed his thick finger within inches of Fatima's face.

Fatima shifted her head from side to side. "You must think I'm Mercy. Bring it if you want but you're gonna get jacked up."

"Don't hit her, Troy."

"I was gonna clock her but Hanif's the one who needs to put her in check. If, he's man enough to do it."

"Hanif knows the deal. He will never lay his hands on me. And he doesn't have to pretend that he's a man. You walkin' around here frontin' like you're a father. Y'all should have given Alexus up for adoption since neither one of y'all wanna take care of her."

"What she talkin' 'bout, Mercy?" Troy asked. "You better be takin' care of *my* baby." He got in Mercedes' face. "You're the mother and that's your job. Get it?"

"And what's your job?" Fatima asked.

"I'm doin' my thing. Workin' and goin' to school and that's all I can do right now," Troy spat out.

Fatima watched as Mercedes wiped Troy's spit off her face. *How stupid can she be? I wish he would spit on me. He would be pickin' all his teeth up off this floor.* Aloud Fatima said, "While you were out tonight takin' care of your so-called manly needs, you should have been here helpin' out with Alexus."

"I work hard and a man gotta hang sometimes. Roll with his boyz sometimes. Otherwise, he'll go crazy."

"That's how I feel too, Troy. But you have a fit when I wanna hang out with my girlfriends, and Fatima wanna keep me on lockdown too. It can't just be all about Alexus. I gotta have a life too," Mercedes said and tears rolled down her face.

"Me and Alexus is your life," Troy said.

"I know but I need more."

"I hope you thought about that tonight as you were sexin' it up. What you gonna do with two babies?"

"She ain't gonna get pregnant again. We know what we're doin'," Troy said and then laughed. "Sounds like you're jealous. You ain't gettin' none from Hanif?"

"Jealous of what? You two sexing it up?" Fatima began and pointed at the couple. "I ain't even gonna lie. We ain't havin' sex 'cause we ain't even ready to be takin' care of no babies. And that includes y'all baby."

Troy stood before Mercedes and squeezed her face. "My baby's mama better get it together. I don't ever wanna hear this crap no more. Are you feelin' me?" Troy asked. The imprint of his thick fingers sunk deeper and deeper into her skin.

"Ouch, Troy, that hurts," she mumbled between scrunched up lips.

"Are you feelin' me, Mercy?" Troy asked again.

Tears streamed down her face and onto his fingers. "Yeah, Troy."

Her boyfriend released his grip. However, the indentations from his fingers remained. "Why you gotta make me go off? Huh? I love you, Mercy. Didn't I show you tonight how much I love you?"

Mercedes did not answer.

"But you've gotta start obeying me, Baby."

Mercedes stood there and massaged her cheeks. Fatima waited for her cousin to retaliate or yell at Troy or something. Yet, Mercedes did nothing. Fatima rolled her eyes at her and turned to Troy. "Look," Fatima began and fingered quotation marks, "'Man', Mercy needs money for diapers and formula for your baby so give it up." Fatima held out her hand and wiggled her fingers.

"I only got enough for the bus home, but I'll try and swing by tomorrow."

"Well, try real hard 'cause that's about all she got left is enough to get through tonight."

"Ain't you workin'?" Troy asked Fatima. "Can't you spring for some?"

Fatima covered her face and exhaled into her hands. "Y'all ain't hearin' me. This is the last time I'm gonna break this down. I ain't Alexus' mama. I ain't her daddy. Y'all wanted to keep her. So y'all take care of her."

"Preach on, Sistah Fatima. Now tell us something that we don't know," Troy said.

Fatima stepped up so close to Troy that she smelled his sour breath. "Okay, Troy, news flash. Instead of trackin' Mercy's every move, start trackin' how many diapers and how many cans of formula *your* baby goes through a week and bring 'em on over here *every week."* Fatima cocked her head. "Are *you* feelin' me, Man?"

DOMINIQUE

HELP!!

I can't take this! Why won't she forgive me? If she can't play again, I will NEVER forgive myself. Isn't that enough payback? Isn't dealing with my father enough? He says that it was just a freak accident & that he isn't holding it against me but I know he is. What's killing me is that I know it wasn't an accident. Well yeah, in a way it was because I didn't crash into Imani on purpose.

See what happened was Ms. Walsh kicked me out of her class for talking. Do you believe that? So I went to the bathroom & smoked a you-know-what & was feeling real good. But by the time I got to practice, my high wore off. I was sleepy, tired, & aggravated. I wanted to sneak off the court so bad & get another hit but before I could, my father called me to lead the team jogging around the gym like a bunch of idiots. I don't know if I was running with my eyes closed or what when I barreled into Imani. If I hadn't smoked a you-know-what, this never would have happened. NEVER.

And my teammates, ohmygod. All of them HATE me! We've lost every game since Imani's been gone. EVERY GAME! They all blame me & I know deep down that my father does too. I can't take this pressure anymore...I just can't take this...

The words on Dominique's monitor were fuzzy from the pool of water in her eyes. As the tears flowed, her vision cleared and she clicked the "send" button. She stared at the screen and hoped Kelli replied right away.

"What am I thinking? Nobody's home on a Friday night but me," she said and the tears built up in her eyes again. "I'll call her on her cell." Dominique dialed the first three numbers but stopped when she heard a knock on her bedroom door.

"May I come in?"

Dominique knew that was not a question. It was a matter of seconds before her mother barged in. She hung up her phone, wiped her eyes and threw the mound of wet white tissues into the wastepaper basket beneath her desk. As she shut down her computer, Mrs. Wilkens entered the room. She frowned and then asked, "What is burning in here?"

Caught up in her message to Kelli, Dominique forgot that she lit incense. A quarter of the cinnamon colored stick remained and charred residue hung from the tip of it. "Spiced Apple," Dominique said.

"My goodness. That aroma is so strong that I smelled it downstairs. Doesn't that scent get caught in your throat?" Mrs. Wilkens rubbed her long neck.

"Nope." Dominique laid across her bed and acted disinterested in whatever her mother said.

"Nope?" Mrs. Wilkens asked.

"I mean no it doesn't," Dominique said. It annoyed Dominique that her mother corrected her English. She caught herself before she rolled her eyes at her mother. That move would have prolonged the conversation. She wished her mother would leave so she could call Kelli.

"What is bothering you?" her mother asked.

"Nothing."

"I can tell by those red eyes and flushed face that you've been crying. So what's going on?"

"Nothing," Dominique said and rubbed her eyes. Had she known they were red, she would have used eye drops before her mother came in. Dominique watched as Mrs. Wilkens fingered through the school papers on her wood desk. Dominique cringed as her mother's brows raised, eyes widened and mouth opened. Mrs. Wilkens' complexion changed from vanilla to strawberry. Dominique closed her eyes. The sound of papers shuffled about intensified. "What on earth is happening here? Red marks all over the place."

Dominique's closed lids could not contain the tears. She did not try to hide them just like she left those papers with red "Ds" and "Fs" on her desk and hoped that her parents found them. "I told you I hate that school. Even those stupid teachers don't like me." Dominique sat up. She looked her mother dead in her light eyes. Dominique felt miserable and she wanted her mother to see it. "Now, may I transfer back to Parker?"

Mrs. Wilkens grabbed a handful of papers and pointed at her daughter. "Are you doing this on purpose?"

"No, Mom. It's not my fault. The teachers are doing it not me."

"So the answers they marked as incorrect on your work are really the right answers but the teachers said they are wrong because they hate you. Is that what you are alleging, Dominique?"

"Nooo, they are wrong. But it's the teachers' fault because they won't help me. I'm tired of raising my hand and watching students look at me like I'm stupid or something. But the teachers should see that I need help."

Mrs. Wilkens threw the papers down on top of the wood desk and waved her hands in the air. "You sit up here in your room all night and do what? Why didn't you come to your father or me for help?"

Dominique did not have an answer because the truth was that she had not studied in weeks. When she excelled in her classes, some students claimed that Dominique thought she was more intelligent than they were. When she slacked off, those same students called her dumb and stupid. That was when she decided not to do anything. Dominique was frustrated and did not know how to explain that to her mom. She waved her hand at Mrs. Wilkens. "You don't understand, Mom. You and daddy never understand."

"What don't I understand? I am looking at an intelligent and beautiful young woman who is determined to have her way or else she is going to deliberately ruin her life. Her excuse is that, 'everybody hates me.' Please explain again why that is so."

Dominique stood and raised her voice. "How many times do I have to tell you? Look at my skin. Look at my eyes. Look at my hair. The only person who doesn't care about my looks is Kelli. I could be purple and she would still be my friend."

"Bingo," Mrs. Wilkens began, "friend, is the key word. Kelli likes you for who you are. However, you have to be your own best friend and love yourself for who you are even if nobody else does. It took me a long time to comprehend that truth."

Dominique stared at her mom and realized that she yelled at the wrong person. She wanted to scream at Imani and every player on the team and every student in every one of her classes. The tears flowed again and her mother embraced her. Dominique cried on her shoulder and asked, "How can people be so mean? It hurts, especially, when another black girl is talking about me."

"I know it does, Baby," she began and patted her daughter's back. "Let's sit down," Mrs. Wilkens said and handed Dominique a tissue.

Dominique never cried so much than in the past few weeks. She hid in her room when the crying spell hit her. Dominique felt like a big baby. She looked at her mother who was strong and successful. Her father was strong and successful. Compared to her parents, she felt like a wimp and a failure.

"I experienced that same type of racism from the black girls in my neighborhood. They called me high-yella and red-bone in the summertime when I had a tan and white girl the remainder of the year."

"I didn't know you went through that."

Mrs. Wilkens nodded her head. "It did not help that I got a lot of attention from the boys. Those girls were deathly afraid that I would take their boyfriends."

"Wow. They haven't thrown that in my face, yet."

"I hope they don't either."

"I'm sure they'll hit me with that one sooner or later," Dominique said. She heard her father as he barked orders at the players on TV as if they heard him.

"Talk to your father about his experiences."

"Why? Anybody can see that he's black."

"Name calling was not limited to light-skinned people. Your father was called blue-black, jet-black, midnight, shoe polish, spook, tar baby, and on and on. So unfortunately, some black people hate on other black people because of the amount of melanin in their skin."

"But why, Mom?"

"Baby, as far as I know, this nonsense began back in slavery. The light-skinned slaves worked in the big house and the dark-skinned slaves worked in the fields. So the perception was that light-skinned blacks were superior to dark-skinned blacks and that type of slavery mentality has carried through to this present day."

"When will it end, Mom?"

"I don't know. I hope that your generation wakes up and realizes that we are all in the same race and no shade of black is superior or inferior to another."

"I hear what you're saying, but it's still happening now so how do I deal with it?"

"You can start by selecting your friends based on who they are on the inside and not what they look like on the outside. That applies to all races not just ours." Mrs. Wilkens paused and pointed at her daughter. "There is something else you must understand."

"What?"

"Consider it a compliment when people tease or talk about you."

Dominique frowned. "That doesn't make sense."

"Well, hear me out because this pettiness goes beyond skin tone. Tormentors will not say exactly what it is. However, they are jealous of something their victim has or does. There is something about you that those who speak badly about you wish they had and it might not be what you think it is."

"Oh come on, Mom, like what?"

"Well," Mrs. Wilkens began as she surveyed Dominique. "They could be intimidated by your height. Perhaps they envy your intelligence or confidence in class. Even in elementary school, teachers commended you on your active participation in class. So maybe those who pick on you lack that confidence to speak before their classmates and hate the fact that you can do it..."

Dominique stared at Mrs. Wilkens and wondered if her mother was psychic. She kept her latest classroom experiences a secret. Yet, her mother zeroed in on it.

"...only the girls who are giving you a hard time know what it is. But believe me, Baby, when people talk about you, that means you are doing something right."

"I haven't done anything right in a while," Dominique said and the tears flowed. She felt safe in the warmth of her mother's arms. Her mother's floral scented perfume was a nice change from the pungent incense. "I feel so stupid, Mom, for making myself act stupid and pretending that I'm dumb just so they will accept me."

Mrs. Wilkens placed her hand under daughter's chin. "Look at me."

Dominique gazed up at her mother and the tears slid down her face.

"Do not dumb down for anyone. You hear me?"

Dominique nodded.

"Do not apologize for being Dominique and do not let people define who you are. Only you can do that."

Dominique closed her eyes, inhaled and released it. "I just wanted them to like me and accept me."

"Answer this. Have you accepted Dominique?"

Dominique's eyes widened. Yet, no answer came.

"Have you forgiven yourself for hurting Imani?"

Dominique shook her head, "no."

"Is Dominique going to cut Dominique a break?"

She hunched her shoulders. "I never thought about it like that."

"And a couple of more questions for you to ponder. Are you willing to do the hard work it takes to remain a starter on your team? Or, will you settle for coming off the bench? Only you have the answers."

Dominque thought about the answers to those questions as she tossed and turned all night. Actually, the entire heavy conversation kept her awake. She rubbed her sore eyes. *Wow, Mom and Dad went through the same things and they made it. I can't let them down. Imma get my grades back up and shut up my teammates too. They'll see how good I am on and off the court.*

Dominique twisted so that she tangled herself up in the white cotton sheet. "Oh forget this," she said and got up and logged-on to her e-mail. She hoped that Kelli responded. One new message appeared on the screen.

I'm picking you up tomorrow night at 7...be ready...Love ya, Kels.

* * *

Dominique inhaled the scent of new leather as she sank in the soft seat. She tilted her head back and gazed at the stars through the opened sunroof. It was twenty degrees outside but the cold air felt good. When Kelli accelerated, the powerful engine rived above the deep bass of the hip-hop beat.

"Isn't this car like, ohmygosh, hot?" Kelli asked.

"Too cool," Dominique said as she grabbed unto a handle on the door as Kelli sped around a sharp curve. "The most expensive present that I've ever gotten was a computer. I can't believe you got a red hot sports car."

"I love it!" Kelli yelled and bounced in her seat. "And we're gonna have fun tonight. Big fun tonight..." Kelli sang. "That's what you need, Doms, big fun!"

Dominique was excited yet nervous. They headed for a party where she would meet Kelli's friends. Some of what her mother told her sank in. Dominique decided that she would be herself. If Kelli's friends did not like her, then too bad.

"You want a joint?" Kelli asked.

Dominique shook her head so hard that it made her dizzy. "Nope. Every time I think about a joint, I remember what I did to Imani."

"That wasn't your fault, Doms."

"It's not just that. Weed makes me too mellow and my brain foggy. I need energy. I have tons of studying to catch up on and basketball practice is Monday."

"Energy, huh? No problem," Kelli said.

Dominique wondered what that meant but she did not ask. She stared at Kelli's face and it looked taut and narrow. She constantly sniffled, rubbed, or picked at her nose. "So is that allergies or what?"

"I dunno. It's grossing me out too."

Dominique nodded. *Me too,* she thought. Aloud, she asked Kelli, "How's your diet?"

"Ten more pounds gone and ten or twenty more to go. Size four jeans now. Size two here I come. Summer will be here before you know it and I've gotta look great in my string bikini. Just picture it, Doms. A hot babe in her hot bikini and she's driving a hot car to the hot beach. That hot babe will be me when I lose ten or twenty more."

"Tell me you're kidding. Don't supermodels and actresses wear a size six or four?"

"Exactly. That's my edge. They will look like whales and pigs next to me. Nobody will want them. All of the designers will beg me to wear their creations down the runway. TV producers will want me on their shows instead of them. See?"

"That's if you don't kill yourself trying to get to size two. Are you still throwing up?"

"Oh, Doms, please. Throwing up has never killed anybody that I know. But no, I don't do that anymore. I just don't eat. I drink water and that's about it."

"What!"

"I get full off partying. I'm a party girl. No time to eat." Kelli released a wild laugh. Her car swerved from the center lane into the right and back to the center lane.

"Are you high?"

Kelli laughed again.

Dominique squeezed the handle tighter and thought about what she would do if Kelli could not drive. Dominique did not know how to drive and did not know where they were.

"I feel sooo good," Kelli began, "you're the one who looks old, tired and totally freaky. Just look at you. Is that ponytail like permanently attached to your head?"

"What?"

"Like all you ever wear is you hair pulled back or up in a bun. Are you 60 or 16?"

Dominique did not want to explain the black history of so-called "good hair" and the resentment that it caused. That was why Dominique seldom displayed her long straight hair. So instead, she told Kelli, "It's convenient since I play a lot of ball."

"You're not playing now, Girlfriend. So loosen up and let your hair down."

Dominique nodded. Kelli had a good point, and Dominique promised herself that she would stay true to herself. She untied the gray ponytail holder and felt the weight of her hair as it dropped past her shoulders.

"Doesn't that feel good? You're beautiful, Doms. The cutie pies at the party will be all over you."

Dominique checked it out for herself. "Not bad," she said as she admired herself in the lighted mirror.

"Now we need to brighten up those dull lips. What color is that anyway? Mud?" Kelli asked and then pulled a gold tube out of her coat pocket. "Try this."

Dominique stared at the scarlet colored lipstick and thought, *I don't know where her lips have been. Her nose is always running so I know snot probably has been on them and this lipstick. Eeelll what am I gonna do?*

"You can wipe it off first if you want," Kelli said as if she read Dominique's mind.

Dominique took a white tissue and scraped the slanted tip of the lipstick. She used a clean end of the tissue and removed her nutty brown lip color. Kelli's creamy red lipstick brightened Dominique's face and her mood. She smacked her lips together. "I like this. I've gotta buy one."

"Trust me, Doms, I know what's best for you," Kelli said as she pulled into a driveway.

Dominique glanced about the complex and all of the buildings looked identical. A short and skinny guy with wire rimmed eyeglasses stood in the doorway.

"Oh, it's you," he said to Kelli.

"Well, thanks for the welcome," she said.

"Sorry, Kels. I was expecting special delivery."

"In that case, you're excused," she said and they exchanged fake kisses on the cheeks. Kelli turned to Dominique. "Doms, Toms, Toms, Doms."

"Oooh, you're tall too. I love tall women. You're welcome here anytime. And by the way, Gorgeous, my name is Thomas not Toms but you know how Kels likes to shorten everybody's name."

Dominique laughed. Not because what he said was funny, but so that she could release nervous energy.

"Come on in and take off your coats and get comfortable. The party hasn't *really* started yet," Thomas said and stepped aside.

Dominique followed Kelli into the living room. The foul stench of marijuana hit her in the face. Dominique wanted to sprint out the door before Thomas closed it but it was too late. She heard the door as it snapped shut, and Kelli grabbed her hand.

"Hey everybody," Kelli said and they all greeted her. "I want to introduce a dear friend of mine."

Dominique jerked on Kelli's arm. She gritted her teeth while she told Kelli, "You're embarrassing me."

Kelli continued. "Make Doms feel welcomed."

Dominique smiled back at the guests. Some of them appeared college aged and others looked younger.

"Let's show her some love," Kelli said.

They all converged on Dominique at once. She endured their hugs and kisses and the smell of alcohol on their breath and pot on their clothes. When they backed off, one guy stood before her and checked Dominique out.

"You're gorgeous. You know that?" he asked. His eyes like most of the guests were blood red.

"Doms, Wills, Wills, Doms."

"It's William and pleased to meet you, Doms."

"It's Dominique," she said.

Kelli giggled and took a step backwards. "I'm gonna chit chat with Toms a minute."

Dominique wanted to follow her but did not want to appear childish. Yet, she felt lost and did not know what to do with her hands, so she extended her right one. "Nice meeting you too," she whispered.

William bypassed her hand and wrapped his long arms around her waist. She closed her eyes. *Ohmygod, can he feel me shaking through my clothes?*

"You wanna sit?" he asked.

Yup, he felt it. Probably figured I'm about to pass out or something. Dominique nodded "yes" and sunk into a black loveseat. She avoided eye contact and concentrated on his other facial features: long straight nose, rusty brown mustache, thin lips, and square chin. She decided that he looked okay. Not fine but not a troll either. Then the conversation with her mother popped in her mind that she should select friends by what's on the inside. So she focused on what William said.

"Can I get you a beer or something?"

"Soda. Any kind," she said. He laughed and she laughed too but did not know why.

"You don't drink. Do you?" William asked.

"No, not really."

William laughed but that time Dominique knew that the joke was on her. She frowned at him.

"I'm sorry," he said. "It's just that you remind me of Kels when she first started hanging out with us. She didn't drink, didn't smoke pot, hell, I don't even think she smoked cigarettes," he said and then chuckled. "Now, Kels will try anything. She's so cool and sooo hot. She's like half the size she used to be."

Dominique surveyed her friend's new physique and agreed that she was super thin. Flat abs, hips, and dierrie. The only body parts that stood out were her new boobs. Dominique guessed that they filled a "C" cup. Even her long stringy blonde hair lacked body. "So a 'hot' girl is someone who's super thin?" Dominique asked.

"Yeah. Gotta be thin to be in," he said and then stretched out his arms. "Look around. No fatsoes in here."

Dominique felt like a buffalo as she surveyed the people. All of the girls appeared anorexic. "Do you think I'm fat?" she asked but regretted that she did because his light brown eyes lingered all over her body.

William scooted over so close to Dominique that she smelled the alcohol on his breath. He lifted his arm and placed it behind her head. That was when she got a whiff of his foul underarm odor.

"Let's put it this way. Your face on Kels' body would make you the hottest chick in here. And by the way, I love your freckles," he said and winked at her.

Dominique nodded. *Get your stinky self away from me. Gonna call me fat and then throw in a compliment. Thanks, Jerk.*

"I'll get that soda."

He rose and strolled away, yet his musty scent remained. Dominique wanted to leave before William returned. As she eased up, another guy sat next to her.

"I thought he would never leave your side."

"Me either," Dominique said and settled back in her seat. She wondered how she became so popular.

"My name's Carl."

"Short for Carlton?" Dominique asked.

"No, just plain old Carl," he said and flashed the brightest smile that she ever saw. His well-defined lips stretched wide and displayed white teeth that played off his dark chocolate complexion. The whites of his eyes were just that–white.

Dominique smiled back at him. *Wow, he is so fine. Imani's boyfriend type fine. He's probably a jerk like William. But oooh, he's fine.*

The doorbell rang and Thomas looked through the peephole. "Special delivery," he said. A chorus of "all right" sounded out from the group.

"This party's about to get started," William said as he handed Dominique a red plastic cup. She inspected the dark bubbly beverage and sniffed it. It looked and smelled like cola so she took a sip.

William winked at Carl. "Isn't she great?"

"If you leave us alone, I can find out."

"Oh, that's cool. It's time to party anyway. See you in the fun room," William said. He followed Thomas, who carried a package, Kelli, and all of the others. They seemed energized and excited. That mood was opposite of their mellow behavior earlier.

"I was expecting a party with loud music and dancing but everybody seems so laid back."

"They've been smoking weed."

"They? You don't smoke?" Dominique asked and looked straight into his jet black eyes.

"Used to. But it doesn't do anything for me anymore other than give me the munchies, a dry mouth and a dry throat. It was time to move on. If I'm gonna get high, I wanna get there quick, still be alert and not groggy. You know what I mean? So what about you?"

Dominique did not know what he meant by "get there quick." Yet, she played it cool. "Kelli turned me on to pot, but I don't think I'll ever smoke again."

"Bad experience, huh?" he asked but continued before she answered. "There was one time that I swore I was gonna die. I smoked this joint and I don't know what that sucker was laced with but my heart was beating triple time. I was dizzy as hell. Do you know how hard it is to get vomit in the real toilet when you're seeing double? I was dizzy and shaking like crazy. When that high finally wore off, I think I slept almost two days straight. I came this close to missing a final exam. I think I got a "D" but I didn't care. I was just glad to be alive."

"Ohmygod, that's scary," Dominique began, "I can't imagine going through that. Thanks for telling me. Now I know I'm not gonna touch that stuff again."

"Glad I could help," Carl said and licked his lips.

Dominique stared at his luscious wet lips as she thought of something else to ask. Then her eyes moved up to his slanted ones. "Sooo, Carl, are you in college?"

"Yes, I am. I'm a crazed pre-med student," he said and then chuckled.

Dominique laughed too.

"But seriously though, the workload is insane. Way too much reading and research and too little time." Carl glanced at his watch. "I should be cramming right now, but I had to take a break and get rejuvenated."

"Me too," Dominique began, "I have so much work to do and so much to prove to everybody. Especially, to my dad and basketball team."

"You play ball? Go 'head, Girl. You're young, beautiful, athletic, and articulate. Wow, what a lethal combination that could crush my heart." He took her right hand in his and kissed it.

Dominique held her breath. The softness of his lips lingered on that hand. *I can't believe this is happening. A super fine college guy interested in me and he understands pressure because he's feeling it too. I wanna hug him or kiss him or something. No, I can't. What if he pushes me away or thinks I'm a slut or something? Nah, I can't do that.*

William's loud voice broke her private thoughts. "Heeey, let's pump up some music in here!"

Dominique watched in awe as the young people paired off and danced. Most of them just jumped about.

"It looks like they started without us. Follow me," Carl said.

"It's all set up for you!" Thomas yelled.

"Have fun, Doms!" Kelli hollered and kissed Dominique on both cheeks. Before Dominique spoke, Kelli took off to the other side of the room and jumped in between another couple. They danced and laughed.

Dominique felt a lump in her throat and a knot in the pit of her stomach the size of a baseball. Carl opened a door and she let go of his hand. He looked back at her.

"I'm not going to hurt you."

Dominique took a deep breath. *Don't let this college guy think you're a baby. Go in.* Dominique tried to smile but her lips would not move. She stepped through the doorway. The first thing her eyes landed on was a bed. "Why are we in Thomas' bedroom?"

"To get rejuvenated and energized, Sweetheart," he said and pointed downward.

Dominique's eyes traced his long arm down to where his finger pointed. Her eyes widened and her jaw dropped. "Is that?"

"Yup. You've gotta try it," he said.

Atop the glass table were four thin lines of white powder. A couple of metal cylinders lay off to the side. A pile of dollar bills on the opposite side. "This will give you the juice that pot couldn't," he began, "come closer."

Dominique backed up. "I can see from here."

"Are you just going to stand there and watch me? That's no fun. All of them out there snorted and they're having a great time. Trust me, if you can smoke weed, you can do this. It's a natural progression."

Dominique shook her head. *I can't believe Kelli's doing cocaine. And she thinks this is what I need? She was wrong about weed. What if she's wrong again?*

"What are you afraid of, Sweetheart?" Carl asked and interrupted her internal conversation.

"I don't think drugs are for me. I couldn't handle pot, so how can I handle coke?"

"Now is a great time to find out. You're here with friends and we won't let anything bad happen to you. Kelli would not bring you here to hurt you. She probably paid for your trip. If she didn't, your first time is on me."

Dominique felt so naïve. She never questioned Kelli about where and how she got the joints that she gave her. Money never entered her mind.

"This is safer than going out on the streets and dealing with those hoodlums directly," Carl said. "I don't even know what our delivery boy looks like. Thomas never lets him in."

That answered one of Dominique's questions.

"Thomas uses the honor system. We come in here, use what we want and pay for what we used. He takes most of the money to pay for more treats for the next party. Cool dude. Not in it to make a big profit. He just wants us to have a good time and that includes you."

"Nooo, not tonight. I don't know how much this stuff costs, Carl, but I can't let you pay for me. I don't have money on me so maybe next time."

"Cocaine is expensive, but the trick is not to sniff more than you can afford. But I can tell that you're worth the investment," he said and then licked those lips again.

Dominique felt weak and leaned against the wall. Her heart raced as she contemplated what to do. The only thing she knew for sure was that Carl was too fine. "I don't know, Carl. I've never even used nasal spray before. Doesn't that hurt?" she asked and rubbed her nose.

"Initially, it may sting but you get high within seconds and forget all about it."

Dominique moved to the center of the room and got a closer look of the drug and paraphernalia. It looked scary to her. "Carl, I'm not being a baby about this. It's just that I'm trying to get my life back on track. I don't wanna blow it."

Carl sauntered over and hugged her. He whispered in her ear. "I promise you that coke will help you get it back together quicker. You'll have the energy you need to make it happen."

"You sure?"

"Sweetheart, when I'm high off this stuff, I feel invincible. It's like nobody's stronger or smarter or better than me. I can stand up against anybody," he said and released her.

Dominique stared at the white powder. She could not believe that something that looked as innocent as winter snow could do all that. "How much does it take to feel like that?"

"Everybody's different. For me, just two or three lines take me to ecstasy."

She walked behind the table and stared at the white lines. "That's a lot. Isn't it?"

"Not really, Sweetheart, but we can start you off with one or two."

"I didn't say yes."

Footsteps neared the doorway. Dominique felt guilty although she had done nothing. She peered at the entrance. "Doms, what's taking so long? Like are you two praying or partying?" Kelli asked.

"I don't know about our friend here, but I'm about to get my party on," Carl said. He bent over the table, placed the metal cylinder to his nose and inhaled two lines within seconds. Dominique stared at the empty spaces where the white lines were and could not believe how quickly he erased them.

"Wooo! Good stuff!" Carl exclaimed.

"Wooo, baby, yes it is," Kelli said. She went up to Carl and kissed him, or did he kiss her? Whoever kissed whom, they both looked as if they enjoyed it.

"Come on back, Kels," Thomas' voice cried out from the living room. "I miss you."

"In a sec," Kelli said and hunched her shoulders. "What can I say, Doms? Men love me."

"Love is waiting for you too. Go for it," Carl said.

"Yeah, Doms, go for it. I'll even hold your hand."

Dominique was too nervous to be mad at Kelli for the love she showed for Carl. Perspiration oozed out of every pore of her body. Dominique wiped away beads of sweat from her forehead. *Okaaay. I'm gonna do this just one time. Just for Kelli. But that's it and I'm never coming back here again. Never. I don't ever wanna see drughead Carl again, either. I'm gonna do this just to shut the both of them up. And if I die, I swear I'm gonna come back and haunt the hell out of them.*

Dominique eased down behind the table. She picked up the metal cylinder that Carl did not use. It slipped through her sweaty fingers and hit the glass top. "Sorry," she said and wiped her hand on her jeans.

"That's okay. You're doing fine," Carl said.

Dominique picked it up again. The cylinder felt cold and hard. She eased the tip up to her left nostril. That felt awkward. She switched it to her right one. She leaned forward and aligned the bottom opening of the cylinder with the line of cocaine. Her hand trembled so that the cylinder moved from side to side.

"Doms, back away. Back away and take a deep breath," Kelli said.

Carl squatted down behind Dominique. She felt the heat from his body on her back as Carl massaged her shoulders. His hot breath touched her ear as he whispered, "Take it easy and relax. You can do this."

Kelli joined them. "You can't hold your breath, Doms. You gotta inhale like you smoked weed. But instead of your mouth, suck through your nose," Kelli said and then giggled.

"Stop laughing at me," Dominique said.

"I'm not laughing at you," Kelli replied and held Dominique's left hand.

"Okay, I'm gonna try again."

Carl moved away. Dominique aligned the cylinder to the coke and inhaled down to the end of the first line as Carl and Kelli cheered. "Ooouch, that burns," she said and pinched her nose. She released it and then sneezed.

"Bless you," Carl and Kelli said.

"Eeelll, I feel it dripping down my throat. Yuck. It tastes like chopped up aspirin or icky medicine. Yuck."

"You're doing fine. Just wait a few seconds and if you wanna stop, I'll snort that other line," Kelli said.

Dominique's nose felt numb. She sat still and waited for something else to happen. Her heartbeat speeded up. She discounted that as fear. Another minute passed by. "Okay, I feel something now," she said.

"What?" Carl and Kelli asked in unison.

"I dunno. It's like I'm in a daze but I'm awake and alert. Everything is so clear and bright like that green bedspread, Carl's blue shirt, and your red one."

"It's fuchsia," Kelli said and then laughed.

"Whatever, it's bright as hell," Dominique said and laughed along with Kelli.

"And?" Carl asked.

"Well, it's kinda like the rush I get before a game but more like...wow. Like I can dunk all game long and go home and read ten chapters of history nonstop."

"History? Yeah, you're high, Girlfriend," Kelli said and they all cracked up.

"You feel alive and totally juiced up?" Carl asked.

"Yeah, that too." Dominique stared at the last line of bright white coke. "Can I do this one now?"

"Go right ahead," Carl said and smiled at her.

Dominique smiled back at Carl and licked her lips. "I feel like kissing you all over your body," she said.

Carl bent down and got close to Dominique's face. "Go right ahead."

TYLER

The voices and music filtered out into the parking lot of Holy Tabernacle Fellowship Center. Droves of people approached the expansive building. There was no apparent dress code. The churchgoers wore everything from suits and dress shoes to jeans and sneakers. The older women wore the most elegant attire with colorful hats of various shapes and sizes. The one thing everyone who approached the building had in common was a sense of urgency. They rushed towards the double glass doors.

"My goodness," Miss Rollins began, "you would think there is a major sale event going on inside. I cannot believe how loud it is already. You can hear the noise from here." She glanced back at Mr. Powers' shiny black luxury vehicle, "I hope it is there when we return."

Tyler tuned her out long ago. She complained about everything: the traffic, the potholes, the bent street signs, the rundown houses, the music, and the safety of the car in the parking lot.

Tyler led them into the lobby. "Wow," Tyler said. He smiled at Imani as she stood at the second set of glass doors. Imani looked beautiful. Her long braids hung loose around her shoulders and curled up at the ends. The ivory colored sleeveless knit dress melted against her milk chocolate skin. His eyes bypassed the white cast on her left arm and roamed down to the curves of Imani's hips. The hemline fell right above her knees. And those legs. Those super long legs worked the black suede boots that he bought her.

Tyler wanted to kiss her so bad that his mouth watered. He sensed his father behind him and decided that was not the time. Imani greeted the threesome and handed them a lavender folded flyer that outlined the order of service. "I'll show you where we're sitting."

Tyler took her right hand and Imani led them down the center aisle. The further down they walked, the more intense everything became. The bass was deeper, the mass choir's vocals were stronger, the drumbeat, organ, keyboard, and guitar acoustics were louder and so were the handclaps. The temperature was hotter and the congregation was livelier.

Miss Rollins must be pissin' in her pants. And dad's just plain old pissed, Tyler thought. He maneuvered his big shoes between the narrow pews and avoided other people's feet. He got to an opening and smiled at Imani's parents. They smiled back at him as they clapped their hands and sang. Tyler looked straight ahead at the raised platform where the choir stood and formed rows of dark purple and gold, their robe colors.

"Hallelujah...thank you Jesus...yes Lord...glory," rang out all about Tyler. Even Imani hollered and waved her good hand. All of a sudden, the music stopped. Yet, the congregation continued their shout and raised their hands. Tyler sat because he did not know what to do.

"Wait until the Pastor tells you," Imani said.

"I wore the wrong shoes," Tyler mumbled as he stood. He tried to wiggle his toes but he had no extra room in his dress black shoes. He had not worn them since the junior prom. Tyler loosened up his gray and black print tie and wiped the sweat off his temples. He heard a strange sound behind him. Tyler turned his head to the right and strained to interpret it. It wasn't English, Spanish, or French but some type of foreign language. *What in the heck is that?* He asked himself and turned his body around.

A woman held her hands out in a pick-me-up position and stared at the ceiling. Tears streamed down her face and her lips moved fast as she spoke in that odd language. Tyler watched her as he wondered, "Is she possessed?" He glanced at the man and the child next to her. They did not seem fazed by it. So Tyler faced forward and watched a man dressed in a white robe trimmed with purple as he stepped up to the podium. He looked like a minister. Tyler's mind drifted back to the last time he was that close to a pastor.

"We are gathered here to celebrate Sister Lorraine Powers' home going. She leaves behind a wonderful husband, Andrew, and a 12-year-old son and future basketball star, Tyler. I've seen you play boy and you're good. And you're gonna be tall too."

Laughter echoed around young Tyler as he wept in silence. The pastor must have thought that comment would get Tyler to smile. However, the smile never came. His heart ached too bad to find the humor in anything. Tyler's eyes remained fixed on the minister. He could not bear another look at his beautiful mother stretched out in the white silk lined casket.

Tyler felt a tug on the hem of his gray suit jacket. "Sit down," Imani said. Tyler took his thumb and dabbed at the corners of his eyes. He wondered how long he had zoned out. He sat down on the cushioned seat and wished he could kick off his shoes.

Imani tapped him, "Stand up."

"What?"

"Stand up. Pastor Mitchell just asked for all first time guests to stand."

Tyler thought that he paid attention. Yet, he missed that one too. He glanced to his right and his father and Miss Rollins were on their feet. He eased out of his seat and a chorus of "amen" rang out followed by applause. As Pastor Mitchell welcomed all of the guests, Deacon Fields, the guard at the recreation center, twisted his body around and held out his massive hand.

"Not again," Tyler mumbled and flexed his right hand. He braced himself as he took hold of the deacon's hand. Tyler was surprised at the small amount of pressure that the deacon applied. *Maybe he wore himself out jumping around,* Tyler thought as he smiled at him.

At offering time, Tyler watched Imani and her parents as they slid money into a small white envelope.

"You need money, Son?" his father asked as he leaned across Miss Rollins with a $20 bill in his hand. Tyler waved it off, reached into his pocket, and pulled out his own money.

"An envelope is in the program," Imani told him and he used it. Before Tyler filled out all the information on the back of it, Imani shoved a large wicker basket in front of him. He dropped his envelope into it and passed it on to Miss Rollins.

"Teen church is cancelled today," Pastor Mitchell announced.

"Oooh, too bad. You would have enjoyed it. We go to another room and have service. We have big fun with the youth pastor over there," Imani said. Tyler's eyes followed where she pointed. The guy appeared no older than 21.

"I cancelled teen church because God gave me a message to deliver to them today."

Tyler shifted in his seat and scratched his head. *God must have known I was gonna be here and gonna get on me about not going to church.*

"The message is, 'Satan wants you. So you better get right with Me'."

"Yup, I knew it," Tyler whispered. He tried to slide down in his seat. However, his long legs pressed into the back of the chair in front of him.

"When I say Satan, you young people may think of this cartoon character with a red face and horns sticking out on top of his head. He has a tail and he's holding a black pitch folk. You're probably envisioning red and yellow flames surrounding him representing HELL."

Tyler nodded his head as he visualized that scene. He watched the pastor as he backed away from the podium and walked to the edge of the platform.

"Naaaw, young people, that's not the form of Satan I'm talking about."

"What you talkin' about, Pastor?" Deacon Fields yelled out.

"The devil disguises himself so he can attack you from many angles. Drugs like heroin, crack, and Ecstasy are Satan. Alcoholism is Satan. Fornication is Satan..."

Tyler sat up straight in his seat as Pastor Mitchell fired off items on his Satan list.

"...and can I keep it real up in here?"

"Yeah," rang out throughout the congregation.

"Walkin' around here callin' young ladies the 'b' word and hos and you young ladies believing that it's okay to be addressed at a level lower than a dog ain't nothing but Satan. If you don't respect yourselves, how can you respect God?"

There was an explosion of handclaps throughout the sanctuary. The people were on their feet and yelled, "say it," and "teach Pastor," and "amen," and "all right now." Pastor Mitchell sipped water from a crystal glass and wiped his face while the congregation settled down.

"Young people. Disrespecting God, yourselves, your parents, your elders, your teachers, and on and on and on *is Satan*."

"Yes, Sir!" Deacon Fields hollered.

"And can I really keep it real up in here?"

"Keep it real!" Deacon Fields yelled along with many others.

"How many of you have the nerve to step up in God's face and tell Him off? Just diss Him right in front of His face?"

Silence fell upon the congregation. Tyler gazed around the church to see if anyone had his or her hand raised. No one did.

"Thank God no one in here is that bold to admit it. However, do you realize that's what you are doing? You are telling God off right to His face."

It was as if the pastor's comment sucked the air out of the sanctuary, and everyone held on to his or her last breath. Tyler held his breath too.

"Young people. Whenever you have sex outside of marriage, you might as well walk up to God and say, 'I know that you said fornication is a sin and that it's wrong. But, I'm gonna do it anyway because having sex feels good'." He paused and gazed about his congregation.

"Some of y'all sittin' there frontin' like you don't know what I'm talkin' about. Even if you're not having sex, how about this one? 'Lord, I know you said thou shalt not steal, but I want that outfit. Since I can't afford it, I'm gonna take it and I'm gonna look good in it. Or, I know you said that I should honor my father and my mother and I will as long as they let me do what I want when I want and give me what I want. Because NOBODY is gonna tell me what I can and can not do. NOT EVEN YOU, GOD'."

As the pastor caught his breath, there was another explosive response from the people. Tyler thought he was at a basketball game and the home team scored the winning basket at the buzzer.

Pastor Mitchell pointed down to a spot below the platform. "I want every teen wrestling with the demon of drugs to bring it to the altar. The demon of alcohol, the demon of fornication, the demon of low self-esteem, the demon of thievery and trickery, the demon of profanity, the demon of disrespect, the demon of..."

Tyler's mouth dropped as he watched what looked like hundreds of teens gathered in front of the altar and overflowed into the center and side aisles.

"I see some teens still sitting in their seats. Y'all must be the kids who are not struggling with these demons. Well, I got news for you. You are Satan's prime target. He's working hard to recruit YOU. God wants you to continue your walk with Him and to be strong and say 'no' to Satan's temptations.

"You know what I'm talkin' about," Pastor Mitchell continued, "'yo man, it's just weed. It won't hurt you. Snort a little cocaine and it'll get you high even faster. Smoke some crack and it will blow your mind. Or, oooh baby, you know I'm clean. I ain't got AIDS. If you love me baby, you'll give me some. Oral sex ain't really sex and everybody's doing it. Oh girl, you know you can't get pregnant your first time'. The devil is a liar! That's why I've got to pray for you too."

Tyler felt Imani grab hold of his hand. He looked at his father for assurance and Mr. Powers patted Tyler on his back as he stepped by him. Once in the center aisle, there was no place to hide. He felt that all eyes were on him because he towered over the other teens. Tyler lowered his head. *Maaan this is embarrassing. I hope nobody knows me or thinks I'm a druggy or alky or something. Let's make this quick, Pastor.*

* * *

Tyler was embarrassed in a different sort of way as he watched the looks of disgust all over Miss Rollins' face. Tyler sat across from her in a dingy white plastic chair. Miss Rollins was close under his father on the couch and fanned herself. The room was hot. Mr. Jackson apologized for it but he said that it was out of his control. Yet, he was glad that the heat worked. A cold breeze flowed through the open window in the kitchen and into the living room. As the wind passed through, it picked up the scent of collard greens, cinnamon spiked yams, garlic, buttery biscuits, and stuffing.

"Sooo, Tyler," Mr. Jackson began and broke the silence, "Imani tells us that you're the star player on your team and pulling high grades."

Tyler smiled and shrugged his shoulders. "Yeah, I'm doing all right."

"Stop being so modest, Son," Mr. Powers said and then turned to Mr. Jackson. "He is the best player, and the captain of the team, and has a 3.8 grade point average. I hear that your daughter is pretty smart too."

Mr. Jackson smiled and said, "Yes, she is."

Mr. Powers looked into the kitchen. "I'm sorry about your injury, Imani."

"Me too," she said and then stared at Tyler. "May I speak with you for a second?"

"That door stays open and hurry back," Mr. Jackson told them.

Tyler did not say it aloud but he figured that his bedroom was four times the size of Imani's. He looked at his beautiful girlfriend and was tempted to close her door. He followed her father's orders and left it open.

"I'm dying out there," Imani said.

"I know," Tyler said and went in for the kiss. Imani backed away.

"Miss Rollins acts like she's scared to death that something's gonna crawl on her and like she's just too good to be here. I hope her nose gets permanently stuck up in the air."

Tyler laughed.

"And your father."

Tyler's smile faded. "What about him?"

"He's no better. I know he feels the same way she does but not showing it."

Tyler stepped back. "I can't believe I'm defending my dad, but he's not frontin'. He knows what it's like to be poor because this is how he grew up."

"W-e-l-l-l, maybe he forgot," Imani began, "and don't you forget not to say anything about me working."

Tyler shook his head. "You know you're wrong, Imani. Your father is gonna freak when he finds out and I don't blame him. I don't like you working either. It's our senior year. Let's try and have some fun."

Imani sucked her teeth. "Yeah, that's real easy for a rich boy to say."

"Wooo, wait, hold up," Tyler said and took a step forward. "Since when have you been referring to me as 'rich boy'?"

"I didn't mean it in a negative way. It's just that your college is paid for. And with your SAT scores, you can pick any school you want."

Tyler nodded. "Yeah, my father can spring for tuition, but he didn't buy those scores for me."

"Still, Tyler, you can have fun and concentrate on winning the state title. You don't have to struggle. Everything comes easy for you."

"Is that right?"

"Yeah, that's right."

"Wow. I guess you don't know me after all," Tyler began, "I'm wondering if I know who you are anymore."

"Dinner's ready," Mrs. Jackson announced as Tyler and Imani stood firm and stared at each other.

"I've lost my appetite," Imani said.

"Not me. I feel right at home. How about you?" he asked and then exited Imani's bedroom.

There were four wood chairs with blue floral quilted cushions tied to them and two plastic chairs around the kitchen table. A spearmint green colored vinyl tablecloth hung halfway to the floor on all sides.

"Tyler and Imani, take one of those other chairs and let the grown-ups have the cushioned seats," Mrs. Jackson said.

Tyler took a seat and noticed items that he did not smell earlier. A golden brown baked chicken, light orange colored macaroni and cheese, yellowish potato salad, beet-red cranberry sauce, and bright green string beans with pieces of smoked turkey wings in it. "Everything looks sooo good, Mrs. Jackson," Tyler said.

"Thank you, Tyler."

Mr. Jackson said grace and it was the longest one Tyler ever heard. Tyler kept his head bowed and eyes closed and waited for that final word. "Amen," Mr. Jackson said and Tyler said the same. He glanced about food and licked his lips. "I wanna try everything."

"Now, Son. Don't act like you've never had a meal," Mr. Powers said.

"He's a growing boy. Let him eat," Mr. Jackson said and handed Tyler a pan of macaroni and cheese.

"So, Tyler, I hear that you're mentoring Tariq," Mrs. Jackson said.

"I'm trying," Tyler said and dumped spoonfuls of the cheesy pasta onto his plate.

"Not that little wild haired sassy boy you brought to the house?" Miss Rollins asked.

"Yeah, and?" Tyler asked.

"Does that mean you're going to be spending even more time on this side of town?"

Tyler glanced at Imani and she rolled her eyes at him. Tyler turned back to his father. "I guess so."

Mr. Powers pointed his silver fork at Tyler. "Well, let me tell you something. If your grades start slipping or you get into trouble with that new car, you will be spending more time at home. As is, you are on the road way too much."

Tyler shook his head. *Maaan, was that necessary?* Tyler asked himself.

Mr. Powers took his eyes off his son's and looked at Imani. "Imani, what colleges are you applying to?"

"My heart was set on Howard but I dunno now."

"Oh, I see," Mr. Powers said and his dark brown eyes shifted back to Tyler. "So, Son, is Imani the real reason why you want to go there?"

Tyler did not answer right way. He exhaled. *Oh maaan, I can't believe we're back to this and why now?*

"Well, Son?"

"Nooo, Dad, we've talked about this before."

"Yes, we did but that was before I knew that Imani wanted to go to Howard. When we get home, we're gonna finish Georgetown and Duke's applications and send them off ASAP."

"Georgetown and Duke?" Imani asked as she stared at Tyler.

"Both are fine universities," Miss Rollins said.

"When were you gonna tell me?" Imani asked.

"That was Coach and Dad's idea. I haven't even applied yet."

"But he will," his father began. "Tyler's having an incredible season and deserves to be at a great university with a nationally known basketball team."

Tyler whispered in her ear. "I was gonna tell you if I was doing it for sure so you could apply."

"I'm not interested. You know I wanna go to a historically black school," Imani whispered back.

"Imani," Miss Rollins began, "I sure hope that you are awarded a scholarship. College is very expensive. Parents should start saving before their child is born."

"My daughter will make it to college even if I hafta work three jobs," Mr. Jackson said.

Miss Rollins' arched brows raised higher. She took a sip of her iced tea and sat as straight as a board.

"Sooo how did everyone enjoy the service?" Mrs. Jackson asked.

"I thought that minister would never stop praying for those teenagers," Miss Rollins said. She frowned at Tyler as he devoured his food.

"As much trouble as these young folks get into today, you ought to be glad that somebody is praying for them," Mrs. Jackson said.

"Amen, Cora," her husband said.

"I guess, Mrs. Jackson. However, the service was still too long for me," Miss Rollins said and then asked, "do you have a tossed salad?"

"Nooo, I'm sorry. I'm out of lettuce. Otherwise, I would make you one. You're not on a diet are you?"

"Oh goodness no. It's just that I have never cared much for soul food. I like to eat light."

"Oh, I see. Well, you could slice off some of that chicken breast. It's light."

Miss Rollins picked up a knife and fork and reached for the chicken. "I'll get that for you, Sweetie," Mr. Powers said and sliced it for her while he spoke to Imani's father. "What do you do for a living?"

"I'm a custodial worker down at the local hospital. I also supervise the custodial crew from time to time."

"He's also the superintendent of this building," Mrs. Jackson added as she smiled at her husband.

"It sounds like you're a leader and a hard worker. I am always searching for good managers for my stores. If ever you are interested, let me know. Have you ever shopped at one of my Power Walk stores?"

"If you don't have one in this town, then I can't say that I have."

Miss Rollins leaned forward and made eye contact with Mr. Jackson. "I think that's a great idea for you to work for Andrew. You can earn more income, find a comfortable place to live, maybe buy a newer car, bigger dining room table with matching chairs, and..."

Tyler turned to Imani and they both looked at Mr. Jackson. He took a yellow paper napkin and wiped the shine off his lips. He placed the napkin back onto the table and tapped the tabletop with his long thick finger. "Ummm, Cora, I counted about five insults in that one statement. How many did you count?"

"I counted about four or five," Mrs. Jackson said in a soprano voice.

"I'm sure Candice did not mean that the way that it sounded," Mr. Powers said.

"Absolutely not. If I insulted anyone, I apologize." She took a deep breath and added, "What I meant was that there is nothing wrong with improving yourself and your standard of living. I can't tell with that beard but I'm guessing that you're around Andrew's age. So you're still a young man. Too young to settle for living a certain way all of your life."

Tyler wrung his hands under the table. *Get her Mr. Jackson. Get her. She talks too much. I hope that he shuts her down.*

"W-e-l-l-l, Dad, she does have a point. If you worked for him, maybe I could afford to go to college without a scholarship and I wouldn't have to wor–"

"What?" her father asked.

"Wor-ry. I could focus on studying and not worry about how I'm gonna make it to college."

"Let's set some things straight. You," he said and pointed at Imani, "don't have to worry about that. You're going to college with or without a scholarship. Just focus on your studies." Mr. Jackson's eyes left Imani and landed on Miss Rollins.

"And you, I read you like a book right off the bat. You looked real smart but I knew you were an uppity..."

Miss Rollins' posture stiffened. She tossed her hair away from her face and gazed at Mr. Jackson. "I am intelligent and I won't apologize for that. I have a master's degree and considering a doctorate and I won't apologize for that either."

"My husband didn't ask you to apologize for any of those things. You insulted him and our family. That's what we want an apology for," Mrs. Jackson said.

"I am entitled to my own opinion. Just because I don't like your church or where you live doesn't make me uppity. I just think that your service is too long and it doesn't take all that hooping and hollering and jumping up and down to get God to hear you."

"So you don't think it takes all that, huh? Let me tell you something, Missy."

"Don't disrespect my lady. Her name is Candice not Missy," Mr. Powers said.

Mr. Jackson bowed his head. "You're right and I apologize to you, Miss Candice. However, the Bible says to make a joyful noise unto the Lord and serve him with gladness and to come before Him with singing. So we praise and worship God and not sit there all dry and dead like we're in a morgue. Our God is alive not dead. It's a time to celebrate what God has done, is doing, and will do. What I have now may not look like much to you but I know how far God has brought me and my family."

"Amen, Robert," his wife chimed in.

"This apartment is small but it keeps us out of the rain, snow, and sleet. My oldest daughter, Roberta, is in college on a full scholarship. Imani is on her way somehow or another. I thank God for my health so I can work two jobs. Some people ain't got one job and God has blessed me with two," Mr. Jackson said and pointed to Imani and her mother. "Does my wife or daughter look malnourished to you?"

"Well, no," Miss Rollins said.

"That's right. So, does it take all that? As for me and my house, yes it does."

It was a while after that statement that anyone spoke. The sound of metal utensils as they struck the white with black trimmed plates filled the small room. Tyler exchanged nervous glances with Imani.

"Mr. Powers."

"Call me Andrew."

"Mr. Powers, you're very quiet," Mr. Jackson said.

"I don't have much to say about religion."

"You're raising a teenaged boy and you don't have much to say about religion? What are you teaching him? I hope that Tyler learned something from the pastor's message today, especially on fornication."

"Mr. Jackson, I've taught Tyler right from wrong since he was old enough to understand. And after that incident last year, Tyler knows he's not ready for sex."

All eyes shot to Tyler and Tyler stared at his father. He was shocked that he went there. Tyler knew that Imani's father would never let that slide.

"What incident last year?"

"Here we go," Tyler mumbled.

"I thought Imani told you."

"No, Mr. Powers, I didn't spread Tyler's business all over the place," Imani said.

"What incident?" Mr. Jackson asked again.

"Last year a girl claimed that Tyler was the father of her baby."

"What!" Imani's parents shouted in unison. Mr. Jackson pressed on. "A claim? Why was a claim made? He must have been havin' sex with the girl if she made a claim like that."

"Calm down, Daddy," Imani began, "it's history."

He pointed a finger right past Tyler and into Imani's face. "First of all, I didn't know anything about Tyler's past. Well, forget that for a second. Your mother and I didn't know Tyler existed until a couple of months ago. And God knows that surprised me because I thought that I could trust my daughter. Now that I know she got a little sneak in her, I've got to keep a closer eye on her."

Tyler backed up as Mr. Jackson's torpedo shaped finger was within inches of his face. "If I ever find out that you were even thinking about having sex with my daughter, there will be a claim all right. Your father will be at the coroner's office claiming your dead body."

"Robert! Daddy! Mr. Jackson!" everyone around the table screamed at the same time. Mr. Powers' voice rose above the others. "You are totally out of line." He stood and so did Mr. Jackson. Both men were eyeballs to eyeballs. "When you threaten my son, you're threatening me. That means you take me on and not him, and I don't back down from anybody!"

"If you had a daughter, you would know that I am not threatening your son. It is a promise of a consequence if I find out that his zipper came down and her dress went up. Tyler may be the man on campus but he couldn't rule as much as a fly in my house." Mr. Jackson glanced at Tyler and then looked dead into Mr. Powers' eyes.

"Imma keep a close watch on your fast-behind son. And if I don't like what I see, he won't be seeing Imani. I am the man in my house and what I say goes!"

IMANI

Pregnant women and other female patients filled the waiting room in Dr. Parker's office. Imani smiled at the women as she rushed past them and headed for her desk. She glanced at the round black and white clock on the wall. "Wooo, I just made it," she mumbled.

"Thanks for coming in on your day off," Dr. Parker said. Dr. David Parker was a handsome middle aged man. Imani was not into gray-hair. However, she liked how it looked on him.

"Thanks for the extra hours."

"Well, you accomplish more with one arm than my last receptionist did with two. Keep up the great work."

Imani smiled. *You just keep those checks coming,* she thought. Each Friday when she saw her name on her paycheck, Imani felt proud. Every penny Imani earned she tucked away under her mattress.

"Hey, Girl," Shonda began, "it's gonna be a long day. Look at them out there. I don't know if they have group sex or what, but it seems like all his patients get pregnant at the same time."

Imani laughed. Shonda was a true relative of Fatima's. They not only looked alike but also their sense of humor was similar. "You know the routine," Shonda said and pointed to the telephone.

Imani strapped on her headset and answered calls. "Dr. Parker's office. How may I help you?"

"This ain't Shonda. Who this?"

"Fatima? Is that you?" Imani asked

"Yeah, it's me. Oh snap, Imani?"

Imani laughed. "See, one day your tacky phone manners is gonna get you into trouble."

"Since when you started workin' on Mondays?"

"They needed help so I'm here. What you want? I got a job. I don't have time to be messing with you."

"Now you think you're grown. Don't make me come over there," Fatima said and both girls laughed. Imani placed Fatima on hold and took another call then got back to her friend.

"Tell me you're proud of me," Fatima said.

"Why?"

"I mailed off community college's application."

"All right! Yeah, I'm proud of you. I sent them mine too. Howard is in the mail but that was probably a waste of time and money."

"Ain't that a trip? You gotta pay the college just to apply to their school and they can turn around and say 'we don't want you', but they still gonna keep your money," Fatima said.

"That is a trip and Tyler's trippin' too."

"What's up with him?"

"He's all mad at me because I didn't apply to Georgetown or Duke. Well, I'm mad at him too because he did apply. I love Tyler and I thought we were gonna go to the same college and live on campus together, not in the same room, but you know what I mean."

"You ain't feelin' either one of those schools."

"I know that, you know that, and Tyler knows that too. So since it doesn't look like we're gonna go to the same school, I applied to Spelman."

"Eeelll who wants to go to college with all girls?"

"It's a great historically black college."

"Whatever. Ain't no men there."

"Girrrl, don't you know Morehouse is nearby and it's a historically black college for men?"

"You lyin'. Stop lyin', Imani."

"I'm serious. Morehouse College is full of brothas and Clark Atlanta University is close by and it's co-ed. So there will be plenty of men around."

"Daaang why you just now telling me? I woulda taken high school more seriously and gotten better grades had I known that..."

Imani placed Fatima on hold again and answered more calls. She returned and Fatima still whined, "I wanna go to Spelman."

"You have another shot at it, Fatima. Just knock out the two years at Bedford Community College with a high GPA and then apply to Spelman."

"Yeah, Girrrl, Imma handle my bizness."

"It's not a big deal for me because if things don't work out with Tyler, I'll never date again."

"Now I know you're lyin'."

"I'm serious, Fatima. I can't concentrate in class 'cause our last argument is always on my mind. Who needs this kind of headache and heartache in college?"

"Crap happens, Girl. Look at Hanif and me. I thought we were gonna hang tight too, and now I don't think it matters whether or not he comes back."

"Don't say that, Fatima. Don't give up on him."

"Sounds like you're drop kickin' Tyler."

"That's different."

"How?"

"I dunno. I guess it's my fault because I was living in a fairytale. Now the real deal has slapped me in the face and it hurts."

A tear caught Imani off guard and rolled out of the corner of her left eye. She looked up to see if anyone noticed and was relieved that no one did. "I gotta go."

"Tell Shonda to call me."

"Okay," Imani said. She closed her eyes as she inhaled. *Hold it together and do your job.* She did just that and worked through the headache that developed as she held in her emotions.

When she left the office, it was dark and frigid outside. Imani stood alone at the bus stop. The 7:30 p.m. bus was 20 minutes late. A gust of wind pushed against her back. The coldness seeped through her gray wool coat. Imani shuffled from side to side. *Call Tyler. Nope, I'd rather freeze. Catch a cab. Nope, too expensive. Call him...*

Imani continued her internal debate and kept an eye on a white car that pulled up near the curb. The horn blew but Imani could not see the driver. The car door swung open. "Hop in," a woman's voice said.

Imani bent over and peeked into the window. "Thank God it's you," she said and got into the vehicle. Whose car is this?"

"One of my male friends let me borrow it while mine is in the shop," Shonda said.

"One of your male friends? How many you got?"

"Ummm about three I see on the regular and another two when the other three don't act right," she said and then laughed.

"Wow. I can't handle one."

"Yeah, Fatima said you're having problems with that man of yours. Now usually I don't check out the sports section. But I flipped through it the other day and Tyler just jumped right out at me. Like, bam! Dang, Girl, that brotha is hot!"

"You and a whole lotta girls at school think so," Imani said and rubbed her temples.

"Look at cha," Shonda began, "that's why I can't get all sprung over one somebody. You've gotta keep a few on reserve to fill in for the main players when they start acting funny and wanna toss you aside like yesterday's newspaper. Well, I got news for you Sistah: men are just as dispensable and replaceable too."

Imani figured that revelation was supposed to make her feel better. However, it confused her more. "It's not that easy 'cause Tyler's my first real boyfriend."

"And he won't be your last. I don't know how many so-called boyfriends I've had. I don't even call them boyfriends anymore. They are just men that I date."

"But how can you love them all?"

"Who said anything about love? I said they are men that I date."

"Oh," Imani said.

"Let me school ya, Lil Sis. That's when you get into trouble when you start throwing that 'love' word around. That's why Fatima's sweatin' Hanif. I told her to forget him and to move on. She met a football player at your party–"

"Erik," Imani said.

"Yeah, Erik. She got his digits and never called him. Now how stupid is that? I know Hanif is kickin' it with some girl where he's at."

"Hanif wouldn't play Fatima like that."

"Tyler wouldn't play you either, huh?" Shonda laughed. "Y'all so young."

By the time Imani reached her apartment door, her head felt like it would explode. It did not help matters that she was fifteen minutes past her curfew and she had to think of an excuse. Imani could not claim that she attended her team's game because her parents knew there was no game scheduled that day.

"You're late, Baby Girl," her father said before she closed the door. "Where were you?"

"Sorry," she said and headed for her bedroom.

"Come back here. I'm not finished," he said.

"Dang it. Now what?" she mumbled.

"I heard that, Imani. What's gotten into you? Your father asked you a question and we've yet to hear an answer," Mrs. Jackson said.

Both of her parents sat on the couch and stared at her. Imani rubbed her forehead. *Are they trying to read my mind? And where is their attitude coming from?* Imani thought as she stared back at them. Both had deep creases formed in the middle of their foreheads. "Practice ran over and I stayed until it ended. By that time, I missed one bus and had to wait for another. And of course, it was late too. The colder it gets it seems like the later the buses run," Imani said aloud and threw her right hand up. "That's why I'm late and got this horrible headache from standing out in the cold so long."

They stared at her.

Imani was surprised as well at how the lies flowed out of her mouth. Unless her parents were psychic, that could not have been the reason why they gawked at her. "What?" Imani asked in a high-pitched voice.

"Where was Tyler?" Mr. Jackson asked.

"Tyler? I dunno. I saw him in the cafeteria today but that was it."

"Oh, really?" her father asked.

"Why you seem so surprised? After the way you showed out–"

"Hey!" he yelled.

Imani's body jerked. He never hollered at her like that before. Her eyes widened as he eased off the couch. She did not know whether to cry, run, or shout.

"Don't you dare speak to me like that," Mr. Jackson said. His wife tugged on the tail of his denim shirt. He sat back down.

"Imani, go and change and I'll warm up some soup for you," her mother said.

Mr. Jackson glared at his daughter. Imani looked at her mom.

"Go on," her mother said.

Imani rounded the corner to her room and placed her backpack on the floor. Tears streamed down her face as she leaned against the wall and eavesdropped on her parent's conversation.

"You scared that poor child to death. Why do I get the feeling that you don't believe her? Imani doesn't have a history of lying to us," Mrs. Jackson said.

"Nooo, but history can start at any point in time. It's just that. I don't know, Cora. It's just a gut feeling that I have and I can't shake it."

"I think you're overreacting, Robert."

"Maybe so, but she has kept a couple of things from us and both of them were about Tyler. So if she wants me to fully trust her again, she's gotta earn it."

Perspiration slid down Imani's temple. She removed her knit cap and listened on.

"Tell me what your heart is saying, Robert."

"What?"

"We've been blessed with a wonderful daughter. Yet, you're beginning to treat her like a criminal. So I want to know what's really bothering you."

"Oh, Cora, I hate when you do this. I have a lot on my mind. Can't we just leave it at that?"

"We could but I don't want to because it's making you miserable and if you're miserable then we're all miserable and I don't like being miserable. Now if you're set on being–"

"Good Lord, Woman, don't say 'miserable' again. I'm not miserable. I'm just concerned."

"About what?"

"You know how I feel, Cora. Why you gotta make me say it?"

"Because you would feel better if you let it out."

There was a pause before he spoke again. Imani heard her father as he exhaled. "I love my baby girl and I would hate for her to suffer the way that I did. You know the story. Here I was an all-state football player with college scholarship offers up the wyzoo and then bam!"

Imani jumped from the thunderous clap of her father's hands.

"My knee snapped and it was over."

"But, Robert, it's different for Imani. You only went to school to play football. Your grades were the pits so you didn't have a chance at getting an academic scholarship. Our baby loves school and she has proved that she's got what it takes to earn good grades."

"Don't you know I know that, Cora? I put on this front like I have everything under control. When the truth is, I don't know how I'm gonna send her to college if she doesn't get a scholarship."

Imani drew a deep breath and covered her mouth with her right hand. *I knew it. I knew it.* Imani was not sure if she wanted to hear more. Yet, she stood still.

"I can *not* let my daughter down. If ever she was disappointed in me, I couldn't live with that. I don't want her to be ashamed of me or think that I didn't fight hard for her," Mr. Jackson said.

Imani felt a lump in her throat.

"So is that what's in your heart, Robert? You think Imani is ashamed of you?"

"Cora, back in high school, I had big dreams. Football was gonna be my way out. I didn't plan on livin' like this. I can't offer her the things that Mr. Powers gives Tyler. You've seen that man's house and cars. Our daughter is getting a taste of what it's like on the other side. And from where she's standing, it's gotta look good."

"I'm sure that Imani is impressed by all the stuff that Mr. Powers has and who wouldn't be? But you have given Imani things that he or Tyler could never give."

"Like what?"

"Like life. You and I brought Imani into this world. And we have provided for her so that all Imani has to do is go to school and get educated so that she can get all of the stuff that we couldn't give her. So, Sweetheart, we have given our daughter life, love, and opportunity."

The salty tears dripped into Imani's opened mouth. She wanted to hug her father and tell him that she was proud of him. When times got tough, he never skipped out on his family. He never punked out.

"We've been through many storms, Robert, and we'll survive this one too."

Imani nodded her head. *Yes, we will.*

* * *

The halls of Westmoore High were abuzz with talks that the girls' team had a shot at the City Tournament. Everyone expected the boys' team to make City. So much of the hype was about the girls and Dominique's remarkable improvement. Her picture was next to Tyler's on the front page of the school paper.

Imani was so enthralled with the article that she bumped into a brick wall. "Daaang!" she exclaimed and grabbed onto her encased arm. It hurt and itched to the point that she wanted to rip the cast off. The paper slipped out of her hand. When she bent down to pick it up, she came face to face with Tyler.

"I heard you holler. What happened?" he asked.

Imani broke her gaze from his hypnotic eyes. "I'm okay." Imani lied.

"I'm not," Tyler began, "I miss you."

Imani pointed to the paper. "It looks like you're doing fine without me and so is my team."

"I can't speak for your team, but I miss you. Can I see you later?" he asked.

"I gotta work."

"I'll pick you up."

"Shonda brings me home."

"Tell Shonda you got a ride."

Imani didn't have a quick answer for that so she looked away from Tyler. The bell sounded for the next period. "I gotta get to gym," Imani said and walked away. She felt Tyler's hand on her good arm.

"We're both under pressure, Imani, but I'm not pushin' you away. Don't push me away."

"I'm not."

"Then what would you call it?"

"I need space, Tyler. Just give me some space."

Tyler released his hold on her. She backed away. "How much space?" he asked.

"I dunno. But right now, I feel like I'm suffocating. I'm on overload and I can't handle another thing."

"The crap that went down with our dads is between them not us. I'm not the enemy, Imani."

"Then give me some space. And if we're meant to be together, we will find our way back to each other."

"Your way back. I'm here for you," Tyler said and pointed to the floor.

"Okay then, my way back to you."

The hurt on Tyler's face ripped through Imani's heart. The pain in her arm could not compare. "See you," she said and then took off down the stairwell and ran all the way to the gym.

"Wooo, Speedy, where's a doctor's note giving you permission to run like that?" Coach Wilkens asked.

Imani felt winded. It had been weeks since she sprinted. She caught her breath and then answered him. "I don't have one."

"Well then, young lady, none of that running in here. And how is that arm?"

"It aches sometimes but mostly it itches like crazy. I can't wait to get out of this stupid cast."

"I know you can't," he said and looked away.

"The good news is that next week I'm going in for an x-ray. If all looks well, the doctor might switch me to a soft cast or maybe even bandages."

Coach Wilkens turned back to her. "Imani–"

"I know, Coach. You've told me a million times."

Coach Wilkens gave a faint smile. "Add another one. I'm sorry."

"I know."

"However, that's not all I wanted to say. I wish you would speak to Dominique. She feels even worse than I do about this. It was a freak accident. Dominique didn't mean to hurt you."

"I know. I was gonna apologize to her today."

Mr. Wilkens smiled. "Thank you."

Imani's arm throbbed and it reminded her of her own freak accident with the brick wall moments ago. She laughed at herself. "Where is she?" Imani asked and glanced about the gym. She spotted Mrs. Daniels, the school nurse, who rushed towards them.

"Hello, Imani. How is that arm?" she asked.

Imani hated to repeat that same information. "Fine. So, Coach, where's Dominique?"

"In the locker room," he began, "take a few minutes with her but then tell Dominique to come out and practice her free throws."

Imani nodded and watched as Mr. Wilkens and the nurse conversed. "Today?" Imani heard the coach ask as she walked off the court.

Imani entered the locker room and stared at locker number 24. The same number as her jersey. She had not opened it since her injury. Terry told her that out of respect for her, no one else used it either. Imani walked up and down the aisles and found no one. She stepped into the bathroom and heard a long sucking sound. Imani bent down and saw sky blue and white sneakers in the last stall. She heard that sound again.

"Dominique?"

Dead silence for a second. Then the sneakers shuffled about and then the toilet flushed.

"Dominique?"

"Yeah. I'll be out in a minute."

Imani walked out and sat down on the bench in front of her locker. "I never thought my senior year would end like this," she said. A couple of minutes later, Dominique ran into the room.

"Who's looking for me?"

The first thing that Imani noticed was that Dominique did not have her hair in a ponytail. She watched her long hair as it flopped up and down as Dominique bounced around. She clutched a bright red cosmetic bag in her right hand. Imani caught hold of her buck wild eyes and Dominique leaped into the air.

"Ohmygod, you scared me," Dominique said and placed her hand over her heart and giggled. "Were you calling me?"

"Yeah, it was me. I wanted to talk to you," Imani said. Dominique shifted and paced so that Imani lost her train of thought. "Come sit with me," Imani said and patted the space next to her.

"Okay." Dominique plopped down next to Imani.

"What I wanted to say was that ummm that I am so sorry," Imani said. She watched Dominique as she half opened and closed the zipper on the bag. Imani placed her hand on top of Dominique's and kept her hand still.

"You tried to apologize to me many times and I wasn't hearing it. I asked God over and over to help me forgive you, and I do forgive you because I know this wasn't your fault. It was just a stupid accident."

Dominique looked up at the ceiling. "Wow, I thought I was gonna lose my mind over this. If it wasn't for my mom and my best friend, Kelli, I would have lost it. But I'm okay now and I got a whole bunch of new friends and life is incredible and I'm sooo happy. Now you forgive me so everything's perfect." Dominique jumped up from the bench and sat back down. She sniffled and wiped the tears from her red eyes. "Wait until I tell Kelli," she said and went to hug Imani then backed away and looked at the cast.

"It's okay," Imani said and received a light hug from Dominique.

"I've been working really really hard trying to please everybody and make everything right. Did you see my picture in the paper?"

"Yeah, nice picture. Terry told me you've been practicing like crazy. I guess it's startin' to pay off," Imani said and tried to control her waterworks.

"Ummm hummm," Dominique said as she rubbed her nose. The tip of it turned crimson. "I've even got a boyfriend. You believe that?"

"Who?"

Dominique smiled. "You wouldn't know him. Carl's in college. Do you believe that? A college guy is into me. And Carl's sooo cute! Tyler is a high school type cute, but Carl is a college *man* type cute."

"Okaaay, whatever that means. Does Coach know about him?"

"Heck no and don't you dare tell him."

Imani understood that because she knew that her father would not allow her to date a college guy. He could not deal with Tyler. She hugged Dominique. "You can trust me. I'm happy for you."

"I'm finally happy too," Dominique said and patted her red bag.

"I hate to spoil it for ya, but your dad told me to tell you to come out and work on free throws."

"That's cool," Dominique said and then leaped off the bench.

Imani wrapped her arm around Dominique's shoulder as they strolled out of the locker room. Coach

Wilkens met them halfway and he smiled. "Looks like you ladies worked things out."

"We're cool," Dominique said.

Coach Wilkens hugged both girls. "While you were in there making up, you both missed an important announcement that I made to a couple of the other players. Nurse Daniels just informed me that all athletes must take a drug test."

"What!" Dominique exclaimed.

"I don't have to go. Do I?" Imani asked.

"Technically, Imani, you are still on this team. So yes you do."

"When!" Dominique yelled.

Imani and Coach Wilkens stared at Dominique. "Why are you screaming?" her father asked but his daughter never answered. "Both of you need to report to the nurse's office right away."

"Now? Right now? How can I go now, Dad? I gotta ummm I've gotta practice those free throws and we've got a big game coming up Daddy so can I go tomorrow or Friday or something but I can't go today..."

Imani listened in amazement at how fast Dominique talked. She worked up a sweat and her ears were as red as her nose and eyes.

"Calm down. Let me call the nurse to see if we can reschedule." Dominique followed her father to the black telephone on the wall. When Coach Wilkens shook his head, Imani knew what that meant.

Imani led the way and Dominique mumbled the entire time. Imani turned into the office and Terry met her in the doorway.

"I can't believe we hafta do this," Terry said.

"I'm not playin' and I have to do it. Dominique's behind me freakin' out."

"Come on, ladies," Nurse Daniels said as she waved them in.

"Eeelll, I hate coming in here. It smells like the stinking hospital," Imani said.

"I've made a pee donation. I'm outta here," Terry said and left the room.

"Just pee?" Dominique asked. "No blood?"

"Just urine, ladies, so can we get started?" the nurse asked.

Rows of small plastic cups filled with urine in various shades of yellow covered a table behind Mrs. Daniels' desk. She handed Imani and Dominique an empty plastic cup.

"I need you to fill it up to that top line and bring it back to me. I will put a label on the cup that has your name on it. Then you can fill in the information on this form and sign the release agreement. If you refuse to sign it or to provide a urine sample, you can not play any sport here at Westmoore. Have I made myself clear?"

"Yes," Imani said.

"I didn't know you wanted urine," Dominique began, "I can't do this today because I'm on my period."

"That won't affect the test results. The lab is looking for illegal drugs in your system not blood in your urine. So one at a time, go use the bathroom in the back."

"To save time, can I use the girls' bathroom down the hall and Imani can use the one here?"

"Sorry, Dominique. I must see you walk into that bathroom and then walk out of it. These are not my rules but I must adhere to them."

"I'll go first," Imani said and walked a few paces to the tiny bathroom. She examined the cup and realized that she did not have to pee. The sink next to the toilet gave Imani an idea. "Water," Imani said and turned on the faucet. She hoped that the sound of water would coax her to urinate. She squatted and waited.

"If I was walkin' in the rain and four blocks from home, I bet I would have to go." She envisioned that scene and peed but some of it missed the cup. "Eeelll all over my hand." She looked again and saw that enough urine was in the cup. "Yuck," she said as she washed her hand and exited the bathroom.

"This cup thing may work for boys but not girls. There has got to be a better way," Imani said as she handed the warm container to the nurse.

Mrs. Daniels laughed and placed Imani's sample on the table. "Do you know what medications you were taking for that injury?"

"Not by name."

"Wait one second," she told Imani. "Dominique, go on in," she said and pointed to the bathroom and then looked back at Imani. "Is your mother home?"

"Should be."

"Let's give her a call because I want to list what you've taken to alert the lab just in case it registers," the nurse said. Imani followed her to a side room.

Moments later, Dominique called out, "I'm done."

Imani looked at Dominique's beet-red face.

"You had to strain to get that out, huh?" Imani asked and then laughed.

"Hush," the nurse said as she held the red receiver against her ear.

Dominique stood in front of them and held the cup like it was a time bomb about to explode.

"Ain't it gross?" Imani asked.

"Shhh," the nurse said and asked Imani's mother to hold. She glanced at Dominique. "Do me a favor. Put your label on it and place it on the table. But don't leave.

I need you to complete the paperwork. I'll be out in a second," she said and then retrieved information from Mrs. Jackson. Imani watched as the nurse recorded the names of the medications. Imani tried to sound out the long words but gave up.

"Thank you, Mrs. Jackson. There is nothing for you to be concerned about. I doubt if these medications are still in Imani's system. However, I wanted to inform the lab so that they wouldn't make a big stink about it."

The nurse gazed up at Imani. "Okay, I think we have everything. All I need is your signature and then you may go."

Imani left Dominique in the nurse's office and headed for her locker. From the end of the hall, Imani saw Tyler surrounded by three girls. He seemed amused by the ladies as they all laughed. Imani wanted to turn back but decided to walk by them. "Act like you don't see them," she told herself. As Imani neared Tyler and his groupies, she focused straight ahead.

"Imani, wait up," Tyler said.

"I can't. I gotta go," Imani said and did not look back at him. Imani thought that Tyler would follow her. She was wrong.

FATIMA

The weather did not cooperate with Fatima. She hoped for clear skies and a warm March night. Instead, she got a cold rainy night. Fatima changed outfits five times and still was not satisfied.

"I can't wear my black leather pants. Erik saw those at Imani's party and I can't wear suede in the rain," Fatima said to Mercedes.

Mercedes sat silent as she fed Alexus.

Fatima skipped over everything brown in her closet. Brown reminded Fatima of her Chicken Shack uniform. She frowned at the black jeans and turtleneck that she had on and decided the outfit needed something that said, "Fatima." She went to Grandma Rose's closet and pulled out a red crochet shawl with fringes on the edges. Fatima folded it diagonally and slung it around her waist. She sashayed into the kitchen and asked Mercedes, "Is this hot or what?"

Mercedes rolled her eyes at Fatima and then placed Alexus on her shoulder.

"Well, you don't have to say it 'cause I know it's hot," Fatima said. She sat at the kitchen table and painted her nails with a fresh coat of red polish. "I can't believe I'm buggin'. That's what I get for being outta the game for so long."

Mercedes remained silent. She rocked Alexus back and forth.

"Let's see. I haven't had a date with a guy other than Hanif since I dated that jerk, Money. Now you know that is not like me. Shonda had to remind me who I was," Fatima said and then laughed.

Mercedes still rocked her baby.

"I hate first dates. Too bad you can't start with date number two. I hope Erik doesn't get lost. I did tell you his name is Erik, right?" Fatima waited for an answer. One never came so she continued. "Anyway, he's a football player at Imani's school." Fatima stretched out her arms. "Big, Girl, he's real big."

Mercedes jumped up from the table, laid the baby on the couch then proceeded and changed her diaper. Afterwards, Mercedes marched into the kitchen and dumped the soiled diaper into the trashcan.

"You're droppin' some pounds, Girl," Fatima said.

"Who has time to eat?" Mercedes asked.

Mercedes transferred to Culver High School where they provided child daycare services. Fatima was happy about that but she was more thrilled that Mercedes took better care of Alexus. Yet, Mercedes lacked the spunk and sense of humor that she once had. She seldom spoke to

Fatima or Grandma Rose. Troy was the only person she communicated with most often.

"So where y'all headed?" Mercedes asked.

"Probably to the movies and then grab something to eat. If the weather wasn't so icky, we could hang outside. But it's a freebie for me so I ain't complainin'."

Mercedes sucked her teeth as she filled the baby's bottles with formula.

Fatima sucked her teeth too. "Why she asked that question if she was gonna catch an attitude?" Fatima mumbled. It was a Saturday night and no teenager wanted to be in the house. However, Fatima felt that there was no reason why she had to be on lockdown just because Mercedes was confined. Whether Mercedes liked it or not, it was all about Alexus. Her baby needed care 24/7. There was a knock on the door and Fatima hurried and answered it.

"Hey, you made it," she said.

"Can I leave this out here?" Erik asked.

Fatima noticed the drenched umbrella that Erik laid against the wall. "Yeah," she said and opened the door wider. Erik's large frame made it through the narrow doorway. Erik was 6'4" and 240 pounds. His thick eyebrows stood out against his bald head. When he smiled, Fatima noticed his dimples. She displayed her own. Moments later, she broke away from his gaze and introduced Mercedes.

"Nice meeting you," Erik said to Mercedes who was now in the living room with them. "You wanna hang with us?" he asked.

"I can't. I hafta baby-sit," Mercedes said and then pointed to Alexus.

Fatima watched as Erik's eyes widened and bushy brows raised. Fatima shook her head. "She's not my baby. That's Mercy's baby, Alexus."

"Oooh," Erik said. He appeared relieved. A sheepish grin crossed his face. "She's cute."

Fatima nodded. *Yeah, she's cute but you would have been outta here if she was mine,* Fatima thought. She picked up her black bomber jacket and Erik helped Fatima put it on. Fatima opened the door and turned back to Mercedes, "Tell Grandma I'll catch her later." Her cousin rolled her eyes. Fatima turned around, bumped right into someone and looked up. Her mouth flung open, yet no words came out.

Hanif peered over Fatima's head and stared at Erik. His eyes lowered and met Fatima's eyes. "Going somewhere?" he asked.

"You should have called first," she said over Mercedes' voice as she laughed in the background. Fatima reached around Erik and slammed the door shut.

Erik bent down and picked up his long stick umbrella. "Is this a problem, Fatima?" he asked.

Hanif flexed his fingers and made a fist. However, Fatima knew he did not stand a chance against Erik who was twice his size. "Erik, why don't I meet you at your car. I'll be down in a minute."

"Are you sure? 'Cause if you two got something going on, I'll step back."

"Yeah, Man, step back," Hanif said.

"Nooo, no, I'll meet you downstairs," Fatima said and stared at Hanif. She waited until Erik left before she spoke. "You've got some nerve."

"Me? No wonder you didn't care whether or not I came back. You're playin' me, huh, Fatima?"

"Oh, like you weren't seein' some girl down south. Don't even front like all your time was spent takin' care of your mama."

Hanif shook his head. "Is that what you really think? Or, do you need an excuse to cheat on me?"

"I ain't cheatin' on you."

"What do you call it?"

Fatima thought about that for a second. "I call it ummm hangin' out with a friend who ummm just happens to be a guy." Fatima slapped her forehead. "Hold up. Why am I trippin'? You left me, remember?"

"I didn't leave you, Fatima. I never called you and said 'hey, I don't ever want to see you again.' I never said this relationship was history. I never cheated on you."

Fatima looked down at her red leather boots. *He's got a point. Especially, if he ain't lyin' about cheatin'. Ouch. That hurts. But it also hurt when he wouldn't come back when I needed him,* Fatima thought. However, Shonda's advice rang in Fatima's ears too. *You gotta have backups. Don't put your heart into one guy.*

Fatima zipped up her jacket. "I'll holla at you tomorrow 'cause tonight, I'm hangin' with Erik." As she marched off, her high heels clunked against the floor.

"Who said I'll wanna talk to you tomorrow?"

Fatima heard that question. She also thought she heard Hanif's voice everywhere: on the radio in Erik's car, from the guys who sat behind her in the movie theatre and even through the voices from the actors on the screen. Fatima tried to shake it off and to relax. She laid her head back on Erik's muscular arm that stretched across the back of her seat. His body twisted towards her. She figured at some point he would try to make a move on her in the dark theatre. Yet, he never did.

They left the theatre and arrived at an upscaled soul food restaurant. Fatima figured that the romantic setting in the restaurant would turn him on. The lights were dim, a candle glowed in the center of their table, and jazz flowed through the speakers. Fatima gazed across the table and replaced Erik's face with Hanif's face. Erik spoke and broke her trance.

"The problem with the movies is that you can't talk to your date," Erik began, "but maybe now, I can find out more about you. So let's start with Hanif."

Fatima sipped her soda before she responded. "What about him?"

"I don't like dissin' another dude by goin' out with his woman. But ummm, Hanif looked at me like he wanted to start something and that kinda ticked me off."

Ummmp, teddy bear got a little attitude, Fatima thought as she drank the last of her beverage.

"So are you sittin' here trying to make him jealous or are you really feelin' me?"

Fatima propped both elbows up on the table and leaned forward. "You kinda bold, huh? Well, let me be bold right back at cha. I don't know if I'm feelin' you. That's why I'm hangin' with you so that I can check you out. And no, I'm not tryin' to make Hanif jealous. I don't know how I feel about Hanif, but I'll let you know the deal when I know for sure. And another thing," she said and lowered her voice, "if you think you're gettin' some just 'cause you took me to this nice restaurant, then I suggest you save yourself some money. Call that waitress over here and cancel the order so we can bounce."

Erik looked as if he was in shock. His eyes were wide open and he did not blink. All of a sudden, Erik released a deep laugh. It seemed like it came from his gut. When he finished, Erik gulped some tea and shook his head. "Fatima, we need you on our football team. I would put you on defense too. You got more juice than some of those sorry guys."

Fatima laughed. "I've been known to rough up some folks."

"I believe it," he said. Erik leaned back in his chair. "Thanks for takin' the pressure off me."

"What?"

He inched forward and whispered. "Whenever I go out with a girl, especially if she knows I play ball, it's like she expects me to ask for sex. And look at me," he said and pounded his broad chest, "I've gotta go for it. I've got a rep to live up to."

Fatima was guilty of that expectation too. The difference was that Fatima knew the deal. Her last boyfriend, Money, tricked her and she vowed that would never happen again. "That's why sistahs like me have to keep brothas like you in check. You ain't gotta step up to me talkin' that let's have sex yen yang just to prove that you're a man. Havin' sex don't make you a man. Dogs have sex. Does that make them men?"

Erik chuckled. "I never thought of it like that."

"Take it from a sistah who knows. If you got it goin' on and treatin' a sistah with respect, she'll wait on the sex."

Erik nodded as if he agreed with Fatima. "I know one thing I can't wait on," he said.

"What's that?"

"Food. I'm ready to throw down!"

Fatima's cell phone rang and interrupted their laughter. "I meant to turn it off. Sorry." She checked the caller ID and it was her home telephone number. "What's up, Mercy?" Fatima asked then rolled her eyes.

"What! When! Where are they takin' her!"

"What's wrong?" Erik asked.

"Go with her stupid! Hanif?" Tears poured out of her eyes. "I gotta get to Bedford Hospital," Fatima said. Her hands trembled as she grabbed her coat. Erik threw money on the table and they took off.

* * *

Fatima jumped out of Erik's car before it came to a complete stop. She ran into the emergency room and up to the nurse's station. "Where's my grandma?"

The woman did not answer. Fatima banged on her desk. "Where is she!"

A security guard approached Fatima and told her to calm down. "Who is your grandmother?" the nurse finally asked.

"Rose Jacobs. Where is she?"

The nurse checked the computer. "She's still here in ER. Go down the hall to the next station."

Fatima ran to the next station and asked to see her grandmother. She turned around to see who called her name. It was Hanif. "Where is she?"

"The doctors are workin' on her and runnin' tests and stuff."

"What happened?"

"I dunno. I was talking to her and then she started gasping for air and passed out."

"Just like that?" Fatima asked.

"Yeah. It scared the heck out of me when I couldn't wake her up so I called 9-1-1."

"I'm so glad you were with her," Fatima said and fell into his arms and sobbed. Hanif squeezed her so tight that Fatima could hardly breathed. Yet, she did not care because she felt safe.

"Hang in there," Hanif told her and led her to a plastic chair. "C'mon, sit here a minute."

Fatima's legs wobbled as she sat down. She searched her bag for a tissue and found none. Hanif got a handful from the nurse's station and gave all of them to her. "Thanks," she said.

"Is she all right?" Erik asked.

Fatima hunched her shoulders.

"You want me to wait for you?"

"Naw, Man. I got this," Hanif said.

"I was talkin' to the lady, Man."

"The macho crap has gotta stop. Both of y'all are my friends. Okay? So you can both hang with me if you want." Fatima looked at Hanif and his mouth was open but then he closed it.

"Is there a Fatima here?"

"That's one of the doctors," Hanif said.

Fatima stood and raised her hand.

"Hello, I'm Doctor Wyatt. Your grandmother is conscious and she is asking for you. I will let you see her for a minute. But first, let me tell you that she is a very sick woman. We almost lost her."

Tears streamed down Fatima's face. She was in a daze as she stared at the doctor's mouth. To Fatima, his lips moved so fast.

"She suffered a heart attack and possibly a stroke. When the test results come back, we will know how much damage that caused and whether or not she will need surgery. But right now, our biggest battle is lowering her blood pressure."

"If you can't, is she gonna die?" Fatima asked.

"We are going to do everything that we can to keep her alive," he said and touched Fatima's shoulder. He smiled and then added, "The good news is that your grandmother seems to be a fighter."

That last comment gave the young looking doctor credibility. Fatima never saw Grandma Rose back down from a challenge. "Can I see her now?"

"Let me forewarn you that she will have a lot of tubes and wires connected to her. Don't let that upset you because if she sees you upset, that will only increase her pressure. Can you do her a favor and stay calm?"

"I can do anything for her."

"You want me to go with you?" Hanif asked.

"Sorry, Son, only the next of kin is allowed."

"I'm all right," Fatima told Hanif and then she followed the doctor. Fatima took a deep breath as he pulled the curtain aside. If the doctor had not forewarned her about the gadgets connected to her grandmother, Fatima would have passed out.

"I'm not gonna bite ya," Grandma Rose said and then showed Fatima her pink gums.

Fatima felt bad for all the times that she teased Grandma Rose about her dentures. She inched up to her bedside and kissed her grandmother's cheek. "Sorry I wasn't there."

Grandma Rose whispered, "Thank God for Hanif."

"I'm sorry," Fatima said again.

"Who knew? Not even old Doc Floyd. So stop being sorry and listen to me while I got breath left."

"Two minutes," the doctor said as he checked one of the many monitors. They beeped too loud for Fatima.

Fatima lowered her ear and it touched Grandma Rose's lips. Fatima did not want to miss a word. "If they lose me again, I may not come back. Do you remember where my important papers are?"

"Why? They're not gonna lose you again. You're not going anywhere," Fatima said as she cried.

"One minute," the doctor said as he shook his head at Fatima.

Fatima used the balled up pink tissues and wiped her eyes.

"The money I hid is all yours. You hear me?"

Fatima nodded.

"I wish I had a house to leave ya. You can have my old car. Find somebody to fix it for ya."

"I'll get it fixed so you can drive it," Fatima said.

"And you and Mercy go live with Aunt June. I took care of hers so she can take care of you. You hear me?"

"You're not goin' anywhere, Grandma."

"And if I find out that you didn't graduate, I'm gonna haunt you for the rest of your life. You hear me?"

"Visit's over, ladies," the doctor said.

Fatima ignored him. "You'll be at graduation."

"I love you just like my own daughter," Grandma Rose said. She took a deep breath and closed her eyes.

Fatima's heart raced. "Grandma. Grandma," she said as she shook her.

The doctor grabbed Fatima's hands. "Calm down. She's just sleeping."

"Oooh," Fatima said and then swiped at her tears.

"Does she have family nearby?"

"A sister."

"You should call her," the doctor said.

Fatima reached the waiting room and Grandma Rose's sister was already there. Fatima went straight to Aunt June and cried on her shoulder. When she settled down, Fatima repeated what the doctor told her.

"I didn't know she had a bad heart."

"Me either, Aunt June."

"Bill, let's go find the doctor," Aunt June told her husband. They went in the direction that Fatima pointed.

Fatima looked at her watch. It was near midnight. Erik sat next to her while Hanif paced back and forth. "Some date, huh?" Fatima asked Erik.

"It's a first," he said and they both half smiled.

"Thanks for getting me here so fast. I just knew you were gonna get a speeding ticket."

"That wouldn't have been a first." He laughed and Fatima joined in. Hanif sat down on the other side of her.

Fatima's smile faded. "Erik, you can go on home. I'll call you tomorrow."

"Are you sure, Fatima?"

"Yeah."

Erik went for a kiss on Fatima's cheek until Hanif released a loud sigh. Erik gave Fatima a bear hug instead and said, "Good night." He gawked at Hanif and then strutted away.

Fatima's aunt and uncle returned. "The doctor said it could be a while before all of the results are in. Why don't you go home, get some sleep and come back in the morning. We'll stay here until you get back."

"I can't leave her. What if something happens?"

"We'll call you," Aunt June said.

"And I'll pick you up if I have to," her uncle said.

* * *

It had been a long day and Fatima was exhausted. She hesitated but they convinced her to rest so she could be strong for Grandma Rose. Fatima fell asleep on the car ride home. Hanif offered to walk her upstairs but she declined. Fatima knew that he wanted to talk about Erik and she was too tired to go there again.

Fatima heard Troy's voice from the other side of the door. She walked into the apartment and Mercedes covered her eyes. "How's Aunt Rose?" she asked.

"Yeah. How's the old woman?" Troy asked.

Fatima decided that she was not down with their drama either. "Go and check for yourself," she told Mercedes and then headed for Grandma Rose's room.

"She ain't nothing but an old witch," Troy said.

Fatima stopped. "Now, why he had to go there?" Fatima mumbled. She stood out of their sight and listened to their conversation.

"Troy, you said you would never hit me again."

"I love you so much that it makes me crazy." It sounded like he kissed her. "You know I love you."

"I guess."

"What do you mean you guess? If I didn't love you, would I care where you are or who you talkin' to? Would I have you checkin' in with me around the clock? You losin' that weight and startin' to look good again, so I want every brotha out there to know that you're mine. That's love, Baby." The kissing sounds resumed.

"Are you gonna act right and show me some love? The baby's sleep and hopefully your cousin won't show her ugly face. So no excuses."

"I dunno, Troy."

"Oh c'mon, Baby. Don't you love me?"

"You know I do but I don't feel like havin' sex. I'm tired and I need to put ice on this eye."

"Don't sweat your eye. I'll love that pain away."

"Fatima might hear us."

"Forget Fatima and her stuck up self. I'm your man and you're supposed to obey me. I ain't beggin'. "

"Stop, Troy."

It sounded as if they wrestled on the couch. Fatima rushed into the room. Troy was on top of Mercedes and she tried to push him off. Fatima grabbed the back of Troy's shirt and threw him to the floor. Mercedes sat up straight on the couch. Her blackish purple bruised eye was in full view. She buttoned up her white blouse.

Troy leaped up and lunged at Fatima. She ducked out of the way and he lost his footing and landed on the floor near the door. The commotion must have startled Alexus because she cried out.

"Troy, just go. Go so I can take care of the baby."

"I ain't goin' nowhere until I teach this heifer a lesson," Troy said and pulled out a switchblade.

"Oh, you gonna cut me? You can't take me with your fists, Punk? Come on, Punk, fight like a man."

Troy dropped the blade. "You right. Imma beat you like a piece of meat."

"Bring it," Fatima said. When Troy was within inches of her, she pulled her hand out of her pocket and sprayed mace into his eyes. He screamed and covered his face with his hands. Fatima kicked him in his privates and shoved him to the floor.

"Call the cops, Mercy!" Fatima yelled as she sat on Troy's back.

"Why?" Mercedes cried.

"He tried to rape you!"

"He didn't mean to and he said he was sorry for punching me."

When Troy lifted his head, Fatima smashed his face into the hardwood floor. "Stop being so stupid, Mercy! He tried to kill me! Call them or I will."

DOMINIQUE

Dominique searched under her bed, in between her mattresses, under her dresser, behind the painting on her wall and found nothing. She pulled every shoebox out of her closet and checked each one. She found nothing. Dominique rummaged through every article of clothing that had pockets. She came up empty.

Perspiration formed on her forehead and she felt nauseous. Dominique snatched up her cell phone and called Kelli. "Oh come on, not voicemail," she huffed as she listened to Kelli's recorded message. Dominique tapped her foot on the carpet as she waited for the beep. It sounded and then she said, "I can't wait until the party. Call me back ASAP." Dominique disconnected and then dialed another number. She got Carl's voicemail but did not leave a message for him. In frustration, she knocked over her desk lamp.

"Dominique? What are you doing up there?" her mother asked.

"Nothing."

"Well, come down and eat."

Dominique huffed and mumbled. "Food? Is that all anybody ever thinks about?" She looked about her ivory colored bedroom for a secret spot she might had overlooked. "There has to be some left," she said and felt underneath her desk where she had taped a small plastic bag of cocaine. "Auuug! Nothing!"

"Dominique? We're waiting," her mother said.

Dominique realized at that moment just how much cocaine she snorted that week. No more free rides off Kelli and Carl left her strapped for cash. She joined her parents at the dinner table because she wanted to hit them up for money.

Mrs. Wilkens stared at her daughter and asked, "Are you sick?"

Dominique gazed down at her plate and avoided her mother's eyes. "No," she mumbled.

"I hope not," her father began, "we've got a big game tomorrow. If we win, we're in," he said and then he shook his head. "I can't believe that this time next week we could be in the City Tournament."

Dominique felt the perspiration on her face. Snot ran out of her nose. She could not stand that gross new habit. She wiped the mucus with a napkin. The sight of the mound of mash potatoes with brown gravy that slid into the green broccoli made her gag. "Excuse me," she said and ran upstairs to her bathroom.

Dominique's body jerked as she vomited into the toilet. Sweat oozed from every pore and tears streamed down her cheeks. "I've gotta get some money," she whispered. Dominique's undergarments stuck to her skin as she moved about. She wiped the vomit off her white tee shirt and it left a yellowish stain. "I'll be down in a minute!" she yelled as she crept into their bedroom.

Dominique knew that her father kept his wallet on him. However, her mother's money was in her handbag. Dominique unsnapped the black wallet and was disappointed when she counted only 20 dollars. She wanted it all. Yet, an empty wallet would have made her mother suspicious. Dominique never stole anything and certainly not from her parents. Her hands trembled as she took 15. "I'll bum the rest off Kelli and Carl."

The doorbell rang and Dominique placed her mother's bag back where she found it. She smiled when she heard Kelli's voice.

"Dominique, you have company," her father said.

She ran to her room and threw on her jacket and sneakers. Dominique kept on the same vomit-stained shirt and wet underwear. She did not comb her frizzy hair or put on make-up. "Time to party," she said and then ran downstairs and greeted Kelli. They blew fake kisses at each other.

"Where do you think you're going looking like the flu bug bit you?" Mrs. Wilkens asked.

"She's not going anywhere," her father said.

"Mr. and Mrs. Wilkens, we're not hanging out or anything like that. We're just uh, like going to visit uh–"

"Imani," Dominique said.

Her father frowned. "Why?"

"Because I promised her I was gonna braid her hair since she can't do it herself and I feel kinda bad since it's kinda my fault you know..."

"And like I've never met Imani. I told Doms I would like to since Doms talks about her all the time. I think it would be like totally awesome for Doms' two friends to get to know one another."

"Doesn't hair braiding takes hours to complete?" her mother asked.

"I'm only tightening the loose ones. So it won't take too long."

"You've got two hours. I want you in this house and resting for that game tomorrow," Mr. Wilkens said.

"That's cool. Can I borrow fifty dollars?"

"For what? You already hit me up for an advance on your allowance. What happened to all that money?" her father asked.

"You better learn to budget," her mother said.

"I wanna bring Imani some flowers," Dominique began, "and a teddy bear or something."

Mr. Wilkens reached into his back pocket and pulled out his brown leather wallet. "Here's 20. Get what you can with that."

"Oh come on, Dad. What's 20 dollars?"

"Let me see what I have upstairs," Mrs. Wilkens said and then headed for the staircase.

"That's okay, Mom. This will do."

Once in the car, Dominique doubled over. "I am sooo sick," she began, "thanks for rescuing me."

"Like when was the last time you had a hit?"

"I dunno. Maybe a few hours ago and I freaked out when I couldn't find any. I can't believe I did it all."

"It goes like really fast," Kelli said.

"Pull over!"

Before Kelli's car stopped completely, Dominique opened the door and vomited in the street. She cared less about who saw her. The chilly air felt frigid as the wind met the sweat on her face.

"I feel so bad that I can't keep your supply coming, Doms. I just can't afford it anymore. My dad will kill me if he finds out that I've wiped out my savings account. I've had that account since kindergarten."

Dominique closed the car door and glanced over at Kelli. "Eeelll your nose is bleeding."

"Oh geez not again," Kelli said and pulled out a crumpled piece of tissue that was stained with brownish spots. "I've never had this many nose bleeds."

"I've never been so stuffy and congested either," Dominique began, "do you think snortin' coke has anything to do with it?"

"I'm sure it does. But hey, what a small price to pay for being happy and popular, right?" Kelli asked.

"Money-wise it's become a big price. I took money out of my mother's wallet and still don't have enough. I'm counting on Carl to come through for me."

Kelli laughed. "Good luck. The last time I spoke to Carl he was busted too."

"Oh no, don't say that," Dominique whined. "I can't play like this tomorrow. Maybe Thomas will let me slide this one time."

Kelli laughed so hard that she lost control of the car. It swerved from the right lane and into the left lane.

"Watch it!" Dominique screamed.

"Stop making me laugh, Doms."

"What's so funny?"

"You are if you think that Toms is gonna let you get over. Toms says 'if you can't pay you can't play'. And he ain't bluffin', Girlfriend."

The girls arrived at Thomas' condo. Dominique greeted him with a kiss on the lips and then hugged him.

"My, my, Gorgeous. You're extra friendly today."

"I'm just happy to see you," Dominique said.

"Oh really? Well, give me another squeeze then," he said and Dominique obliged. She was so much taller than Thomas was that his face landed on her chest.

"Ummm, this feels so warm and good." He turned to Kelli. "Why can't you love me like this?"

"Oh, Toms, you know I love you," Kelli said and then embraced him. She added a few tongue kisses.

Dominique nodded. *Imma stick my tongue in there too if he gives me a free ride.* She turned from them and searched around the room for Carl. No one else was there but the three of them. She figured everybody was in the bedroom and that was where she headed.

"You're a pro now. Go help yourself," Thomas said.

"Wait, Doms. Don't you have something to ask Toms first?"

"I'll talk to him after."

"If it's about money, you better talk to me now," Thomas said in a deeper tone.

Dominique closed her eyes. *Oooh, I'm so close to paradise. Don't stop me now.* If it wasn't for the serious tone of his voice, Dominique would have ran and snorted the coke anyway. She forced a smile as she turned to him. "I'm gonna be honest with you. I'm a little short on cash and I was hoping that you would like maybe cut me a break just this one time."

"How bad do you want it?" he asked

"Real bad. I'm sick, Thomas. Plueeeze, can I slide just this one time?"

"I knew you were feigning the second I saw you. Just how short are you?"

Dominique reached in her pants pocket and pulled out the crumbled up bills. Her hands shook as she extended them out to Thomas. "Take it all."

Thomas smoothed out the wrinkled bills as he counted them. He looked at Kelli and she shook her head. "I wish I could add to it, Toms, but I barely have enough for me. C'mon, Toms, be a sweetheart."

He turned to Dominique. "You've got enough for today but what about tomorrow? What are you gonna do when you crash again?"

"I'll deal with that tomorrow. I've gotta get through today," Dominique said. She felt her nose as it ran. The salty mucus dripped into her mouth. Yet, she did not care. Dominique kept her teary eyes on Thomas so that he could see her pain.

"I like to keep my customers happy, especially, the ladies. Therefore, I'm gonna turn both my girls on to something more in your price range."

Dominique and Kelli skipped behind Thomas and into the back room. "Where is everybody?" Kelli asked.

"It's a slow night. I guess everybody's finances are low like the two of you."

Dominique wiped her nose on the sleeve of her jacket. She looked at the glass top table and the usual set-up was there. She stared at the white lines of cocaine and her mouth salivated. Her depressed mood lifted just at the sight of the snowy substance. "Can I get one line plueeeze?" she whined.

"Let's try something else and if you still want a line, it's on me," he said. Thomas went into a closet and returned with a small glass pipe in one hand and vials in the other. He placed the vials in Dominique's long outstretched hands. "You can have all of that for the money you gave me, and I'll throw in the pipe."

"Wow, I wanna try some," Kelli said as she jumped up and down.

Dominique held the vials closer to her eyes. In each was porcelain like pebbles. "What's this?"

"Ohmygosh, Doms. It's crack," Kelli said and then giggled. "You're so silly," she added.

"I can't do this," Dominique said.

"Why can't you? It's nothing but another form of cocaine. They only call it crack because of the crackling sound it makes when you smoke it. It's cheaper and I guarantee you an instant high that will blow your mind."

"Oooh, Toms, I want some," Kelli began, "and look at how much you get for your money."

"It's your choice. Sniff a couple of lines and go home empty handed, or smoke a rock or two and save the rest for another day," Thomas said.

That made sense to Dominique. She decided to try one rock to see if she liked it. Thomas suggested that they sit and then instructed both girls on how to smoke the crack. They placed one pebble in the top opening of the pipe and he lit the rock for them. "Inhale through that mouthpiece just like you're smoking a joint."

Dominique turned up her nose. It smelled weird like burning plastic or chemicals. Yet, she inhaled and the pebble crackled. A warm sensation filled her mouth and throat. She held in the smoke as long as she could and then released it. Dominique continued that process until she consumed the entire rock.

Within seconds, Dominique felt a rush. She leaned her head back and laughed so hard that she fell backwards. Her head hit the wood floor, yet she felt no pain. She thought that she took flight when Thomas picked her up off the floor and laid her on his bed. She looked up at the white ceiling and it appeared so close that she reached up and tried to touch it. "It keeps moving," she said and laughed again.

"How do you feel, Doms?"

"Happy and high as hell. This stuff is dope. Get it? Dope," she said and laughed so hard that she rolled off the bed. A loud thud sounded when she hit the floor.

"Are you okay?" Thomas asked and lifted her back onto the bed.

"What happened?" she asked and looked back up at the ceiling. "Look at those clouds. What are they doing in here? They're beautiful."

"Yeah, she's strung out," Thomas said.

Dominique pointed to the white ceiling. "No, I'm not. I know clouds when I see them."

"Why don't I feel like that? I wanna feel like that," Kelli whined.

"You've been doing coke so long that it's gonna take more for you to get that old time high. Smoke another one," Thomas said.

"So that's what the problem is? It's been driving me crazy. I used to snort once or twice a week and now it's everyday just to try to get that high back," Kelli said as she sobbed. "It's so frustrating."

Dominique flipped over onto her stomach and propped her chin in her hands. She giggled as Thomas consoled Kelli. "I gotta be perfect, Toms. The world expects me to be perfect with blonde hair, blue eyes and big boobs. Look at me. I'm all that and a size two and I'm still not perfect. I don't eat. I can't sleep unless I down some sleeping pills and even then, I don't sleep all night. Look at her," Kelli said and pointed to Dominique.

Dominique grinned at them. She was proud that for once, Kelli envied her. The joy Dominique felt inside showed on the outside and Kelli wanted it too.

"Try smoking a joint or drinking beer or some alcohol to bring you down so you can sleep," Thomas suggested to Kelli.

"But right now, put some happiness in that pipe and smoke it," Dominique said. She leaped off the bed and hugged Kelli. "My turn to cheer you up," she said and placed a rock in Kelli's pipe and lit it for her. Dominique watched and mimicked Kelli as she inhaled and consumed the rock. "You feeling it?"

"Like wooow, this is so rad. I feel like flying."

"Me too. It's like I can do anything. I can see myself flying over everybody on the court and dunking all game long. Nobody's gonna stop me tomorrow."

"Are you happy, Kels?" Thomas asked.

"I love you, Toms. I love you, Doms," Kelli said and then kissed the pipe. "I especially love you."

Minutes later, Dominique crashed. She and Kelli smoked more and more crack until Thomas cut them off. "That's it, Ladies. Kels is driving and I don't want either one of your deaths hanging over my head. You two can smoke all night but not here. Go home, it's midnight."

Dominique's heart raced and she gasped for air. She rambled on as Kelli drove her home. "My dad is gonna kill me. Midnight? Where did the time go? What am I gonna say? I know they're waiting for me at the door. Ohmygod! What if they called Imani?"

Kelli appeared fixated on the road.

"I bet they've left a million messages on my cell," Dominique said as she turned on her phone. She had 13 messages and all but one was her home phone number. "I'm grounded for life if they don't kill me first. Ohmygod! What if they called the police and reported me missing? Here I am walking in the house with drugs on me and the cops can probably just look in my eyes and know I smoked crack. They'll search me and then I'll do time in jail and it's like my whole life is over..."

"Will you shut up! I'm trying to stay in between these white lines but I can't figure out what lane I'm in and if you don't shut up, we're gonna really crash and then you won't have to worry about going home."

"Well, somebody's high wore off real quick," Dominique said and then rolled her eyes.

"That's right so shut up."

"You don't have to be so nasty. Forget you," Dominique mumbled. She pulled down the visor and was shocked at the girl who stared back at her in the mirror. Her eyes were red and watery and her hair was matted. "I look like sin but this could work. I'll just tell them I do have the flu and we didn't get any further than your house and we fell asleep and I didn't want to call so late and scare them..."

"I told you to shut up!"

"You shut up and mind your business! I was talkin' to myself!" Dominique yelled back.

"Well, stop it!"

Both girls remained quiet for the duration of the ride. When they arrived at Dominique's house, Kelli did not pull into the driveway. She stopped her car in the middle of the street. Dominique got out and slammed the car door. Smoke rose from the rear tires as the car sped off. Dominique rolled her eyes then looked at her house. Light shone through every window.

"Thank God. We've been worried sick about you. Where in the hell have you been? We called Imani's house but no one answered the phone. Do you know we called the police and filed a missing person's report? Why didn't you call us? What's the matter with you? Have you lost your mind?"

Dominique could not figure out who asked what question because they both fired them at her simultaneously. Their voices echoed about her as if she was in a tunnel.

"Answer us, Dominique!"

No doubt, that was her mother's high-pitched voice. Dominique told the same story that she rehearsed in the car. Her mother touched her forehead. "She feels warm and clammy and look at those bloody red eyes."

"If you knew you were ill, you should have turned around and brought your silly behind home. How can you be so irresponsible?" her father asked. Before she answered he said, "I'll call the police and let them know that she's back."

"I'll bring you up some cold medicine. But in the meantime, take a warm shower. You smell sour or musty or something," her mother said.

* * *

It was the last game of the regular season for Dominique's team. A win would qualify them for the City Tournament. A loss meant the end of their basketball season. Her mother's loving care calmed Dominique down enough that she slept through most of the night. Dominique felt rested and suited up for the game. Although, she wondered when she would score her next hit more than how she would score in the game.

Both teams ran through their warm-up routine as droves of spectators filled the stands. Dominique smiled when she saw Kelli seated next to her mother. "I guess she's not mad at me anymore," Dominique mumbled. She spotted Imani and figured it was odd that Tyler sat rows away from her.

Dominique felt as if she moved in slow motion as she practiced her lay ups and free throws. She shook her head. *I can't play like this. I've gotta get a hit.* Both teams returned to their benches. "Terry, you're starting and Dominique, you're coming off the bench."

"Why?" Dominique asked.

"You look sluggish out there. That's why," her father said and gave her the eye.

"Daaag, so I'm not imagining it," she mumbled.

Dominique rode the bench the entire first half. Her team had a 10-point lead and all of her teammates smiled as they left the locker room at half time. Dominique felt left out.

"You coming?" Terry asked.

"I'll catch up with you. I gotta go to the bathroom," Dominique said. As soon as Terry left, Dominique got her red cosmetic bag out of her locker and ran to the last stall. She pulled out her crack pipe, loaded it up and smoked as quickly as she could. As the adrenaline jetted throughout her body, she felt invincible. She squeezed drops in her eyes to ward off redness and bolted onto the floor. "I'm ready!" she told Coach Wilkens.

"Where did all of that energy come from all of a sudden?" he asked.

"I dunno, but I'm ready. Put me in, Dad." Coach Wilkens did just that.

Dominique brought the ball down court, outran not only her defender but also her teammates, and scored an easy lay up. Her opponent dribbled the ball and Dominique reached in and stole it. She drove in another lay up. She soaked up the cheers from the Westmoore fans and waved to them. Coach Wilkens called a time-out.

"What are you doing?" he asked her.

"What?"

"Stop waving."

"I'm just having fun." Dominique giggled and looked at her father dead in his eyes. "Lighten up, Dad."

Everyone on the team looked at her and then to the coach. A crease formed in the center of his forehead. That was Dominique's cue that she pushed him too far. Yet, she cared less. "Are y'all gonna stare at me or are we gonna go out there and kick some Landover butt?" she asked and scanned about her teammates.

Sweat rolled down her forehead and dripped underneath her chin. It felt like a heat wave saturated her from head to toe. She pulled the tail of her jersey out of her shorts. "It's hot as hell in here."

"Tuck that jersey in or sit down," her father said.

Dominique sucked her teeth but followed his command. She jogged out onto the court and fanned herself as she waited for her opponent. Her heart raced and she fought for every breath. "You're gonna finish this game even if you have to suck wind," she told herself.

A few moments later, Dominique's legs and feet felt heavy. She thought that she stuck to her opponent. Yet, the girl drove past her and scored. Dominique dribbled down court and her defender reached in and stole the ball. Dominique grabbed hold of the girl's jersey and the referee called a foul. She leered at him. "You jerk. I didn't foul her," Dominique mumbled.

The girl made both free throws. Terry threw the inbound pass to Dominique. Perspiration streamed into her eyes and stung her. She swiped at her eyes with one hand and dribbled with the other. Before she reached mid court, her opponent stole the ball again and drove it in for an easy deuce. "She hit my hand!" Dominique yelled at the referee.

"Calm down and play the game," Terry told her. "Leave the refs alone."

Dominique dribbled with one hand and pushed her opponent's hand away with the other. "Back off," Dominique told her and pushed her hand away again. The Landover High fans screamed "foul" but the referee did not call it. "I said get off me," Dominique told her defender and slapped her hand. Dominique held the ball up in the air with both hands as she looked for a teammate who was open. She spotted Terry. Dominique threw the ball well above Terry's head and it sailed out of bounds. "Damn, Terry! Can't you catch!"

"Do I look eight feet tall to you?" Terry asked and pointed way above her 5'6" frame.

Coach Wilkens signaled for another time out. Dominique bumped into her defender as they crossed paths to their respective benches. "Imma get you," Dominique told her and then strolled off the court.

"Dominique, if you turn the ball over one more time, you're out of there. And leave those refs alone. Are you hearing me!"

"They act like they can't see that girl all over me."

"Play tight 'D' and stop complaining about her sticking to you," Terry said.

"Learn how to catch!" Dominique fired back.

"Learn how to pass," Terry said.

"Enough! This game is slipping away from us," the Coach began, "and this is what we've gotta do..."

Coach Wilken's voice sounded so far away. Dominique did not hear a word of his instructions. The noise from the fans sounded muffled too. Dominique placed her hand on her chest and felt her heart as it banged against it. She squirmed about on the bench. She buried her face in a white towel and rocked from side to side. "If I don't get a hit soon, I'm gonna hit somebody. Everybody's pissin' me off."

Dominique played her opponent tight. "You scared. I know you scared," Dominique told her. The girl smiled at Dominique and then blew past her. She stopped and hit a jump shot.

Dominique could not understand what happened. She thought that she stuck with her opponent. Yet, she found herself flat-footed in the same spot that the girl left her. Dominique's father yelled, "Move it!"

Landover was up by one point and three minutes remained in the game. Dominique shook her head. "I'm not losing this game," she mumbled. She got the ball from Terry and sped down court determined to score. Terry blocked out Dominique's defender. Dominique was free to drive the lane. Landover's tall center appeared out of no where and blocked the lane.

Dominique laughed and said, "She can't stop me. Imma fly right over her." Dominique charged towards the girl. The two collided but Dominique got the shot off and it went in.

The Westmoore fans roared. A whistle sounded and the referee called a charging foul on Dominique. She ran up to the referee and got in his face. "Oh hell no! Are you crazy? Score that damn basket!"

The referee signaled a technical foul.

"What! Forget you, Jerk!" Dominique yelled as she flipped him the bird.

The red faced short referee signaled another foul and pointed towards Westmoore's locker room. He ejected Dominique from the game. She felt like she was bum-rushed. Hands and arms swarmed all over her body and dragged her off the court. Dominique knew her father's voice was amidst the commotion. Yet, no one voice stood out. Her heart pounded so hard that she thought it would explode. From the intense heat in her face, Dominique knew that she was redder than fire.

When her arms were free, Dominique picked up a folding chair and threw it at the referee who called the two technical fouls on her. A sea of "ooohs" drowned her. Someone grabbed her and lifted Dominique over their shoulder. It all felt like an out-of-body experience and she hoped the nightmare would end. When her feet touched the ground, she knew it was not a dream. The assistant coach shook his head or was it heads? She did not know which one of the two to look at.

"I'm speechless," he said and ran his fingers through the brown hair on both of his heads.

Dominique rubbed her eyes. She looked at him again and both of his mouths moved. She walked away from him and went to her locker. When Dominique looked his way again, he was gone. "Good. Leave me alone you two-headed geek," she said.

Dominique peeled off her jersey and flung it. The satiny jersey was so wet that it made a splat sound when it hit the cement floor. She retrieved her red bag from her locker, ran to her favorite stall and smoked another rock. "Everybody's against me. I gotta watch my back. They're all comin' after me."

Seconds later, her spirits lifted. "You stupid jerk ref. I should be on the court right now. I could score a hundred no a thousand points tonight. Nobody can stop me." She jumped when someone called her name. Immediately, Dominique zipped up her bag. She exited the stall and checked out who was in the locker room. Dominique huffed when she saw who was there.

"Are you all right?" Imani began, "what happened to you out there? You acted possessed or something."

"I'm fine. Wanna see?" Dominique asked and then danced about in her sports bra and shorts while she laughed. She stopped and frowned at Imani. "What's wrong with you? You need some cheering up too?" she asked and patted her red bag.

"How can you be pissed off at the world one minute and then clown around the next? Are you high?"

"Why are you here? You spying on me?"

"I came in here to see if you were okay."

"Yeah, right," Dominique said and placed the red bag underneath her arm.

"What's in the bag?" Imani asked.

"Personal feminine stuff."

Imani extended her right hand and asked to see the bag. Dominique clutched it to her chest.

"Why can't I see what's in the bag?"

Dominique laughed. *See what I'm sayin'? I can't even trust Imani. She's tryin' to bust me. She's probably wired and got cops listening in waiting for me to slip up. They must really think I'm crazy or stupid or something. I'm smarter than all of 'em. She ain't seeing jack.*

"Give me the bag, Dominique."

"Why you so nosy? Just say what you really came here to tell me. I know you wanna say I blew the game. So go ahead and say it."

"Yeah, you did. You blew an opportunity that I would give almost anything to have. It hurt like crazy sitting up in the stands knowing I should have been on that court and helping my team win. You had that chance and blew it. I have never seen you act so whacked."

Dominique rolled her light eyes and turned up her nose. "And if you were out there, you never would have lost your temper. We would be ahead by now. Okay, I said it. Are you satisfied?"

Imani exhaled as she shook her head. "You don't get it, Dominique."

"I got it, Imani. You're a great player and I suck. I messed up but it was that stupid ref's fault. Now can you go and leave me alone? I need time by myself before the rest of 'em come in here and beat me down too."

"You still don't get it. It's not about me being a great player. It's about what you did out there. Even if they pull this game out, you're probably suspended for one game or the whole City Tournament."

"I didn't hit the jerk."

"It doesn't matter, Dominique. For God sakes, you threw a chair at the man. You could have hurt him or one of the players."

"Like I hurt you?"

Imani sighed. "That was an accident. What you did out there was intentional and stupid."

There was a loud roar from the crowd. Dominique could not tell whether it was the Westmoore or the Landover fans that cheered.

"Imma catch the rest of the game. Call me if you wanna talk," Imani said and left Dominique alone.

Dominique eased down onto the cold cement floor. She thought about how she let her team down. She imagined the disappointed looks on her parents' faces. Dominique wept as she stared at her red bag. Her lips quivered as she spoke to it. "I gotta stop. No more crack. No more cocaine, no weed, nooo nothing." Dominique shook the bag. "Are you hearing me?"

IMANI

Imani walked through the automatic revolving door of Bedford Memorial Hospital. That stale hospital odor greeted her and caused instant nausea. Imani held her stomach and searched for Fatima. When Imani spotted her best friend, her heart sank. Fatima sat alone in the waiting room. The two girls hugged. "I knew you had my back," Fatima said.

"You know it. Shonda said she'll be over later."

"Aunt June and 'em are coming too."

"Good," Imani said and looked about the room. "Are they operating yet?"

"No, but they're getting her ready. I hope they let me see her before they take her in."

"They should," Imani said and then rubbed her chest. It ached at just the thought of open-heart surgery.

She tried to think of something that would cheer up Fatima and herself.

"My team is going to the City Tournament."

"That's cool. Too bad you can't play," Fatima said and took a second look at Imani's arm. "Hey, a soft cast. That's good, right?"

"Yeah, it's healing and pretty soon I can start therapy and get this sucker back in shape."

"Fatima Russell."

"That's me," Fatima said and then walked over to the person who called her.

"You may see Rose for a minute or two."

"I'm coming with you," Imani said.

"Are you immediate family?"

"Yup. She's her granddaughter too," Fatima said.

The nurse looked at them as if she searched for a family resemblance. She could have studied them all day and not found any.

"Imani's from the tall side of the family."

"Oh. I apologize. I didn't know," the nurse said and then led both girls to Grandma Rose's room.

Imani followed Fatima into the room. It felt as if the french fries Imani ate for lunch swam up her stomach and lodged into her throat. Imani swallowed hard and thought back to when she laid in a hospital bed. She remembered the sorrowful faces of her parents and Tyler as they looked down at her. *Dang, they must have felt as helpless as I feel right now. I don't know what to say.*

"Y'all look scared to death. I'm the one goin' under the knife," Grandma Rose said.

Imani rubbed her chest again.

"You're not scared?" Fatima asked.

"Once this medication knocks me out, I won't be. And if I don't make it through–"

"Don't say that," Fatima said.

"I'll be at peace and in heaven with my daughter braggin' about my grandbaby Fatima."

Imani cleared her throat and said, "I'll be praying for you, Grandma Rose." Imani wiped her eyes and then passed a tissue to Fatima.

"God knows what's best, Baby. If He has more work for me to do on this earth, I'll be here. If He needs me up there, that's where I'll be."

"Raisin' me is work. So he's gotta keep you here."

Grandma Rose smiled. "I got you through the toughest years. Now both of you girls got work to do."

"My work will be taking care of you," Fatima said.

Grandma Rose moved her head slow from side to side. "No, Baby. He ain't put you here to baby sit me. God put you two beautiful girls on this earth for a bigger purpose. And your purpose ain't to be drug addicts or alcoholics or locked up or knocked up."

Imani walked over to the other side of the bed and kissed Grandma Rose. "I love you," she said.

Grandma Rose smiled. "I'm leaving Fatima in good hands. Your people did a fine job raisin' you and I know y'all will help this chile out when she needs it. Make sure she finishes school. I done told her I'll haunt her for life if she doesn't."

"Yes, Ma'am," Imani said.

"And take her to church even if it means draggin' her out of the bed kickin' and screamin' the whole way."

"Yes, Ma'am." Imani chuckled as she shook her head. *Here we are supposed to be cheering her up and she's making us feel better.*

"Fatima," Grandma Rose began, "you don't have to question if I knew you loved me. I know you do. God gave us 18 wonderful years together. Be grateful for them."

For once, Fatima was speechless. Imani never saw her without a quick word or words on the tongue.

"I told Fatima the funeral's already paid for. I don't want y'all cryin' and fallin' out and cuttin' the fool. Celebrate my going home to be with the Lord."

Imani nodded.

"Don't invite folks that ain't bothered to call or visit us in the past five or ten years. I don't want no fake and phony people there." Grandma Rose sighed. "Wooo, I'm tired. Baby, if you've got something to say, hurry up 'cause I'll be sleep in a minute."

Fatima leaned over and whispered, "Thank you."

Grandma Rose smiled. "Enough said, Baby."

Back in the waiting room, Fatima paced the floor and watched the clock. The doctors told them that the surgery would take hours. Only 10 minutes passed by since they took Grandma Rose into the operating room. Yet, it felt like an eternity.

Imani knew one question that would spark a conversation with her teary-eyed and quiet friend. "What's the latest with Troy and Mercy?"

Fatima's red eyes lit up. She sucked her teeth and then said, "That stupid girl wouldn't press charges. She wouldn't slap a restraining order on him. Nothing!" Fatima yelled and threw her hands up. "The cops said I couldn't file a restraining order on him because we weren't married or datin' or livin' together or have a baby together. Ain't that a blip?"

"That is messed up."

"What's really messed up was that I was gonna file charges against Troy for attacking me since I couldn't hit him with a restraining order."

"And what happened?" Imani asked.

"That nitwit cousin of mine said she wouldn't testify against him so it would have been his word against mine. The cop straight up told me not to waste my time since Troy ain't got no criminal record."

"Daaang, Fatima. Is she waitin' for him to rape her or beat her down some more before she presses charges? What's up with that?"

"Who you askin'? I live with that nut and don't understand her." Fatima shook her head. "I guess some girls like getting beat down."

"I don't believe that."

"I don't get it then." Fatima plopped down in the plastic seat next to Imani. "I am too through with her."

Imani leaned over and whispered, "I don't think Tyler or Hanif would try to beat on us."

"As mad as Hanif was about me goin' out with Erik and then Erik being here at the hospital with us, he didn't go off like that stupid Troy. And Troy is just assumin' that Mercy's playin' him."

Imani nodded. "That's like when I told Tyler I needed space. He was hurt and all but he didn't try to swing at me."

"Hanif was here for Grandma Rose and he's not even blood. He stayed with me even while Erik was here." She paused and then added, "He ain't go off and start actin' crazy."

"Sooo what you think about Erik?"

"He's cool."

"Cooler than Hanif?"

"He's cool enough to be my friend, but now I know for real that Hanif's my man."

Imani hugged her. "I'm glad it's him."

"That's if he's still talkin' to me," Fatima said.

"Yeah, that's if Tyler's still talking to me," Imani began, "senior year really got me buggin' and I took it all out on him."

"Most of that crap started with Dominique. She ain't nothing but a druggy," Fatima said.

"I don't know for sure if she's doin' drugs."

"After what she did at that game you told me about, I know the girl's brain is fried."

"If you're right, she's gonna fail that drug test."

"She ain't hafta piss in no cup for me to know the deal. I don't know who's dumber, Mercy or Dominique."

"Dominique's not dumb," Imani said.

"Doin' drugs is dumb and lettin' some punk beat you down with his hands or his big mouth is dumb too. I refused to be owned by drugs or any dog-gone body!"

Imani patted Fatima on her back. "All right. I hear ya, Sistah. Me either but chill out."

"I can't believe you're takin' up for Dominique after what she did to you."

"Dominique may have started my drama but I kept it going to the point that I've probably lost Tyler. Word got around school that he's available and the girls are swarming around him like bees."

"Pssst. Sting their behinds so they'll back off. I can clip a few of 'em for ya," Fatima said and then laughed.

Imani smiled. "Yup, my girl's back."

* * *

News about Dominique's suspension from the City Tournament was one of the topics that floated about the noisy cafeteria. The hottest item was the rumor that a few athletes failed the drug test. Imani sat with Terry and talked about the same things.

"I bet one of those people is Dominique," Imani began, "and I hear she's been out sick this week."

"Maybe Coach knows the deal and is makin' her stay home," Terry said.

"Why didn't he see it sooner? Why didn't we?"

Terry hunched her shoulders. "I wouldn't know what to look for. I don't know anybody who does drugs, and she doesn't look like the drug addicts you see on TV or in the movies."

Imani agreed with Terry. "If people can walk around looking normal and still be high, that's scary. What about the people we depend on like bus drivers, train operators, and the cooks in the cafeteria?" She pointed to her arm, "And doctors, ohmygod, they could do major damage if they're high while treating patients."

Grandma Rose came to mind. She survived the operation but was in critical condition in the intensive care unit. "I just hope that the people at the hospital taking care of Fatima's grandmother are sober and–"

Imani did not complete her sentence. Her eyes followed Tyler as he walked to an empty table in the back and sat down. Two girls joined him before he took his first bite out of his sandwich.

"Why don't you talk to him, Imani?"

Imani sighed. "Every time I want to, Terry, other girls are around him."

"So? You go up to him and look the other girls straight in their eyes and say, 'S'cuse me but I need to speak to Tyler.' Then you take his fine self by the arm and go somewhere you can talk."

"I don't want to seem all possessive and jealous."

"You don't seem too happy without him either but you're not letting that stop you."

"Dang, have you been hanging out with Fatima?"

"No, but I should. She's so crazy."

Imani made an eye connection with Tyler and he stared back at her. Imani thought that was a good sign. "Imma go over there. Thanks, Terry."

"Go on. I'll dump your tray."

It seemed like a mile from where she started to the back of the cafeteria. Imani was self conscious about the way she walked. Was it too bouncy or too stiff? Did her hips sway too much? Did she walk too fast or too slow? Did she look desperate or cool? By the time she reached his table, "Hi," was all that squeaked out of her mouth. Imani saw both of the girls out of the corner of her eye. Their smiles faded.

"How you doing?" Tyler asked.

"Fine."

"Good." Tyler turned from Imani and looked at the two girls. "Do you know Imani?" he asked them.

Both girls nodded.

"It's been a while, friend, or is it girlfriend? I'm confused," Tyler said.

Imani's mouth was dry. Her lips felt paralyzed. She forced them to move. "That's what uh I wanted to uh to talk to you about. Can we uh go somewhere else?" Someone tapped Imani on the shoulder and she jumped. She turned around and it was Coach Wilkens.

"I need to speak with you," he said

Imani looked at Tyler and then her coach. "Now?"

"Right now," he said and then marched away.

"What's going on?" Tyler asked

"I dunno. Wait for me. I'll be right back." Imani took off behind Coach Wilkens. "Where are we going?"

"Principal's office."

"For what?"

Coach Wilkens never answered. All Imani heard was the sounds of the soles of their sneakers as they squeaked against the shiny floor. Imani picked up her pace and kept in step with his long strides. As Imani neared the principal's secretary, the white-haired woman shook her head at Imani. Coach Wilkens opened the principal's door and Imani's heart skipped a beat.

"What are y'all doing here?" she asked.

Imani's parents sat straight and stiff in the burgundy leather chairs. They looked as uncomfortable as Imani felt. From kindergarten until her senior year in high school, her parents never met with a principal.

"I got a call from Ms. Washington asking me and your father to come in today."

"I don't like leaving work early," Mr. Jackson said as he looked at Ms. Washington.

"Have a seat, Imani," the principal instructed as she pointed to an empty chair.

Imani eased down in the leather chair. The seat was hard. Coach Wilkens stood against the wall behind her parents. Nurse Daniels walked in. "Sorry I'm late."

Principal Washington nodded and slipped on the silver rimmed glasses that hung on a gray cord. Somehow the glasses stayed put on the tip of her nose. She read a piece of paper that the nurse handed her. Ms. Washington peered over the rim of her glasses. "Are they absolutely sure?" she asked the nurse.

Mrs. Daniels brows raised as she nodded.

Ms. Washington removed her glasses and stared at Imani. Then she addressed her parents. "I am sorry that I had to call you in here today. However, this is a sensitive and extremely serious matter that could only be handled in person."

"What? What did I do?" Imani asked.

"Imani, would you like to come clean and tell your parents what's going on with you?"

Imani's brain went numb. "Huh?"

"Imani, please cooperate. Do not make this any more difficult than it already is," her principal said.

Imani scratched her head as she searched for an answer. *Did the principal find out I have a job? Why would she care? What does it have to do with the nurse? This doesn't make sense but what else could it be?* Imani cleared her throat and said, "I don't know what you want me to say."

"The truth, Imani." Ms. Washington said.

Imani's brows raised. *It's gotta be the job. What else could it be? Dang it. Here goes.* "Okay, okay. I'll tell them," she said aloud. Imani took a deep breath and looked at her parents. Both appeared traumatized. However, Imani predicted that her father would erupt first. So Imani stared straight into Mrs. Jackson's brown eyes and spoke to her. "I know it's not going to help to say I'm sorry. Actually, the truth is that I'm not sorry. I did what I thought I had to do although it meant disobeying you. But, Mom, I had to do something to help myself."

Imani stopped to see how her mother handled the word "disobeying." Mrs. Jackson's face was like stone. No expression whatsoever. Imani took a deep breath and then continued. "Sooo, what I've been keeping from you is that I wasn't attending the games and practices like I told you. What I was really doing was working."

"What!" Mrs. Jackson and everyone in the room hollered. "Imani Coretta Jackson," her mother continued, "you've been lyin' to us all this time? How could you?"

"Your daughter is still lying," Mrs. Daniels said.

"Maybe not," the principal began, "she must be getting money from somewhere to support this habit."

Mr. Jackson stood. He caught a hold of Imani's eyes and she thought he would never let go. Then he stared at the nurse, then the principal and then back to Imani. "Where are you workin'?"

"It's great experience, Dad. I'm working in a doctor's office and you know I was thinking about going into sports medicine so it's really great experience."

"Who's the doctor?" he asked.

"Dr. Parker."

"Ummm hummm. And how did he hire a minor without something from us in writing saying that it's okay for you to work for him?"

Imani turned to her mother. "Well, I kinda forged your signatures."

"Kinda? Either you did or you didn't, Imani," her mother said.

Imani rubbed her forehead. *At least she didn't use my full name. I hope that means she's calming down.*

"Did you?" Mr. Jackson asked.

"Yes, Sir."

"Imani Coretta Jackson. How dare you do such a thing?" her mother asked.

"I'll fix it. Imma call Dr. what's his name and tell him that you won't be back."

"No, Dad. Don't do that. I like my job."

Mr. Jackson looked at his wife. "Do you see what I mean? I can't trust this girl anymore. Let's go, Cora."

"Wait," the principal and nurse said in unison.

"Mr. and Mrs. Jackson, we didn't know that Imani was working. Even if we did, we would not have called you in for that."

"Then why on earth are we here? And what else are you lyin' about, Imani? I knew that Tyler was no good. You never behaved like this before," Mr. Jackson said as he sat down.

"Mr. Jackson, from your reaction to that news, I may need to call security before I share this with you," the principal said.

"If you tell me that my daughter's pregnant, you better call the armed forces because I will tear up this school searchin' for that fast-behind Tyler. And as God and all of you are my witnesses, I will kill him."

"Robert!" Mrs. Jackson yelled.

"Daddy! I'm not pregnant and I wanna keep my job!" Tears streamed down Imani's face. Imani pointed a finger at her principal. "Stop torturing me and tell us what's goin' on," Imani told her.

"I don't think I like your tone," the principal said.

"I know I don't like it," Mr. Jackson began, "and I don't care how loud you say it, that job is history."

"We're all upset, Ms. Washington, and anxious to find out why we're here," Mrs. Jackson said.

"I understand because this is a stressful time for not only me but also Nurse Daniels. And most of all for Coach Wilkens who appears to be in shock."

Imani gazed at Coach Wilkens. He stood against the wall like a statue. His red eyes would not make contact with Imani's teary eyes.

"I won't prolong this any further," the principal began as she looked at Mr. Jackson. However, Sir, please try to control yourself or I will call security."

Mr. Jackson exhaled.

"Unfortunately, it has come to my attention that Imani tested positive for marijuana and cocaine."

Imani and her parents' mouths flew open. It was as if they gasped for air. Ms. Washington continued, "I know this comes as a surprise to you. However, the parents are usually the last to know."

"Did that bastard turn you on to drugs?" Mr. Jackson asked.

"What! Dad, c'mon. Mom, I swear to God that I don't do drugs. I hated taking the painkillers that the doctor gave me. C'mon, Mom, you know me."

Mr. Jackson shook his head. "You've been lying so much lately that I don't know–"

"Now wait a minute," Mrs. Jackson said as she stomped her foot. "I know my daughter better than that. I know there is no way she's doing drugs. Something is wrong here. Maybe the medication she was on had something to do with those results. Maybe whoever did that report is doing drugs because there is no way that this girl here is smoking pot or sniffing anything up her nose. I can't even get her to try nasal spray when she gets a stuffy nose."

"Mrs. Jackson," the nurse began, "I was as shocked as you. I had the lab run the test again. They reported the same results. As I figured, the pain relief medication that Imani took was no longer in her system. That is why it wasn't detected in her urine."

"There are other ways to use cocaine other than sniffing. She could be smoking crack or free basing and injecting it into her veins," Ms. Washington said.

Mr. Jackson leaped to his feet. He grabbed Imani's good arm and rolled up his daughter's sleeve. "I don't see any track marks on this girl's arm. And as far as I know, she's never even smoked a cigarette. Now somebody in here is lying and I wanna know who it is!"

"I'm telling the truth, Dad. I don't do drugs." Imani broke down and sobbed.

"I know my daughter has been acting besides herself lately, but she ain't crazy enough to be messin' with drugs. Now y'all are gonna collect urine from her today even if we all gotta stand here and watch her pee, and you're gonna run another test even if we have to pay for it. I don't want Imani graduating from here with this nonsense on her records," Mrs. Jackson said.

Imani gasped for air. "Ohmygod. No college is gonna accept me if they find out about this."

"Well, you young people ought to think about consequences like that before you act and–"

Imani stood and glared at her principal. "I *don't* do drugs," Imani forced out between clenched teeth.

"There goes that nasty tone again. Please have a seat and do not interrupt me when I'm speaking," Ms. Washington told Imani and then focused on Mrs. Jackson. "I sincerely think that another test would be a waste of time and money because her cocaine level is so high. I can't imagine her coming up with a clean report."

"You are sincerely entitled to your own opinion. However, we know for a fact that Imani is not smoking, shooting, or snorting any type of drug."

Ms. Washington exhaled and then nodded. "Okay, Mrs. Jackson. Mrs. Daniels, collect another urine sample and tell the lab that I want the results back ASAP."

"Thank you, Ms. Washington," Mrs. Jackson said.

"I hope that I won't regret it," the principal said and then stared at Imani. "You're an honor roll student with a bright future. I would hate to revoke your scholarship here so close to graduation."

"You can't do that!" Mr. Jackson exclaimed.

"She's a great student," Mrs. Jackson said.

"Yes, she is. However, Imani is here on an athletic scholarship. If the results come back positive, she cannot participate in sports at this school," Ms. Washington said and threw up her hands. "Those are the rules."

Imani threw her head back and closed her eyes. "This can't be happening. Just when I thought my senior year couldn't get any worse. How can I face anybody here? Everybody is gonna be talking about me and laughing at me. I can't take it," Imani said and buried her face in her hands.

"What we're discussing here is confidential. No one will know," the nurse said.

"There are no secrets here. Somebody will find out," Imani said.

"I can assure you that they won't find out from anyone in this room," Ms. Washington said and looked at the nurse and Coach Wilkens. Her eyes landed back on Imani. "Let me ask you something. If you're not working to support a drug habit, why did you get a job without your parents' permission?"

"I'll tell you why," Mrs. Jackson began, "Imani was counting on an athletic scholarship to Howard. She couldn't finish the basketball season so she feels that the chances of that happening are next to none. She panicked and took matters into her own hands."

"I was just trying to help Daddy."

"Even after I told you that no matter what I have to do, you're going to college?" he asked.

"Why do you folks feel that the only way for Imani to finance her college education is through an athletic scholarship?" Ms. Washington asked.

"Well, that's how her older sister Roberta got in," Mrs. Jackson said.

"Roberta Jackson?"

"Yes," Imani parents said in unison.

"I didn't know that she was your daughter. As I recall, she was an excellent student and athlete."

"Still is," Mr. Jackson said.

"Glad to hear it."

Imani cleared her throat. "Ummm, what were you saying about financing college?"

"Oh, yes. Mr. and Mrs. Jackson, with Imani's grades, second set of SAT scores, and extra curriculum activities, she shouldn't have much of a problem landing academic scholarships. I don't know your financial situation, but there are grants available for students from low-income households. Grants like scholarships are monies that you do not pay back. I suggest you meet with our guidance counselor and get the details from her."

"Sounds good," Mrs. Jackson said.

"Imani, I'll take your parents to the guidance office while you go with the nurse."

"You folks are doing the right thing. If that was my daughter, I would demand another test too," Coach Wilkens said.

Imani turned her head and gawked at the person who spoke for the first time since the meeting began. "Did Dominique pass?" she asked.

"Of course, Imani," Coach Wilkens began, "why wouldn't she?"

TYLER

It was an unusually warm March day. People hung out in front of the doorway of Tariq's apartment building and along the sidewalk and down to the corner. Sound systems blasted from cars that cruised by, from pedestrians who toted boom boxes, and out of tenant's apartments whose windows were open.

"Can I get in or what?" Tariq asked.

Tyler unlocked the passenger door and Tariq hopped in. The two hung out more since Imani and Tyler separated. Imani lived near Tariq. Many times, he was tempted to visit her. Yet, he did not.

"I ain't about to sit here and listen to no R & B. Hit me with my rap, Man," Tariq said.

"Go ahead and change it but don't ever tell me again that only soft brothas write poetry," Tyler said.

Tariq laughed. "How can you be hard and write that sissy stuff?"

"Rap is nothing but poetry set to a beat."

"Get outta here, Tyler."

Tyler turned up the volume and moved his head to the beat. Then he rapped to it. "Most of the lines...in poetry rhymes...and the rhythm rolls...by how you let your words flow. The lyrics in rap...are right on time...to a beat designed...to blow your mind."

Tariq covered his face as if he was embarrassed. "Maaan, stop. Next time, just say what you gotta say. Don't try to rap it."

"Don't give me no flap...about my rap."

Tariq covered his ears. "Stop rhymin'."

"I can't stop my flow...once I'm on a roll."

Tariq pressed some buttons and an R & B tuned filled the car. "Maybe this will disrupt your flow and get your mind off rap. Either way, I'm gonna suffer. But I'd rather hear this than...oooh, check out that ride," Tariq began, "he swiped another one. That dude's so smooth he could steal your car with you sittin' it in." Tariq laughed.

"Would it be funny if he stole your ride?"

"Check it. If I had a ride, I would sit and profile in it so everybody on the block would know it's mine and to back off. They're scared of me anyway," Tariq said. His head turned again. "Oooh snap, there's JT workin' that corner. He be dealin' around my school. I gotta hook up with him and see if I can get a piece of that."

"Dealin' what?" Tyler asked.

"If I gotta tell you, then you don't need to know."

"Ha, ha, real funny. Let's see how funny it is when the cops bust you for selling drugs and stealing cars."

"Sometimes you sound so corny, Man. I'm too smart and too slick to get busted."

"I bet that's what the guys doin' time in prison said before they got busted."

Tariq sucked his teeth. "Maaan, they stupid. Stupid or one of their boyz ratted them out. My brotha Big Mike is gonna school me just like he taught me how to handle the ladies. That's why I had to cut Imani loose."

Tyler caught himself before he laughed aloud. He liked that Tariq expressed himself so openly around him. Although Tyler disagreed with some of the things Tariq said, at least he talked to him. "So how's your girl?"

"Which girl?" Tariq asked.

"The one you brought to Imani's party."

"Oh, Vicki? She's his-to-ry. Vicki started actin' too possessive like Imani. I got girls now who know they're sharin' me and they ain't makin' a big deal about it."

"None of them are special to you?"

"All the ladies in the world are special to me," Tariq began, "I love 'em all."

"Should all of us fellas have as many ladies as we want and love 'em all?"

"Yup."

"Does your mom date?"

"Don't be talkin' about my momz."

"All I asked was does she date?"

"She's seein' this dude named Clarence. He's the twins' daddy. He all right."

"That's it. She's only hanging out with him?"

"Yeah, just him. So what you tryin' to say about my momz? She don't be creepin' and sleepin' around."

"That's not what I'm saying, Man. But what about that dude she's seeing?"

"What about him?"

"Does he have a lot of women like you?"

"How would I know?"

"Let's say that he's a major playa like you and your brother. Is that cool with you?"

"I don't care what he does as long as he doesn't hurt my momz."

"You don't think it would hurt her if she found out that Clarence has a whole bunch of women on the side?"

"I told you I'm not stupid. I know where this is headed," Tariq began, "if only one person is a playa, then the other person is gonna get hurt. But if both of 'em are playas, then everythang's cool."

"Yeah, something like that. But check this. What about treating women the way you want your mother and your sister to be treated? I don't have any sisters and I'm glad 'cause I would be fightin' knuckleheads all the time."

Tariq was quiet. Tyler figured that was a sign that some of what he said sunk in. Tyler pulled into his driveway. When the two reached the game room, Tyler set up the video system. "Start without me while I make us some sandwiches." When Tyler entered the kitchen, he was surprised that Miss Rollins was there.

"Where's Dad?"

"He stepped out for a minute."

"And left you alone in our house?"

Miss Rollins sliced a red tomato and then placed the knife on the tan chopping board. She sat on a barstool and stared at Tyler. "I'm glad your father's not here because we need to talk."

"I don't have time to talk. Tariq's in the game room," Tyler said and went to the cabinet. He pulled out a loaf of bread.

"May I have just one minute of your time, Tyler?"

Tyler huffed. He had two choices. Deal with Miss Rollins one-on-one or deal with his father after she complained to him that Tyler ignored her. Tyler sat on a stool on the opposite side of the counter.

"Thank you," she began, "Tyler, your father is very special to me. I admire him as a man and a father. He worked his way up from nothing and did a great job of raising you ever since your mother passed away. He brags about you all the time."

"And?"

"And I'm not here to come between the two of you. I do not know where our relationship is headed, but I do know that you must be included."

"Are you finished?" Tyler asked.

"No. And that's another thing, Tyler. I get the feeling that you dislike me and I don't know why. However, I am not trying to take your mother's place."

"You could never take her place and you're right, Candice, I don't like you."

Miss Rollins leaned back. "Wow, that's being honest." Her light brown eyes glazed over. She cleared her throat. "Can you tell me why?"

Tyler looked down at the counter. *Wooo, maybe that was too direct,* Tyler thought. *The ice lady looks like she has a heart after all.* "It's just that, ummm, you remind me of a girl I hooked up with last year. She was fake and phony and swore that she was better than everybody else was and she hated Imani."

"I don't hate your girlfriend."

"Thanks to you, Dad, and Imani's father, she may not be my girlfriend anymore."

"Tyler, I am so sorry about the way that dinner turned out. It was a nightmare. However, I will not apologize for who I am. I am not pretending to be Candice Rollins. I am Candice Rollins. Even if you dislike me, I hope that you can respect me."

Tyler shook his head. "I can't respect anyone who doesn't respect my girl and her family. Just like Dad must see something in you, I see something in Imani. Don't put her down and I won't put you down."

"Wow. You certainly are your father's son. Both of you are straight forward and to the point."

"And?"

"And I hear what you're saying and it sounds fair." Miss Rollins extended her hand. "So, can we shake on it?"

Tyler took hold of her hand and was surprised that it was warm and soft. He was glad that they agreed on that issue. "How's my favorite son and lady," Mr. Powers said as he walked into the kitchen.

"I'm your only son."

"And I better be your only lady." Miss Rollins hugged Mr. Powers. He whispered something in her ear and she giggled.

Tyler watched them. He knew that his father was an intelligent man who made major decisions all the time. Since he invested so much time in her, Miss Rollins had to be at least a little for real.

"Oh, Son, I almost forgot. This letter was in the mailbox." Mr. Powers handed it to Tyler.

Tyler looked at the return address and it was from Howard University. His first thought was not whether or not he was accepted but rather he wondered if Imani got in. "I can't open it right now."

"Why not?" his father asked.

"I gotta call Imani."

"What's up with the food, Man!" Tariq yelled from the game room.

"Why don't you go and call Imani and we'll feed and entertain Tariq," Miss Rollins said.

"We will?" Mr. Powers asked.

Miss Rollins nodded and waved Tyler on. For the first time in weeks, Tyler gave her a genuine smile. He dashed up the steps to his room and headed straight for the telephone. Tyler pressed the speed dial button. On the first ring, he hung up the receiver. "What if she wasn't accepted? What else am I gonna say other than 'sorry'?" His telephone rang before he figured it out. Imani's number appeared on his caller ID.

"Hey, Imani."

"Did you just call me?" she asked.

"Yeah. I uh just wanted to see how you're doing. I waited for you in the cafeteria the other day but you didn't come back so I figured that you changed your mind about wanting to talk to me."

A gush of breath sounded through the receiver. Tyler heard Imani sniffle. "I was so embarrassed that I didn't wanna show my face at Westmoore ever again."

"Why not? What happened?"

She told Tyler about the whole ordeal that took place in the principal's office. Tyler's mouth was open but no words came forth. He pressed the hard plastic receiver against his ear so not to miss one word. Imani's voice shook as she spoke. He wanted to hug her through the telephone. "I wish you had called me."

"I told you, Tyler, I was too ashamed. I didn't even tell Fatima. She has enough to worry about with Grandma Rose still in the hospital."

Tyler took a deep breath and shook his head. "You don't get it, Imani. You keep shutting me out when all I want to do is be there for you. Why do you feel like you have to take the world on all by yourself? You are always there for your family, for Fatima, and for me. Why won't you let me help you? I told you this once and Imma say it again, I am not the enemy."

The line went silent. Tyler laid down on his bed and looked up at the ceiling. He closed his eyes and rubbed his hand across his forehead. Tyler did not know what else he could say to prove his love for her. He opened his eyes when she spoke again.

"Before this went down, I was determined to set things straight with you. Then this happened and I thought 'here's another strike against me'. I know you're under pressure too and I didn't want to add to it."

"But if we hang tight, it's two people carrying the load instead of one and that takes some of the pressure off. We can help each other get through senior year."

"I never looked at it like that. I always thought that asking for help was a sign of weakness. Like you can't handle your own business. You know what I mean?"

"So when you pray and ask God for help, do you feel the same way?" Tyler asked.

"No."

"Well, didn't he put us here to help one another?"

"Dang. What's up with Fatima and you sounding grown? I used to come up with all the answers."

Tyler laughed. "Was that a compliment? Man, I hate to think that I'm startin' to sound like my dad."

"Yeah, I've slipped a few times and sounded like my mom," Imani said and they both laughed. "It feels good to hear you laugh," Imani began, "and I am miserable without you."

Tyler sat up and smiled. "Whatcha sayin'?"

"Fatima and I were comparing you and Hanif to some other guys we know. Both of us realized just how special and for real you two are."

"And?"

"It's true what old folks say, 'you never know what you've got until it's gone'."

"And?"

"And I'm sorry for pushing you away when all you were trying to be is my friend."

Tyler stood. "Sooo, whatcha sayin'?"

Imani giggled. "What I'm trying to say is that when you introduce me to people, especially girls, tell them that I'm your girlfriend."

Tyler smiled and pumped his fist in the air. "So when can I see my girl?"

"How fast can you get here?"

"I'm out."

* * *

Tyler's stomach churned. Pre-game jitters took hold of him. Tyler walked, ran, and jumped but nothing worked. Tyler paced back and forth in the locker room like a boxer in the ring prepared to pounce on his prey.

"Listen up," the coach said and the players huddled around him. "I'm proud of you guys for making it to the City Finals, but we're not here just to fill a slot. We're here to win!"

A roar from the players filled the locker room.

"I know there are college scouts in the stands. Two are definitely from Georgetown and Duke."

Tyler swallowed hard and tried not to puke over everybody. Sweat slid down his back and chest.

"Seniors, you will get the minutes but you gotta produce. Understand?"

Tyler and the other senior players said, "Yeah."

"If you play within your game and ignore the scouts and photographers, you'll be all right." The coach held out his fist. All of his players laid their hand on top of it. "All right, men, let's get out there and take this!"

The echo from the roar in the locker room followed Tyler out onto the hardwood. The first person he searched for was Imani. He spotted Tariq's wild Afro and Tariq spotted Tyler too. Tariq pointed at Tyler and pounded his small chest. Tyler laughed. Imani sat next to Tariq and with a simple smile from her, Tyler felt a thousand pounds lighter. It looked like she mouthed the words, "You can do it," and then blew him a kiss. Tyler motioned with his hand as if he caught the kiss and pounded his chest and pointed at her.

Mr. Powers and Miss Rollins sat a few rows up from Imani. His father gave him the usual thumbs up sign and Miss Rollins waved at him. Tyler smiled at them. He missed Fatima and Hanif but understood that they wanted to stay at the hospital with Grandma Rose.

"You heard the coach. Seniors gotta produce. Otherwise, you'll be ridin' the bench," Paul told Tyler. He walked away and avoided a verbal war with Paul. Tyler saved his energy for the game. Moreover, Tyler knew that Paul was right.

The importance of the game and all the pressure that came with it affected Tyler's performance. Tyler played tight in the first half. When Westmoore went into the locker room, they trailed by 12. Of course, Paul spoke out. "Hey, Coach, why don't you put in some fresh blood? Put me in for Tyler. He's chokin' out there."

Everyone looked at Tyler. It had been a year since Tyler heard the word "choke" directed at him. It stung now just as it did then.

"Tyler, do you think you can loosen up out there and play your game?" the coach asked.

"Yeah." Tyler bent over and tied his laces.

"See, Coach, that's the danger of running 80% of the plays through one person," Paul said.

"Paul, shut up and let me run my team!"

All of the players headed out of the locker room and Tyler lagged behind. He felt the weight of the coach's arm across his shoulder. "This is what I want you to do. The first chance you get to dunk, I want you to slam harder than you've ever done before."

"But, you said 'no showboating'."

"But, I also want to win. And if slamming will loosen you up, then slam on," the coach said and patted his star player on the back. "Just play your game."

Tyler obeyed his coach. On his first possession, Tyler rose above Cliffside's center's outstretched hands and slammed on him. The Westmoore fans went ballistic. Light bulbs from cameras flashed from every direction. Tyler flexed his fingers as he got back on defense. His legs felt lighter and his feet quicker. He glided across the shiny floor.

Tyler forgot about the scouts and the media. All he wanted was that round ball back. He reached in and stole the ball and there was no doubt in his mind what he would do next. The light bulbs went off again as he slammed down another deuce. Cliffside called time out. Tyler tried to block out the screams from the Jaguar fans but the volume was so high. The coach gave Tyler a nod.

Tyler played tough defense and his shooting game was on fire up through the fourth quarter. One minute remained and Westmoore was up by six. Tyler played the entire game and thought the coach would take him out. Yet, he left him in there. Before Tyler ran onto the court, his coach whispered, "Now seal the deal."

Tyler was not sure if that meant run up the score or impress the scouts to the point that they had no doubts about his game. Whichever, fun was on Tyler's mind. Westmoore inbound the ball. Tyler dribbled around his defender. He had an open shot. The fans yelled for him to shoot, but instead, Tyler tossed an "alley-ooop" pass to his center. He caught the ball with one hand then slammed it. The Westmoore fans went crazy. Again, Tyler wanted the ball back. He pressed his man until he turned the ball over. Tyler picked it up and was ahead of the field. He could have laid it up or dunked. Instead, Tyler made a no look pass over his shoulder to his teammate who trailed him. He dunked it.

Cliffside called time out with 30 seconds left in the game. The Jaguar fans were on their feet. The players on Westmoore's bench swarmed their teammates who came off the court. Tyler felt hands all over his head, shoulders, and back. "Way to go, Captain," most of them told Tyler. "Show Time, you're out. Paul, you're in," the coach said.

"What am I supposed to do in 30 seconds?" Paul began, "let 'Show Time' finish the game."

"If you don't play now, you're not playing in the State games," the coach told him. Paul ripped off his warm-ups and checked in at the scorer's table.

After the game, Tyler galloped into the locker room. His teammates sprayed soda in his face and over his head. The fizz stung his eyes but it was a good type of pain. Westmoore Jaguars were City Champions. The players hollered, high-fived, and bumped chests. The coach tried to quiet them long enough to make a speech but he gave up. "See you in practice Monday!" he yelled.

As much as Tyler enjoyed the celebration with the fellas, he rushed to hook up with Imani. After a 30-second shower and a quick change, he was out the door. Tyler maneuvered through several Jaguar fans, the entire cheer leading squad, and reporters.

"How does it feel winning City two years straight?" a reporter asked.

"Great," Tyler answered as he peeked over the reporter's head and searched for Imani.

"It was no secret that college scouts were here tonight. Did that affect your game in the first half?"

"Yeah, a little. But I bounced back."

"Yes, you did. Were you trying to impress them?"

Tyler looked down at the reporter. "I was trying to win the title. And if I impressed them, then that's cool."

"Let me ask you another question," the reporter began but Tyler waved him off.

"Yo! Tyler!" Tariq yelled. "That's my boy. Tyler's my boy," Tariq said to everyone who walked by him.

Mr. Powers and Miss Rollins congratulated Tyler. "I'm proud of you, Son."

"Me too," Miss Rollins said.

"Yeah, me too," someone behind him said.

Tyler turned around and hugged Imani. He could have stood in that spot and held Imani until Monday if people would have left him alone.

"Dinner on me tomorrow night. The restaurant of your choice," Mr. Powers told Tyler and Imani.

"Like a double date," Miss Rollins said.

"Can I come? I wanna come," Tariq began, "I gotta a girl too."

"All right, little man. You can come if your mother says it's cool," Tyler said.

"Yeah, and we better get you home," Imani said.

The threesome got in Tyler's sports car and cruised through the quiet streets of Hillsdale. He caressed Imani's hand. The cast was gone and it felt good to feel her soft hand again. "Am I hurting you?"

"No. Massage is good therapy for it. This whole arm is stiff and weak."

"After we drop him off, I'll see what I can do to speed up the healing process," Tyler said.

"All right now, Doctor Powers." Imani leaned over and kissed him. "I love you."

"Love you too, Boo."

"Oh, Man, don't start that weak rhymin' rap crap," Tariq began, "and cut out all that smooching. Y'all makin' a brotha jealous back here."

"You could have brought a friend," Tyler said.

Imani turned around. "Where's Vicki?"

"Don't go there, Imani," Tyler said.

"Yeah, plueeeze don't get Tyler started. One sermon from him on how to treat women was enough."

"I hope you took notes," Imani said.

"Yeah, yeah, whatever, whatever."

The quiet atmosphere changed as they entered Bedford. There were groups of teenagers on the corners and in front of Chinese fast food joints. Tyler drove below the 35 miles per hour speed limit because some strolled in the middle of the street. Imani grabbed his hand before Tyler pressed the horn.

"That's only gonna piss them off. When we get to the corner, turn left on Grove and it shouldn't be as many people over there."

"Imani ain't lyin', Man. I heard about this dude who blew his horn at them and he and his car got a beat down," Tariq said and then chuckled.

"That's not funny," Imani told him.

"Well, how stupid can you be?"

Tyler double parked in front of Tariq's building. There was a lot of activity there too. "Imma walk Tariq inside. You gonna be okay out here?" Tyler asked Imani.

"Maaan, I don't need no escort," Tariq said. He hopped out of the car and walked over to JT, the drug dealer Tariq pointed out to Tyler once before. As Tyler closed his car door, three guys surrounded Tariq and JT.

"How many times we gotta tell you to stay off our turf?" one of the guys asked JT and then pushed him into another guy.

"And who is this little punk?" another asked.

"I ain't no punk!" Tariq yelled.

"Shake 'em both down," the third guy said.

Tyler looked back at Imani and told her to stay in the car. "Hey!" Tyler hollered, "back off him!"

One of the guys snatched Tariq up and pointed a gun to his head. "Is this one yours?" he asked.

"Oh my God!" Imani screamed.

All eyes turned in the direction of the scream. "Hey!" Tyler yelled and diverted their attention away from Imani. He raised his hands. "I'm not packin' and neither is the kid. Do what you want to that guy but let the kid go."

"Let's deal. The kid for your leather jacket, your sneaks, and your ride."

"Don't give 'em jack!" Tariq screamed.

"You got a lotta mouth for someone who's about to have his brains spray paint the ground," the guy who held Tariq said.

"Maaan, this dude was loaded down with crack and weed," one of the guys said. He and the other guy filled their pockets off what they took from JT.

"Your turn," the guy with the gun told Tyler.

"I ain't givin' up nothing until you let him go."

The other two guys grabbed onto Tyler's jacket. They pulled and tugged on it. Tyler fought back.

"Get off him! Somebody help!" Imani screamed.

That time when Imani got their attention, Tyler's eyes zeroed in on the gun. The barrel pointed towards the car and not Tariq. Tyler mouthed "run" to Tariq. Tyler lunged at the gunman and knocked him and Tariq to the ground. The gun flew out of his hands. Tariq scrambled for it while Tyler pounded the guy's face.

"Don't shoot him!" Imani cried out and sounded the car horn. Yet, it was too late.

* * *

It was a hectic night in the emergency room at Bedford Hospital. The automatic doors opened and shut as people streamed in and out nonstop. Police officers accompanied paramedics and the wounded.

"What do we have here?" a doctor asked as he ran alongside the stretcher.

"Black male with bullet wounds to the chest..."

Tyler was in shock. His body ached but he did not know where the pain originated. Tyler heard Imani's voice. Yet, he could not comprehend. Every sound seemed far off in the distance.

"Miss, we're gonna need a statement from you," an officer told Imani.

"Can I do it later? I wanna make sure he's okay."

"The sooner we get a description of the guys who shot him, then the quicker we can start lookin' for them."

"We're not getting anything out of him tonight," another officer said in reference to Tyler.

"It's my fault," Tyler said as water filled his eyes.

"Don't say that," Imani said.

"If Tariq dies, it's my fault. Damn that was stupid!" Tyler said and then kicked a plastic chair. It flew across the room and slammed into a wall.

"Wooo, Son, calm down, calm down," a cop said. He made Tyler sit. Blood seeped through the bandage wrapped around the knuckles on his right hand.

"How is this his fault?" another cop asked Imani.

Tyler listened as she recounted the ordeal and the police officers took notes. Tyler shook his head the entire time. When she finished he said, "If I had given them what they wanted, Tariq would be home and not here."

"Unfortunately, you all got caught up in a drug situation that could have turned out worse than it did," an officer said.

"Yup. It could have been worse," Imani said.

"What you did may not have been the smartest move. However, I suspect that your adrenaline was pumping and you didn't have time to stop and think through the situation. I hope you never find yourself in a similar incident. But if you do, just give them what they want. Your clothes, money, car, jewelry, or whatever can be replaced," an officer said.

"Tariq's life can't be replaced," Tyler said and then popped up out of his seat. An officer restrained him.

"Let a doctor take a look at that hand."

Tyler waved off the officer. He cared less about his aching hand or his ripped leather jacket. All Tyler wanted was for Tariq to live.

"We're gonna wait for the boy's mother. I want both of you to call your parents and have them come down too," an officer said and then signaled a nurse. "Get a doctor over here to take a look at his hand."

Within minutes, Ms. Greene came through door and she was hysterical. "Where's my baby!" she yelled until a doctor took her to another room. Mr. Powers and Imani's parents arrived together.

"Son, are you all right?" Mr. Powers embraced Tyler before he responded.

Mrs. Jackson was in tears and Imani fell into her arms. "Thank God you're okay," her father said and wrapped his arms around his wife and daughter.

After the parents seemed satisfied that Tyler and Imani were fine, their interrogation began. The adults bombarded Tyler and Imani with questions. Tyler gave them as many details as he could. Imani picked up where he left off and finished the story.

"I was afraid that something like this would happen. That's why I didn't want Tyler spending so much time over here," Mr. Powers said.

"Drugs and crime happen everywhere not just in Bedford. These kids just happened to be at the wrong place at the wrong time. Thank God, they're okay. And we need to be praying for Tariq," Mrs. Jackson said.

Mr. Powers huffed. "You're right. It's not going to do anybody any good to start placing blame. But when I think of what could have happened to my son–"

"But it didn't," Imani's father began, "and I ask God everyday to protect my family because I can't watch over them every second of the day but He can."

Ms. Greene walked into the waiting room. Tyler looked into her red eyes and his emotions surfaced. Tears rolled down his face as he told her, "I'm sorry."

The short brown skinned woman hugged him. "Do you think that I blame you for what happened? Before Tyler answered she said, "Well, I don't."

"I should have just given them my stuff."

"And who's to say they would have left it at that? You can't predict what drug heads and drug dealers are gonna do. I know you care about my boy. And as tough as he acts, he's crazy about you and Imani. Tariq could have ran into the house, but instead, he went for the gun and tried to protect you." Ms. Greene touched the red swollen bruise on the side of Tyler's face. "I thank you for not running away and leaving my boy to fight alone."

Tyler and Ms. Greene held on tight to one another. The pain throughout his body lessened. When he glanced up, Tyler saw that Fatima and Hanif walked in their direction. The couple's eyes were beet-red.

"What's going on?" Fatima asked.

"Why are you on this floor?" Imani asked.

"She's back in surgery. They might hafta put in a pacemaker," she said and glanced about the room. "What are all y'all doin' here? Did she die and nobody told me?"

"Wooo, Fatima, hold up. This has nothing to do with Grandma Rose. Tariq's in surgery," Imani said and then wrapped her arm around Fatima shoulders and took her to another corner of the room.

The only noise in the waiting room came from the television that hung from a corner in the ceiling. Tyler slumped down in the plastic chair, laid his head back, and closed his eyes. *God, I know it's been a long time since you've heard from me. I don't know if this is how you pray but please let Tariq live. He's only 12. I know he can be a pain in the behind, but deep down, he's a good kid. Don't make him pay the price for my mistake.*

I promise to go to church more often if you save his life. Amen. Oh yeah, thanks for keeping Imani safe. I love her big time but you probably know that already. Amen. And oh yeah, I don't know Grandma Rose that well but she needs your help too. Amen.

Moments later, two doctors dressed in their surgical attire came through the doorway. Tyler and everyone stood and faced them. "We're sorry, but we did all that we could."

FATIMA

As the days passed, Fatima felt that life moved on without her. Aunt June and Uncle Bill dealt with the funeral home. Imani and Mrs. Jackson bought Grandma Rose a new dress. Imani cleaned the apartment and cooked while Mercedes took care of Alexus. Hanif picked up and dropped off Fatima's schoolwork. He stayed with Fatima most of the day but never stayed the night. Fatima knew that Grandma Rose would not have allowed that. So, Imani took the overnight shift.

Fatima sat on the front pew with Hanif on one side of her and Imani and Tyler on the other. Mercedes, Alexus, Shonda, Aunt June, and Uncle Bill completed the row. Fatima's dark eyes stayed fixed on the only mother she ever knew. Grandma Rose looked beautiful in her royal blue dress. Fatima's lips curled up. She was surprised that a smile slipped through. Fatima covered her mouth. *Grandma never slept so quietly. Maaan, she could snore.*

Fatima suppressed a laugh that threatened to surface. She figured if she let that out, somebody would have thought that she had a nervous break down. *They're not yankin' me outta here in a straight jacket,* she thought. As Fatima imagined that scene, she covered her mouth and concealed her smile. She also remembered that Grandma Rose told her not to cry at her funeral but to celebrate her home going. Fatima cried for days after her death and figured that there were no tears left. However, she held pieces of balled up tissue in her fist just in case.

Fatima took a deep breath as the choir sang what she considered the saddest song ever, *Amazing Grace*. It was Grandma Rose's favorite and the choir dragged out every syllable. There was a surround sound of sniffles about Fatima. She shook her head. *Come on y'all, speed it up!* Fatima screamed inside. *We'll all be dead by the time y'all finish.*

When the choir strung out the last word, Fatima exhaled. She felt the touch of Hanif's hand. She squeezed it but avoided his eyes. "Okaaay, that was the worst part. It's almost over," she mumbled.

Fatima watched Tyler as he walked across the platform. She was impressed with how sharp he looked dressed in a black suit, black shirt and black tie. She leaned forward and squinted. *How did he hook up all that black like that?*

Tyler stood behind the podium and adjusted the microphone. He was so tall that he bent forward as he spoke into the mic. "Fatima, uh, asked me to ummm write a poem. At first, ummm, I didn't want to do it because I don't like speaking in front of an audience. But uh, sometimes you do things for friends even if you're scared, you know. So ummm, that's why I'm doing this.

"I didn't really know Grandma Rose. But I know what it's like to lose a mother, and that's what Grandma Rose was to Fatima." Tyler glanced down at the podium. He slid a red ribbon off a scroll and unrolled the paper. "This poem is called, 'It's Never Goodbye'." Tyler cleared his throat before he read:

"It's never goodbye because when I close my eyes, I see your loving eyes, beautiful face, and warm smile. When I want to smell your scent, I inhale and remember resting my head on your shoulder as you stroked my face real slow and tender.

"When I want to feel you, I recall how your soft hands comforted me and patched me up after a fall. How you massaged my chest with menthol to loosen the phlegm or rubbed my back and told me to try again.

"When I want to talk to you, I just open my mouth and speak. I recall your voice and put that tone to words so sweet. I ask for advice and know what you'll say 'cause your ideals and morals rubbed off on me in a big way.

"So you see, it's never goodbye because you forever reside in my heart and in my mind's eye."

Tyler exhaled and a chorus of "amen" rang out from the congregation. He rolled up the paper, slid the ribbon onto it, and exited the platform. When Tyler reached Fatima, he handed the scroll to her.

She stood and gave Tyler a big hug. "Thanks."

"Anytime," he said.

Fatima took her seat and ran her fingers across the smooth paper. She turned to the side and saw Imani as she stood. "Dang it," Fatima said and dabbed at her eyes. "It's over now," Fatima mumbled as Tyler escorted Imani up the steps and onto the platform.

"Hang in there," Hanif whispered in Fatima's ear and squeezed her hand.

"I don't like speaking in public either. But uh, I'll add to what Tyler said. As long as it's legal, you gotta do for your friends even if it takes you out of your comfort zone. And trust me, my standing up here is waaay out of my comfort zone."

A few people in the audience laughed.

"Fatima is more than a friend to me. She is my best sistah-friend and Grandma Rose was like my grandmother too. She had my parent's permission to beat my behind and because of Fatima, one time she exercised that right," Imani said and rubbed her hip.

Fatima smiled and nodded in agreement as the congregation chuckled.

"I don't know if you remember, Fatima, but Grandma Rose gave my parents permission a long time ago to keep you in check too. And trust me, now they are really gonna take that role seriously."

"Amen," rang out again.

"I want my bestest friend to know that she's not alone. You have for real friends and family members who will always have your back."

Aunt June and some of the others yelled out, "amen" and "that's right."

Imani's smile faded. "I will miss Grandma Rose," she began and tears streamed down her face. "But she still lives on in my heart, and her personality lives on through Fatima. So like Tyler said, it's never goodbye. See you later, Grandma Rose. God Bless."

Fatima met Imani at the bottom of the steps and hugged her. Fatima did not know if Imani held her up or if she held Imani up. They both leaned on one another.

Love filled the air at Imani's apartment, too, as well as the aroma from the food that cluttered the kitchen table. Fatima knew that Grandma Rose would have loved the spread that Imani's mother created. However, Fatima could not understand how anybody could have an appetite after a funeral. Hanif, Imani, and Tyler watched as the adults ate nonstop.

The doorbell rang and Fatima answered it. Erik stood in the doorway. He bent over and hugged Fatima. When he released her, Erik handed Fatima a yellow envelope. It felt bulky as if money was inside. "It's not much but I had to give you something," he said.

Fatima hugged him again and then invited him inside. Hanif eased off the couch. Erik stepped back. "Hey, Man, Fatima told me straight up that we can only be friends because you two are back together and I respect that," Erik said.

Hanif nodded. "Thank you, Brotha. And she told me that she's keeping you as a friend and I have to respect that too." Hanif extended his hand to Erik.

"Oooh, we're all friends," Imani began, "we can all hang out together sometime."

"Are you cool with that, Hanif?" Erik asked.

"As long as you bring your own lady, it's cool."

"No problem, Man," Erik said and looked in the direction of the kitchen. "Something sure smells good."

"Go and help yourself," Imani told him.

"So much for leftovers," Tyler said. "That boy can throw down!"

"He was a vacuum cleaner at your party, Imani. Y'all dining room table still standin', Tyler?"

Everybody laughed at Fatima's question.

"Y'all kids better get on in here and eat," Mr. Jackson said and watched big Erik headed his way. "That's right, Son, show 'em how we do it."

"Eeelll," Fatima whispered. "Don't you hate when old people try to sound cool?"

Everybody nodded and laughed again.

"Since you're crackin' everybody up, there's a couple of things I wanted to tell you. It's good news and I didn't wanna look happy around you when you were so bummed out but I just have to tell–"

"Dang, Imani, just say it," Fatima said.

Imani took a deep breath. "Oookay, the first thing is that Tariq's doing well and should be home soon. Only one bullet went into his chest and that one went clear through his back. The other two were flesh wounds."

"Thank God," they all said in unison.

"What other good news you got?" Fatima asked.

Imani smiled. "I passed the drug test."

Fatima sucked her teeth and waved her hand. "That test was whack anyway. How you gonna fail and that drug head Dominique passed?"

"After that last game she played, something is definitely up with her," Tyler said.

"Yeah, waaay up like sky high up," Fatima said.

"I wish I could have seen that," Hanif said.

"We can't prove it and I'm not wasting my time tryin'. I got a whole lotta scholarship applications to fill out because–" Imani paused and then sang, "I was accepted into Howard!"

Fatima jumped up and hugged Imani. "I knew it! And there you was tryin' to punk out and not take the SATs again, but I wasn't hearin' it."

"I know I know but hold on. They can't give me a b-ball scholarship. I can try out for the team and if I make it, maybe I can get one next year."

Fatima placed her hands on her hips and frowned. "So how you gonna go this year?"

"The guidance counselor worked with me and there are hundreds of different scholarships out there. Private companies, minority organizations, and even some fast food chains have scholarships."

"Not the Chicken Shack," Fatima said.

"Okay, well maybe not the Chicken Shack but there are others out there. You have to search on-line and there are books available too."

"Imani," Hanif began, "why didn't you ask me? I could have told you all that. I checked out just about every scholarship and federal and state grant out there."

Tyler nodded his head. "See, Imani. I keep tellin' you to ask people for help and stop tryin' to do everything by yourself."

Imani nodded back. "Okay, okay, I've learned my lesson. I even went to my minister for help. He reminded me that our church offers a book scholarship award so I applied for that too."

"Wow, that's cool," Tyler said.

"Yup, and once I get my Student Aid Report back to see how much my parents are expected to contribute, then I'll know how short we'll be and hopefully the grants and stuff will cover it. If not, Pastor Mitchell said he would ask the congregation for a donation since I volunteer at the recreation center."

"Dang, Girl, Imma hafta check out your church."

Imani sucked her teeth at Fatima. "Like you've got a choice. You heard what Grandma Rose said. Just be ready on Sunday."

"We'll be there," Hanif began, "but back to the funds. If you still come up short, maybe you can talk your dad into letting you get into a Work-Study program. You work on campus and the money you earn goes towards tuition and fees."

Everyone stared at Hanif and said, "Yeah, right."

Hanif stared back at them and hunched his shoulders. "What's wrong with that? Imma check into it next semester."

"Oh, so you don't wanna work with me down at the Chicken Shack? You were the one who said 'it's not so bad'," Fatima said and everybody laughed.

"Hanif, my last resort will be to take out a student loan, which I could do in my name, and somehow I'll find a way to pay it back."

Fatima's brows raised. "So you're *really* headed to Washington, DC?"

"Yup. I think so."

"What about Spelman?" Fatima asked. She leaned over and whispered in Imani's ear, "And all of those brothas at Morehouse?"

Imani scrunched up her face. "W-e-l-l-l, I haven't heard from Spelman yet 'cause I applied kinda late."

Fatima smiled at Tyler. "Where you headed?"

"I dunno. I should be hearing from Georgetown and Duke soon. I'm in Howard too if I wanna go."

Fatima's brows inched up as she stared at Imani. She mouthed the word, "if."

"I know what you're thinking but I thought about it and it's not fair to make Tyler feel guilty if he decides not to go to Howard. That was my dream, not his. Plus, I know that their basketball program can't compare to Georgetown or Duke."

"Ouch, that hurts. That reminds me of how I tried to make Hanif feel guilty for takin' care of his own mother. I didn't get it until Grandma Rose got sick 'cause I would have gone anywhere to be with her."

"I'm sorry that you had to understand it that way," Hanif said.

Everyone nodded.

Hanif clasped his hands. "Sooo when do you want us to help you pack?"

Fatima hunched her shoulders. "I dunno. All I know is that I ain't livin' with Aunt June and crazy Mercy. I'm sick of the drama with her and Troy. I'm not feelin' how she lets him beat her and stomp all over her ego in the name of love. If that's love, hate me dang it."

"That ain't love," Imani said and the guys shook their heads in agreement.

"That's just straight up foul," Tyler said.

"How you gonna call yourself a man and beat up on a woman? He jumps on Mercy because she lets him. Put Troy up against another man and I bet he'll back down," Hanif said.

"Shhh, we're talkin' about Mercy and Troy like she's not even here," Imani said.

Fatima glanced into the kitchen. Mercedes sat in a corner as she fed Alexus. Fatima turned her attention back to her friends. "I hope she can hear us. Something other than Troy's fist needs to sink into her thick head. And don't get me started on Troy. It's like he blacks out or get amnesia or something and steps up to me like I'm Mercy. Do I look like a punching bag to you?" Fatima asked no one in particular. Yet, everyone nodded "no."

"I'm back now. So from now on, he's gotta come through me to get to you," Hanif said. He hugged Fatima and then added, "As far as living arrangements goes, I can get a place off campus and you can live with me."

Fatima kissed his cheek. "I love you and all but I ain't about to have Grandma turnin' over in her grave 'cause I'm shackin' up with you."

Hanif chuckled. "You're right, she wouldn't go for that," Hanif began, "but where else can you go?"

Fatima glanced over at Imani's parents and then Imani. "W-e-l-l-l, I was thinkin' that since Imani's going to DC or Atlanta, then she'll need somebody to take care of her room and stuff."

Imani stretched both hands out straight. The left arm did not extend as far as the right. Yet, its flexibility improved since Imani began physical therapy. "Wooo you wanna live under my parents' roof?"

"Are you sure you wanna do that?" Tyler asked.

Imani bumped into him and they both laughed.

"I think I can handle them bossin' me around for two years until I graduate from Community College."

"If you think Grandma Rose rode you like a jockey, wait until they ride you little filly," Imani said.

Everyone laughed except Fatima. "You know what, y'all? I just wanna see what it feels like to have a mother and a father. It might work out and it might not, but I wanna go for it."

Hanif patted her hand. "Sounds good," he said.

"Yeah, Fatima. Great idea," Tyler said.

"I'm sure that my parents won't mind. Hummm, so that would make you my what? Step-sistah-friend?"

"Works for me," Fatima said.

DOMINIQUE

"Psst. Psst, psst. Hey, Dominique, over here." She turned in the direction of the voices. Two pebbles with little beady eyes and round mouths spoke to her.

"Follow us," they said and rolled across the floor and into her closet. They peeked around the corner and shifted their yellow eyes upward.

Dominique shook her head, "no."

"Your parents are coming to get you. They called the cops too. Everybody is after you but you're safe in here with us. C'mon."

Dominique stared at the rocks as their ivory faces changed to fiery red. Their mouths moved again. "Hide in here with us. Bring your pipe and a lighter and we'll all protect you."

Dominique arose and stepped towards them.

"And cell phone in case we need reinforcements."

Dominique forced her eyes wide open and then realized that she was already awake. It was just dark inside the walk-in closet. A tiny bit of light filtered in between the two sliding doors. The red glow from the crack she smoked produced little light. She finished the last two rocks and remained crouched down in the far corner of the closet.

Dominique gasped for air. She muffled her cough so that her parents would not hear. Dominique clutched her chest from the pain. Perspiration glued her satin pajamas to her body. She feared that her parents would catch her if she bolted out of the closet and hollered for help. "How could they keep me locked up in here like a caged animal?" Dominique whispered. "I gotta be free."

The silver cell phone trembled in her hand as she pressed the buttons. "Hurry and rescue me before they find me," she told Kelli. "Don't let 'em get me. Hurry!"

Moments later, Dominique listened as the loud doorbell rang and rang and rang. She wondered why no one answered it. That nonstop sound drove her mad. On all fours, she eased the sliding door aside and poked out her head. No one was in the room. Dominique crawled to her window and peeked over the sill. She spotted Kelli's red car in the driveway and it was the only car there. That meant her parents were not home.

Dominique dashed downstairs and swung open the front door. Kelli's face was blood red. "How could you leave me out here like this?" Kelli asked and then glimpsed over her shoulder. "People are after me too."

Dominique grabbed her hand and pulled Kelli through the doorway. "Hide in here. I'll be right back." Dominique jetted to her room, wiggled her feet into her sneakers, and threw on a trench coat over her pajamas. She ran into her parents' room and was relieved that her mother's handbag was there. Dominique snatched the bag and ran out of the house with Kelli. Before she knew it, they were at Thomas' condo.

"You two look tore up!" he exclaimed.

"The hell with you, Toms. Let's party," Kelli said.

Dominique marched to the back room. "Wooo, slow down. Where's the cash?" he asked.

Dominique opened her mother's brown bag and emptied all of the contents out on the floor. She squatted and picked up the wallet and opened it up. "Payday! Lots of party money here!"

"Unfortunately, I don't have much to offer. My supplier couldn't make a run today."

"We'll take whatever you got," Dominique said.

Dominique and Kelli smoked crack like a chain smoker puffed cigarettes. Rather than feeling high, the girls became more irritated and paranoid. "What kinda weak crap are you sellin' us?" Dominique asked.

"Yeah, Toms, you trying to rip us off?"

"He's probably working with them to set us up. Where's the hidden camera, Jerk?" Dominique asked and then she pushed Thomas.

He rubbed his chest. "See, that's why I don't like dealing crack to my friends. You guys are hooked and I'm not selling to you anymore."

"The hell you're not," Kelli said. She shoved him so hard that he fell back against the wall.

He regained his balance and extended his hands. "I'm all out."

"What!" Dominique yelled and stepped up to him.

"But, hold on. I can tell you where you can go and smoke all you want."

Dominique grabbed him by his neck. She used her thumb and pressed hard on his Adam's apple. Within seconds, his pale complexion turned crimson. "You betta not be settin' us up," Dominique warned.

"That's right. If we go down, you're going down," Kelli said and then spat in his face.

* * *

Kelli parked her red sports car in front of the address that Thomas gave them. It looked like an old abandoned building. Brown boards covered every window of the red brick five-story structure. There was a blockade on the front entrance as well. "Like no way. This can't be it," Kelli said.

"I told you that sucker is tryin' to trap us. Let's go back and kick his butt," Dominique said.

"Well, wait. He did say that we couldn't get into the front of the building and to go around the back. So let's see what's back there," Kelli said.

Kelli set the alarm on her car and then led the way down the narrow alley and around to the rear of the building. A board covered that entrance too. Kelli banged and kicked the wood. Seconds later, a round hole appeared above her. Dominique peeked over Kelli's head and saw an eyeball through that hole.

"Thomas sent us!" Dominique yelled.

The board slid to the side and the girls squeezed through the narrow opening. Dominique's mouth flew open when she saw the massive size of the person that eye ball belonged to. She guessed he was 6'11" and over 300 pounds. A toothpick hung out the side of his mouth.

Another man about his size held a puny teenaged looking guy by the arm. He knocked him to the cement floor. "Get up and get outta here," the man said and then kicked him in his ribs. The young guy screeched as he grabbed his side. The man who kicked him turned to his partner. "This sucka gotta show his money up front."

"I'm good for it, Man," he cried out from the floor.

"Right now you're good for nothing, Sucka."

"One more hit and I promise I'll get your money. I can deal, steal, kill...whatever you want, Man. Just give me one more hit."

The biggest guy picked the boy up by his collar. "You can go mug your mama for all I care. Just don't come back here empty-handed." He shoved the thin boy past Kelli and Dominique.

Dominique scanned the pimple-faced boy up and down. She frowned and pressed her mother's handbag against her body. *Mug his mother? I would never do that.*

He placed the board back, threw on some locks and instructed his partner to, "Pat 'em down."

Dominique gasped as his partner's big hands slid under her pajama top. The rough texture of his palms and fingers scratched her skin as he groped her body. "Get off me!" she yelled.

He laughed and tugged on the waistline of his jeans. "You'll be singin' a different song later," he said and licked his lips. When he groped Kelli, she did not complain. He adjusted the black bandana on his head before he snatched their bags. He searched through them and then nodded to the guy with the toothpick.

"What you want?" he asked.

"What you got?" Dominique asked and snatched her mother's bag out of the other guy's hand.

"Whatever and how much you can afford."

"Well, let's party," Kelli said.

"You got the right attitude. Follow me, ladies."

Dominique looked about the first floor and it was vacant. They ascended the wood steps that crackled as the big guys stepped on them. They reached the top of the landing and Dominique could not believe what she saw right in the center of the large room.

"If you want your own private party, it's gonna cost ya," the biggest guy said. He opened a side door. On the floor in the tiny room was a tattered yellowish mattress. Brown stains covered it as if they created a pattern. Dusty syringes laid about the thin mattress. A kerosene lamp and used candles were in a corner.

"I didn't come here for a room," Kelli said.

"Me either," Dominique began, "just the crack."

"So the ladies wanna socialize with the other clients up in here."

"Who said we're stayin'?" Dominique asked.

"You look like you're dressed for a sleep over," the guy who searched her said. He ran his hand down the front of her satin pajamas.

His partner removed his toothpick. "Leave her alone, Man. Just give the ladies what they want."

"She's gonna want some of this," he said as he clutched his private parts, "before she leaves." He laughed all the way out of the room. When he returned, he waved to Dominique and Kelli. "Follow me."

They followed the bandana-wearing guy into the doorway of a large room. Dominique gagged from the stench in the air. It smelled like urine and feces mixed with vomit and underarm funk. Dominique stumbled over something and then felt a kick on her leg.

"Watch it!"

She glanced down and saw a girl who looked about 15. "Sorry," Dominique said.

The girl ignored her and wrapped a vanilla rubber hose around her bony arm. She tied it so tight that it creased what little brown skin she had on her bone.

Dominique's mouth dropped as the girl injected herself with the same type of dirty needle she saw in the side room. Dominique watched in horror as the girl's eyes rolled back. Her head flopped back and her black matted hair pressed up against the beige wall. Saliva oozed out the corner of the girl's mouth as her dark brown lips curled up on one side.

"What's up with her?" Dominique asked as she pointed to the girl who looked limp and lifeless.

"Strung the hell out on heroin. She takes care of me real good to get it. You know what I mean?" he asked and then blew a kiss at Dominique. He smiled and stuck his pinkish red tongue through his wide gap.

"Eeelll not in this lifetime," Dominique said.

"I've heard that before from every female in here," he said. His partner handed him vials of crack. He held one up in Dominique's face. "Is this what you want?"

Dominique salivated at the sight of the rocks. She reached for it and he withdrew his hand. "Money first."

Dominique opened her mother's handbag and retrieved the money. Kelli pulled out a few crumpled bills. He counted the money that Kelli gave him. "I guess you don't smoke much unless your friend here is gonna spot you a few bills."

"I got her covered," Dominique said. She handed him more money.

"Pipes and lighters cost extra."

"We got our own," Kelli said.

"Then I guess we're straight," he began, "make yourselves at home."

"We're not stayin'," Dominique said.

"What's the rush?"

"Yeah, Doms, what's the rush?" Kelli asked. She already had the pipe in her mouth.

"It stinks in here," Dominique said.

"It's funny how after a while you don't smell it. You smell anything, Man?" he asked his partner.

"Naw, I don't smell nothing."

"Come on, Doms, lighten up," Kelli said and then took a long drag off her pipe.

They looked for a corner that did not have a body slumped in it. There were none. The girls tiptoed over legs and feet and arms and hands in search of an open spot on the floor. The body parts were shades of white, yellow, brown and black. They found a vacancy in between a girl who looked like a teenager and a woman who appeared old enough to be her mother.

Hours slipped by as Dominique and Kelli chain-smoked crack. With each rock consumed, they yearned for that indescribable high that they experienced their first time. It never came and Dominique was frustated. Frustrated and hot. She pulled off her pajama top and sat there in her white bra and satin pajama bottoms.

"I'm goin' to Thomas'. His stuff is better than this."

"Wait, Doms, let's see what else they got here."

The woman next to them laughed. She appeared so happy. Dominique and Kelli watched as the woman took the same needle she just used and handed it to the girl next to Dominique. The woman laughed again. Her red eyes landed on Dominique and then Kelli. "You two don't know what you're missin'. I used to smoke all night long. That damn crack kept callin' my name. You know what I'm talkin' about?"

Dominique shook her head because it happened to her that morning.

"It be callin' you and you smoke it and then nothing. But, I found the secret."

"What?" Kelli asked.

"You gotta mix it up."

"Mix what up?"

"They call it Speedball. I dunno what they put in it. Just ask the man for it. He'll give it to ya."

"I want some," Kelli whined and then rummaged through her bag and every pocket. Yet, she came up empty. "Give me some money," Kelli said as she held her bony hand out to Dominique.

"No–" Dominique choked and then gasped for air. She covered her mouth as she coughed. Dominique hacked so hard that she thought she had vomited. When she inspected her palm, she saw blood. "Eeelll," she said and smeared the blood down her pant leg.

Kelli did not ask Dominique if she was all right. She asked for money again.

"No. I only got enough for me."

Kelli pushed her. "How can you be so freakin' selfish? What about all the times I covered you?"

Dominique shoved her. "Go home and get money."

"Like money's just lying around. Imma see if the nice big guy will let me slide until tomorrow." Kelli stood and looked down at Dominique. "C'mon!"

Dominique and Kelli knocked on the wood door where the two guys retreated. The bandana then the face appeared through the cracked door. He gawked at Dominique's white lace bra and then at her. "What can I do for you?" he asked and then licked his chapped lips.

Dominique rolled her eyes and sucked her teeth. "Nothing." She pointed to Kelli. "My friend needs a favor." Dominique proceeded and told him the story.

"What you got to sell?" he asked.

The guy laughed as Kelli unfastened the pink plastic band of her silver-faced watch. "You're kiddin' me, right?" he asked as he held it in his hands.

Kelli glared at Dominique. "I was rushin' to rescue your sorry behind so I didn't have time to put on my good stuff." Kelli stomped her foot. "Damn it! I should have worn my diamond earrings. You'll like those. I can bring them tomorrow." She smiled at the guy.

He laughed. "Then you can get a hit tomorrow."

"Oooh, c'mon. I promise I'll come back."

"I promise we'll be here tomorrow when you come back with some money," the guy said as he opened the door all the way. He reached for Kelli. "If you ain't got nothing to sell, you gotta go."

She jumped back. "No. Wait. Let me think."

"Hurry up," he said.

"Okay, ummm, okay uh, what about my car?"

"What!" Dominique screamed and then coughed. She held her throat and whispered, "You can't do that."

"Is that your ride out front?"

"Yeah, the red one."

The guy shook his head. "Daddy laid down some mad cash for that sweet ride."

"So can I like rent it to you for like a day and then pick it up like tomorrow?"

He mimicked Kelli. "Like, no."

"Oh c'mon," she whined.

"Here's the deal, Blondie," he said back in his natural voice. "I'll hook you up with as much as you can handle all night long but that ride is mine. Ain't no pickin' it up tomorrow 'cause it won't be here. Got it?"

"Even that speedball stuff?"

"Whatever you want, Blondie. I'll spring for your friend too," he said and blew a kiss at Dominique.

"Now that's a good deal," Dominique said as she looked at the last of her mother's money.

"You ladies are outta here in the morning unless you find something else to sell," the guy said. He turned to Dominique and stroked her flat abdomen and around to her back. She did not push him away that time.

They returned to their spot and the girl who sat next to Dominique was about to shoot up. The girl jabbed the needle into her arm and blood squirted onto Dominique's white bra and on her lips. "Eeelll!" Kelli and Dominique screamed in unison.

Dominique picked up her pajama top and rubbed the blood off her lips. The red spots on her bra seeped into the material and turned a deep burgandy. Kelli stared at her syringe filled with a clear liquid. "Doms, I want those guys to show me how to do this."

Dominique jumped up. "I wanna get outta here."

"Let's get a room," Kelli said.

The guys escorted them to a private room. Dominique sat on one end of the filthy mattress and Kelli the other. "C'mon, Blondie, let's do this," the guy with the bandana said. Kelli held out her pale and bony arm.

Dominique cringed and turned her head. "I can't watch. Y'all crazy."

"Aw, just a little pinch. I hear it's worth it," the biggest guy said.

Kelli moaned and Dominique shook her head. "Imma try just one more rock. I'm just one hit away from paradise. Just one."

The guys left the room and closed the door. Dominique smoked her pipe and stared at Kelli. She appeared plastered to the ivory wall. Her eyes looked like the eyes of the young girl that Dominique tripped over. Except, Kelli's eyes were blue. Kelli's mouth was wide open. Saliva dripped down her chin.

"Kelli? Kelli? Are you sleep with your eyes open?"

Kelli did not answer. She did not move.

"Oh forget you then." Dominique turned her back to Kelli and smoked one rock after another until her heart raced. She fought for every breath. "Kelli, I gotta get air," she said and spun around in Kelli's direction. "Ohmygod!" Dominique yelled and her body trembled.

Neon colored bugs crawled out of Kelli's mouth. They scampered up into her hair. So Dominique thought. She jumped about and shook herself off as she imagined that they crawled on her too. "Help me!" Dominique screamed as she picked at her skin.

No one rescued her. Dominique figured that they were all out to get her. "They set me up!" she hollered.

"Who?" Kelli asked.

"Get 'em off you! Get 'em off me!"

"Get what?" Kelli hollered back as she examined herself and the room. "No one's in here but us, Doms."

The two guys busted through the door. "Who's freakin' out in here?" the guy with the toothpick asked.

Kelli pointed to Dominique who slumped down in the corner.

"Is she hallucinating?" he asked.

"I guess but I'm feeling like real mellow."

He left the room and when he returned, he approached Dominique with a syringe in his hand. She did not move. He injected the needle into her arm and she did not flinch. "That will chill her right out," he said.

"Doms needs air. Can we get some air?"

"Take 'em to the roof," he told his partner.

Dominique was so relaxed that she smiled at the guy who groped her. He scooped her up into his arms. Kelli laid Dominique's coat on her lap and then her mother's bag on top of the coat. Dominique felt like they ascended a million steps. They reached the roof and the cold air caressed her face. He lowered her down on to the black surface.

"She should be all right," he told Kelli. "Come back down when you're ready."

Dominique watched as Kelli twirled about with her arms spread out. She was too tired to join in.

"Look at me," Kelli said.

Dominique squinted. Kelli seemed so far away.

"I'm 99 pounds and still not perfect. But right now, I feel sooo light. Look at me, Doms. Light as a bird. Birds can fly because they're light."

Dominique squinted again. *Is Kelli flappin' her arms or is that a huge bird?* After the bugs that Kelli said did not exist, Dominique no longer trusted her eyes. She closed them and listened to Kelli's voice.

"Look at them, Doms. See how birds fly together? They don't pay Toms or those guys downstairs to be friends and to be together."

Dominique gazed up into the empty sky. Tears filled her eyes. *All I wanted was to fit in like those birds.*

"I wanna be a dove, Doms. They're beautiful and perfect. Everybody loves doves. Right, Doms?"

Dominique closed her eyes and saw a white dove. It was beautiful as it soared towards the blue sky. Other birds stopped in mid flight and admired it. All of a sudden, the dove exploded. The dove's body turned into white powder. It trickled down from the sky. Dominique sniffed as if she snorted cocaine.

"I wanna fly like a dove. I wanna fly..." Kelli said.

A moment later, Dominique opened her eyes and cleared her throat. "Me too," she whispered and looked where Kelli last stood.

SURVIVORS

Fatima, Tyler, Hanif, and Erik sat on boxes in Grandma Rose's apartment. Imani sat on the hardwood floor and her friends clung to her every word. Imani reported everything that Mr. Wilkens told her and her parents. Mouths dropped as Imani continued with the story. "...and then Kelli jumped off the roof because she thought she was a dove or something like that–"

"Wooo, and she died?" Hanif asked.

"Yup."

"Daaang," Fatima said.

"When the cops raided the crack house, they found Dominique up on the roof with a cell phone in her hand."

"How did they end up in a crack house, anyway? I can't believe they let teenagers in there." Hanif said.

Fatima shook her head. "Y'all so naïve. They'll let kindergarten kids in if they showed them the money."

"But get this. Dominique and Kelli were buying drugs somewhere else before then. Dominique ratted on a guy named Toms or Thomas, or something like that. Anyway, the cops busted him at a condo in Spring Lake."

"Get out," Hanif began, "Spring Lake has more rich folks than Tyler's hometown."

Fatima sucked her teeth. "Rich people be doin' drugs too. They just don't get busted as much."

"If I had caught Dominique doin' it, I would have told her father," Imani said.

Fatima sucked her teeth, again. "Oh, like he was gonna believe you?"

"No way, Imani," Erik began, "especially when Dominique passed the drug test and you failed."

Imani snapped her fingers. "Thanks for reminding me. Y'all know how I failed that test?"

"How?" they all asked.

"Check this out," Imani began and took a deep breath. "Dominique confessed that she switched our urine samples in the nurse's office."

Everyone shouted, "What!"

"Daaang, that's messed up," Fatima said. "I knew something was up. You failin' that drug test was bogus."

As everyone shook their head, Tyler stood and paced about the room. He stopped and looked at Imani. "Queen, that *was* messed up. I can't believe she did that."

"Maaan, I've seen people do some foul stuff when they're high. It's like the drugs take over their mind and body and make 'em do crazy things," Erik said.

"Actin' all possessed and crap," Fatima added.

"I thought Coach would never stop apologizing. He had my parents on that phone for hours," Imani said.

"She's the one who needs to be suckin' up to you. Here you were tryin' to be her friend and she stabbed you in the back," Fatima said.

"Is she gonna be all right or what?" Hanif asked.

Imani hunched her shoulders. "Who knows? Her father said that she has crack lung."

"What's that?" everyone asked.

"I don't know all the medical technical details about it but she has burns on her larynx from smoking crack." Imani continued as Fatima frowned and stroked her neck. "And her father said for the amount of drugs she had in her system, Dominique's lucky to be alive."

"She could have jumped off that roof," Tyler said.

"Yup, and I think this whole drug thing has scared Mr. Wilkens to death. He said they're going to get family counseling. And he's gonna put Dominique in a drug rehab program to work through whatever issues caused her to turn to drugs in the first place."

"Drugs didn't solve her problems," Hanif said.

Imani shook her head. "Nope. And check this out. Her father said that her addiction started with one joint. Just one joint and look at where she is now."

"And where her friend Kelli is," Tyler said.

Fatima rose and gazed about the half empty apartment and then she addressed her friends. "This whole year is so messed up. I feel like we've been in a smack down. Battles with Mercy and Troy, Grandma dyin' and I almost lost my boo," she said as her eyes watered. "It's been a trip."

Hanif wrapped his arm around her. "My mom was sick and I had to be away and then I come back here and Erik's pushin' up on my woman." Everyone laughed.

Hanif held his hand up, "Just kiddin', Man."

"You're right. That's what I was doin'," Erik said.

"I could have gotten Tariq, Imani and me killed," Tyler said and then shook his head.

Imani shook her head too. "Don't even get me started on my drama."

"Please don't," everybody said.

"But somehow, we survived," Imani said.

"Speaking of surviving, I gotta go and get ready for the game tonight."

"State championship!" Fatima began, "hook us up with some good seats."

Imani reached for Tyler. "Wait. Before you go, tell them about you-know-what."

"Oh yeah. Well, y'all, I didn't get into Duke."

"Good," Fatima began, "that's because your behind is supposed to be at Howard with Imani."

He looked at Fatima and said, "Georgetown said 'yes' and they're offering me some scholarship money."

"Hey, Man, that's great," Erik said.

"Yeah, Man, congratulations," Hanif said.

"Sooo?" Fatima asked as she gawked at Imani.

"Sooo, Fatima, he's going to Georgetown," Imani said and hugged Tyler.

"And that's cool with you?" Fatima asked.

"Yeah, because Georgetown is only three or four miles from Howard."

Fatima plopped down on a box and pouted. "So everybody's really leavin' me."

Hanif rubbed her back and said, "I'm still here."

"And we're not that far away. You and Hanif can drive down on the weekends," Imani said.

"Or you can drive yourself," Hanif said.

Fatima perked up. "I can borrow your ride?"

"You can drive your own."

"Car? What car?"

"Let's show her," Imani said.

Fatima leaped to her feet and followed the crew outside. They stood near a cherry red four-door car. Fatima glanced up and down the street. "So where is it?"

Hanif leaned against the red car, crossed his arms over his chest, and smiled. Fatima walked around the entire car and ran her hand over the smooth surface. "No way! This ain't even Grandma's old ride."

"Yes, it is!" Imani exclaimed and jumped about.

"Oh snap!" Fatima covered her mouth and the tears flowed from her eyes and onto her hands.

"Hanif got it runnin' and we all chipped in for the paint job and new stereo," Imani said.

"Oh snap," she repeated and kissed everyone.

When Hanif handed her the keys to the car, Fatima hopped into the driver's seat. "It smells like new leather up in here," she said.

"It's called an air freshener. We couldn't afford the real thing," Imani said and everyone laughed.

"Start it up," Hanif said.

"Does she know how?" Tyler asked.

"Ha, ha, very funny. I got this," Fatima said and then turned the key in the ignition. The engine purred.

"Sounds good, Man," Tyler and Erik told Hanif.

Fatima cared less about how the engine sounded. She turned on the radio and pumped up the volume. "Aaah, yeah, that's my song!" She looked at her friends. "Who's gonna teach me how to drive?" Fatima asked as she moved her head to the rhythm.

Everyone mumbled, "Not me."

"We may be survivors, Girl, but we're not crazy," Imani said. The crew walked away and left Fatima in her car as she bobbed on to the beat.

Message from the Author

Dear Reader:

Imani in Never Say Goodbye is a work of fiction. However, the dangers of using drugs are REAL. If you or someone you know is using illegal drugs, please STOP. Drugs do not solve problems. They only add to them.

Help is available. Find someone who you trust (minister, teacher, coach, relative, friend) and tell her/him that you need HELP. Check your local telephone directory for available resources. Or, call one of the organizations/hotlines below. They are available 24/7 and the call is toll-free:

Covenant House NineLine..........	(1-800-999-9999)
Alcohol and Drug Helpline.........	(1-800-821-4357)
National Youth Crisis Hotline...	(1-800-HIT-HOME)

Stay strong, be positive, and keep it real.

Peace & Blessings...Jackie

TALK ABOUT IT...

1. Rather than turning to drugs or alcohol, discuss some positive ways teens can deal with their problems?

2. Why do you think that teens try illegal drugs?

3. What are the financial, physical, mental and social consequences of using illegal drugs?

4. How did Dominique's behavior and appearance change during the progression of her drug use?

5. What advice will you give to someone who is using or thinking about trying illegal drugs?

6. What should Mercedes' role be in raising Alexus? What should Troy's role be in raising Alexus?

7. What is date rape? Was Mercedes almost a victim?

8. What is verbal, mental, and physical abuse? Why do victims of such abuse tolerate it?

9. How do you feel about Mercedes not pressing charges against Troy?

10. Who or what defines how women should look? Did Kelli buy it? Do you buy it?

11. What are positive ways of dealing with the death of a loved one?

12. How can teens & adults show one another respect?

13. How are you preparing for the SATs? How will you obtain scholarship & financial aid information?

14. What are the benefits of a college education?

ABOUT THE AUTHOR

Born and raised in Newark, New Jersey, Jackie Hardrick still makes the East Coast her home. She holds a BS degree from Seton Hall University.

Ms. Hardrick's first contemporary young adult novel, *Imani in Young Love & Deception*, was recommended reading by *EBONY* magazine. Featured in the *New York Times (In/Person),* Ms. Hardrick is dedicated to giving back by writing "what's happening now" novels for teenagers that are positive, inspiring, entertaining, and enlightening. She enjoys sharing her knowledge and wisdom with teenagers one-on-one or in a group setting as in her *"Keepin' It Real" Program*.

The *"Keepin' It Real" Program* is a rap session and book discussion that provokes lively conversation regarding the hot topics addressed in the novel. This Program, as does the novel, stresses the consequences of actions. *"Keepin' It Real"* is perfect for middle & high schools, youth groups, youth ministries, & book clubs.

For more information about the author and her Program,
log-on to: www.authorsden.com/jackiehardrick
or e-mail her at: jackiehardrick@hotmail.com